THE RIVER BRINGS THE SEA

Ali Thurm is originally from Newcastle-upon-Tyne but now lives in London, and spends her time between Ealing and Cumbria. Her first novel, *One Scheme of Happiness,* was shortlisted for the Daniel Goldsmith First Novel Prize in 2017, the Cinnamon Debut Novel Award in 2018, and was published by Retreat West Books in 2020. Her unpublished novel, *Jacob's Ladder*, was longlisted for the Bath Novel Award in 2017. *The River Brings the Sea* placed third in the Daniel Goldsmith First Novel Prize in 2019.

the RIVER BRINGS the SEA

ALI THURM

LENDAL PRESS

First published in 2025 by Lendal Press
an imprint of Valley Press
Woodend, The Crescent, Scarborough, YO11 2PW

ISBN 978-1-915606-63-1
Cat. no. LP0022

A CIP record for this book is available from the British Library.

Epigraphs by Philip Hoare and Maura Dooley are reproduced by kind permission of the authors. Maura Dooley's extract is from *The Silvering* (Bloodaxe Books, 2016).

Cover and text design by Jamie McGarry.

Printed and bound in Great Britain by
TJ Books, Padstow, Cornwall.

for Joe, Frankie and Martha
and in memory of my father

Our melting, shifting, liquid world won't wait
for manifesto or mandate, each
warning a reckoning.
— 'Still Life with Sea Pinks and High Tide', Maura Dooley

London is an illusion; it only floats on sand and clay.
Nowhere is beyond the tidal reach;
the river brings the sea into the city.
— *The Sea Inside*, Philip Hoare

For a while the skies were clear and we could breathe; birdsong made us happy again. Trees put out their leaves as usual, and this time we noticed. Everyone clapped and cheered. We said; we like this, let's not go back to the old ways. But money had a louder voice. Money said we have to. You want to. So, not much later, clouds covered the sun and the rain began. The sea battered the cliffs and the soft sediment of the estuaries; it crept along the rivers and into the cities. It was too late for flood defences. The sea would not hold its boundaries; it washed back up the rivers and took the land.

PART ONE

One

Sometimes now we relax enough to enjoy a meal. But vigilance is necessary, because once it's happened it can happen again, and someone is always posted to keep watch. I'd hauled myself high into the tree at the lookout, feeling the sway of the branches echo down through the trunk, through my body. So, long before they arrived, I knew about the woman. By the time she knocked on our door we had finished eating, but there was enough even for a whole new family. I helped them to find a place near the fire. A bowlful of something hot to eat. Like children after a day out playing, they arrived exhausted and all they wanted was food, shelter, somewhere to sleep. I asked Tracey to make up beds, put the warming bricks in. Extra covers.

Ghosts of the past circle here, where the River Cocker tumbles down through a slate cleft in the rocks to join the Derwent. Gushing together like a reunion, then tamed by the slower flow of the other river. When someone arrives we all sense it again, what has been lost.

In dreams, I go back. It was cold and dark, and there was the overwhelming need to find my way. To get there. And to get away. Darkness so thick you could touch it if you put your hand out. Rough blankets chafing my face and body as we bumped over ground never designed for vehicles. The smell and sound of water. I was being carried and there were cries, a voice shouting. Something pulling at me, wrenching me so much I cried out. Then I was here.

I wake to a sense of foreboding that lingers when I blink the sleep out of my eyes. Something has gone. Tears gloss my pillow, the stripes of the ticking are darkened. Dread. A tight feeling of sickness in my throat as if all night something has been sitting on my chest. Squatting on top of me, compressing my ribs towards the bed. I can't move or breathe. Sometimes I catch it, as my eyes open: weighing down, pinning me like a dead moth in a case, hidden from the light and air. When I call out, my voice is dust dry, a whisper of sand. And I picture myself: '*soft sift in an hourglass*'. Time trickling down through the narrow opening in the glass. Running out.

Then I turn and Robbie's there. His breath going in and out easily. I interlace my legs with his and reach for his warmth, let my breathing settle until I slide back into sleep, the whispers of the river threading through our dreams. Water flowing away from us, down to the sea, letting us feel safe.

Today the soil is beginning to warm up, so it's time for sowing the seed in long rows. Potatoes will soon be growing; tender green leaves pushing up to the light, and we'll earth them up as Daniel taught us when we first found our way here, as he teaches all new arrivals, drawing the soil up to protect the delicate shoots. We make the best of this thin, sandy soil, but the crops are meagre. This year the food has lasted well over the winter, stored in the sheds and in the ice house; although onions are beginning to sprout and the apples are softening and wrinkling, the stocks are edible. If we're lucky, we snare rabbits. We're always hungry.

It's months since anyone came, and years since anyone stayed. This time the new arrivals are a whole family; there are children. When I say whole, I mean each individual part is present: a mother and her two children: a girl and a baby. (We don't expect the fathers. We don't want there to be men.) But each part isn't whole – it's obvious when they speak – each part is damaged and broken, hardly fitting together. A clock that has worn down and will no longer tick out time, let alone chime. How could it? But it will get better for them, through simple repetition. They'll find that out for themselves, once they settle in. The soothing of basic chores and routine. Hypnotic. Meditative. Sowing seed, digging and weeding. Human company. Others with the same beliefs and values. Friends. Lovers. If we let them stay. Robbie takes their temperatures. We can't risk TB or one of the new viruses latched onto micro plastics, swilling around in the floods, floating invisibly in the damp air.

When I bring the family fresh milk, they look at me suspiciously. Their skin is lustreless, their hair long and lank. They've not had milk for weeks, the mother tells me. Tomorrow I'll let them watch me milking the goats and show them how to do it. They can collect the eggs. Everyone has to help. Now we have six female goats we make yoghurt and cheese. Everything is stored. We grow fruit and vegetables, harvest herbs. Anything edible. All the old skills and knowledge we thought had gone or been forgotten. The newer ideas of forest gardening that Daniel is trying to establish. In the winter, we freeze food in the old ice house once we've extracted enough ice from the river. And Daniel has made a bee hive. 'The land of milk and honey,' he jokes. One day, he hopes, he'll track down some bees, I tell the girl. Like all of us, she must crave sweetness. We long for summer when the earth will warm up enough to produce fresh growth. We're sick of musty bottled plums and mouldy vegetables.

A woman with children is something to celebrate, but each in our own way we're unsettled and keep our distance. We know nothing about them. Today the girl is up early and comes with me when I go to milk the goats.

'Does it hurt them?' she asks.

'It would hurt them more if we didn't,' I say.

'My mum hasn't got any milk. That's why my brother is so small. That's why we call him Tiny.'

In the early morning light her teeth are stained. Her skin looks flaky. How long must it have been since they had a proper meal? Her brother has none of the folded fat and clefts of flesh you'd expect of a baby. But he looks up at me and smiles.

'The men stopped us. Mum didn't eat,' she says quietly. 'They wouldn't let us go.' She points at the metal hooks on the wall of the milking shed. 'Have you got guns too? Or only those things?' The spades and forks hanging on the hooks.

'They're for gardening. Or for cutting down trees. Chopping up wood. We don't need weapons. We don't fight.'

One day, when she's older, I'll show her where the lost people are buried, on the other side of the hill, where the last rays warm the earth as the sun sets.

'Can they find us here?' She speaks in a whisper. 'I don't want them to hurt me again. Or my mum.'

When I move to put my arm around her, she flinches, as if my touch could injure her. She has suffered, the whole family has, and we need to ask questions. To find out what level of threat we could be facing. Who it could be. I bite my tongue. It's her mother we need to speak to, not this girl. I let it go, but I won't forget. People say how flexible young people are, how easily they adapt; they don't want to admit how easily they can be damaged too. I do my best to comfort her.

I pat the goats and feel their steamy warmth as they tug and nibble at my clothes. Their coarse hair. Soft ears.

'Would you like to stroke them? They're very gentle.'

She gives a half-smile, showing her damaged teeth again, and tentatively puts out her hand.

I find Robbie up to his waist in water, working on the mill wheel. He doesn't see me and, for a minute, I allow myself to watch him. Whatever he does he's determined to finish it; if there's a problem, he wants to solve it. Looking at him braced in position, hauling on a rope as if this is the kind of work he's always done, you'd never imagine those hands giving injections or changing bandages, comforting the distressed. But that was a long time ago, before all this happened. He's changing the filters that take out all the plastic that washes down the river. It has to be done every week, all year round, otherwise the wheel will stop turning. That would be a disaster. It's bad enough if the river freezes over, which it often does now, although it was rare only ten years ago. The plastic gets into everything. He turns, looking for Daniel, who must have gone for other tools. When he sees me, his face changes and he smiles. The smile that melts me a little and softens the hardness I carry with me.

When Daniel gets back and they secure the rope in position, Robbie wades out and stands on the bank, breathing heavily. Icy water drips down and puddles at our feet. I tell him about the woman. Her name is Nula. Her daughter is Jamila.

'Give it time, Anna. We can question them in a day or two. They've only just got here.'

He's preoccupied with keeping the mill wheel working smoothly, and turns back to look at Daniel adjusting the rope, anxious to get back and help. I know we need it for flour and what little electricity we can generate.

'Anyone who's made it this far north and gone through the camps will be traumatised,' he says. 'Let them settle in. Make them comfortable. I think they're OK, but keep an eye on them.'

With so many tasks there's never time for a proper conversation, and at bedtime we're too tired to talk. As I'm falling asleep it comes back to me again. Our own arrival.

'Get down!' A strong hand pushed me into the bottom of

the boat, down where the oozy smell of sewage and rotting wood made me gag. The light went out and we were in a darkness so thick it blanketed my nose and mouth, filled my ears. The other man pulled the oars to, and we were still, rocking with the waves. In the distance, a sound I'd hardly noticed grew from the angry buzz of a caught fly to the roaring of an outboard motor.

'It's them. Curfew,' he whispered. 'Can't be here after dark. Don't move.' His hand on my back.

Eventually the sound faded away, then he released me and I pulled myself up to sitting again.

'It's safe, Dad. Let's go.' The younger man rubbed his hands together to warm them, then picked up the oars.

'I'm Ewan,' he said, and started rowing. 'And this is our dad, George.'

There was no moon to guide us or keep us company in the immensity of that night. A thick covering of damp cloud. I shivered myself to sleep and woke to another grey dawn, Ewan carrying me.

'I'm OK. I can walk,' I said, struggling out of his arms. But I couldn't. My legs were weak. I couldn't make them do what I wanted. Ewan laughed and picked me up again. Robbie limped along next to us, helped by old George.

I remember the sound of water flowing. A river.

Ahead of us, surrounded by trees and low hills, a gaunt building rose up. Grey stone walls. The rhythmic beat and creak of a mill wheel turning.

'Welcome to the Mill,' said Ewan.

Two

I'm the first to notice. Something about the way Jamila walks makes me look more closely. The way her mother guides her, takes extra care of her, as if she's as vulnerable as her baby brother.

I'm up in the tree again watching, feeling the movement through my legs, arms, stomach. The wind pushing against the tree trunk. Sap rising into my tongue. It shivers like someone knocking against a bowl of water – ripples on the surface. A trembling in me. Robbie says it's a psychological weakness, that's all. Since I was ill. It's the kind of thing he knows, as a psychiatric nurse. Colours, sounds, smells set it going – the ripples over the water. As if I'm stepping with a fragile glass bowl full of water. A moment of stillness when the surface of silver liquid becomes a mirror, a camera obscura, and there I see it. A screen, like a scan, but clearer; none of the grainy features, the buzzing of the machines, the bleeping of measurements. Cold gel on my belly and the radiographer pushing down. Curve of a spine, limbs curled, a muscle twitching, beating. The kernel of the nut tucked into the shell of the ribs. Beating. Then, a blank. And it's gone. I'm back on the earth, the tree pulling up above me. My fingers on rough, fissured bark, my feet on fallen leaves. Smell of rotting leaves.

I need to let Robbie know. I need to tell him now. I try to run, but stumble, of course: my legs don't keep up with my brain. He's at the edge of the tenter field, where they used to stretch out cloth to dry. Today he's fixing the signals. His hands tightening the wires and feeling for breaches in the circuit. I know what he'll say. How he'll look. I stop and wave. Try to slow my breathing, but he's already seen it – he can read me too well.

'You're sweating. Your hands are cold. What's wrong?'

'Been walking fast to get warm. I'm OK.'

'Sure?' Ever since I was ill he wants to protect me.

I nod.

'You're not breathing properly. Take a deep breath.'

'I'm OK.' I pull away from him and lift up a heavy drum of wire to put away.

'Let me.'

I'm too quick for him and pile it up with the rest before he can grab hold of it.

'Jesus, Anna! What's wrong with you? I'm only trying to help.'

I put my arms around him. 'Everything's fine. I'm good.'

His lips are warm and soft against mine. His body relaxes. I find myself thinking how lucky I am, to have found a tall man. I'm only an inch or two shorter. When you're built like a hockey player people think you're invulnerable, as if body size were inversely proportional to the capacity to feel sad or afraid. But Robbie knows that conflict, even a raised voice, makes me shrink inside. Now his need to protect me makes me want to hang on to what I think I've seen a little longer. I hate being the one to cause disagreements in our precarious, small community. And I'm scared of his reaction to my visions, dreams, call them what you will. I don't want to feel like I'm going under again.

It's much later, a few days or even a week, when the girl finally allows us to help her bathe and change into a fresh set of clothes. By then we've both noticed. We women. Tracey and I.

Late winter sun is filtering through broken cloud, catching

on the river as it rushes over the weir. Jamila is watching the mill wheel turning, as the corn is ground into the rough meal we use to make bread. Not the fluffy, white loaves old George remembers, fresh from the bakers and supermarkets of his childhood, crusty bread that soaks up stews or soup. You have to chew this dark, grainy bread until it makes a thick porridge in your mouth. It's hard to get all the stones out but we're used to it now; we eat carefully, slowly. Nobody wants to break a tooth. We're proud of what we do here. How we keep ourselves alive on the edge of a precipice. But there are limits to how many we can feed.

Now that Jamila is eating better, her eyes have started to shine. Her long, braided hair has regained its sheen; it already looks thicker. But she's slight, so small and underdeveloped, how can it be true? She can't be more than fifteen, or sixteen at most. Her mother, Nula, has left the baby asleep in a corner of the mill, surrounded by empty sacks, a safe cocoon, and helps to fill sacks with flour. She's a hard worker. Sinewy. Lean. Not an extra ounce of flesh. Strong. I think she knows about her daughter, but I'm not sure; this needs to be handled carefully. She's a stranger; I've no idea how she'll take it.

It's been a good day, a filling meal for a change. Stew made with the last few rubbery carrots and stringy leeks floating in a skin of fat. The usual unidentifiable threads of meat. Rabbit, most likely. Trying to stay close to the fire, candle flames leaping.

Nula rubs her eyes with one hand. 'Is this the only light you've got?' she says. 'Even in the camps you get electricity. I can hardly see what I'm eating.'

Daniel laughs. 'We get power from the windfarms off the Solway coast, between here and Ireland, but it's intermittent. We'd like our own solar panels, but who's making them? No infrastructure, steel industry, chemical industry…'

'We've got paraffin for the storm lamps. For emergencies. We keep the wind-up dynamo lamps for the bedrooms. Candles are too dangerous for the kids,' I say. 'To be honest, it's best not to see what you're eating!'

'Aye, you'll have to learn not to twine about it,' George says. 'In the war you had to eat what you were given. I don't know where you've been for the last few years, lass! Them Flood camps must be better than what Anna told me.'

Daniel winks at me. George has a habit of talking about the Second World War as if he had lived through it; he wasn't born until the 1950s. He's inherited his grandmother's memories and sayings as well as some of her wartime recipes... *make do and mend... walls have ears. I was four years old when they took bacon and meat off the ration, you know.* It's a running joke. But there is a truth in this that no one wants to talk about. *Walls have ears.*

Jamila's plate is full. She yawns, pushing down her spoon, then leans on her mother's shoulder, tickling Tiny's feet. I'm sure I heard her in the latrines today, throwing up. She came out looking drawn, wiping her mouth with the back of her hand, holding on to the door frame to steady herself. Now in the flickering candlelight she's smiling, almost relaxing.

To leave food these days is a sin. I'll never forget how a child in one of the Flood camps was punished for taking a few apples.

George clears his throat and tuts.

"Eat up, Jay,' Nula says, and Jamila wrinkles her nose, shakes her head. 'We can cover it and keep it for later,' her mother says. 'You need to eat, love.'

Jamila sighs and spoons down the food. Daniel is tapping his fingers on the table, then picks up his violin. He always has music going through his head – it helps us relax in the evenings.

Tracey nods at me. We discussed it by the mill pond, the

wooden wheel creaking its familiar rhythm as the water rushed over it, masking our conversation. I'm the one who has to talk to Nula.

'Can you help me bring in more logs, Nula?' I say. 'Jamila can look after Tiny.'

'But he's getting whingey. I can't make him stop once he starts.'

Jamila takes her baby brother out of her mother's hands roughly and he starts crying. She jiggles him until he stops. She does know what to do; she's obviously used to looking after him.

Outside there's a hard frost, the moon hanging in the branches of the trees like a bright pearl. It's too cold to speak. We each take a basket and walk around the side of the building to the wood store. After the warmth inside, my body shudders before I touch the metal latch. When we're inside, under shelter, I reach down and put my hand on her arm, as she reaches for the logs. She turns as if she's been stung and looks around wildly, into the corners of the enclosure as if there might be danger hiding there, then turns her face up to mine and smiles nervously, pulling her blanket closer round her shoulders. When she smiles her face is transformed. Not a face you'd call pretty, but one you want to look at, to find out what it is, in the distance between nose, eyes and mouth, in the colour of the brown eyes, that makes it compelling. Something about the way she walks and holds herself. A controlled elegance. I've seen how the men can't help themselves, drawn to look at her, even Robbie. I can't help staring at her.

'What's wrong? You scared me.'

'Nula. I need to ask you –'

'I already know.' There's no hesitation.

'But does Jamila…?'

Her basket clatters to the ground, crystals of ice catching

the moonlight like shattered glass. She puts her head in her hands and shakes with noiseless tears, willing them not to fall, not to show weakness. But she lets me comfort her. I can feel the skin stretched over her starved body, the hard muscles and the knots in her shoulder where bones have healed.

'She's too young. I don't know what to do.'

I offer the warmth from my arms, but I don't speak; then she draws a breath and tells me, her voice a monotone.

'We thought we'd got away, but then they came. After the camp. Five of them. My Jamila. They took turns while I screamed for them to stop. The baby crying in my arms. He wouldn't stop crying. One of them. Fair-haired, he was. A young face. I begged him not to. When he said he wouldn't take me instead, I kicked him as hard as I could. Then he took me anyway.'

She pulls away from me, her eyes glittering. 'I want to kill them all.' She starts throwing logs back in the basket. 'I want them dead.' Her voice a mutter: 'And I want to get rid of it.'

'Of course you don't.' I take the basket out of her hands. Compared to her dark, finely shaped fingers, mine are cumbersome and blunted; large, but also weak. 'Listen, Nula. You'll tell her. Help her understand. That's what you need to do. Look after her. We all will.'

'We need to get rid of it,' she says.

As if it's a matter of choice, here in the black nights of winter. As if she could simply choose to abort this baby. Without pain relief. We're lucky if we can get paracetamol, let alone antibiotics. Herbal remedies are all we usually have.

'Their dirty hands and stinking bodies. I don't want to be reminded of their faces every time I look at it.' She coughs and spits away into the dark.

'No one's got the medical equipment,' I say. 'It's too dangerous. Please don't make it worse for her.'

'How can it be *worse*?'

She's a snarling animal. And I have no answers. No way of reassuring her.

'You have to tell her. She needs to know what's happening to her body.'

Nula starts sobbing. A terrible, raw sound. I reach down to touch her, but this time she pushes me away.

'If you want me to…' I start. 'If you think it might come better from me, from another woman.'

She sweeps the tears away with both hands. The flicker of a smile. 'You're not a mother. You're young too, late twenties, right?'

I nod.

'I'll tell her my own way, OK?' She turns to pick up the basket of logs. 'I'll speak to her tonight.'

By the time we get back, everyone has left the kitchen and the heat is already dissipating. Ewan and his father to the lookout. Everyone else to their rooms. In the fading light of the fire I see playing cards spread out on the table, as if someone has started a game then given up. Even the kids are too tired. We're all exhausted. Early nights in winter to save on heating.

Daniel's dog, Victor, gets up, wagging his tail, and I give him a pat to settle him. Having dogs gives us some feeling of safety. I light a candle and walk up the stone steps to our room. In the shower, Robbie is singing to himself. I'll shower in the morning. All I want to do is get warm, so I take off one layer of clothes and get into bed. We're so different: I laugh at things as a defence against our grim lives, but underneath I don't feel it. I do it for everyone else. He's naturally cheerful. He comes into the room, towelling himself vigorously. 'I never thought a cold shower would be the height of luxury.' He shakes his head like a Labrador, drops the towel and rubs his head where his hair has receded so much he's taken to shaving it close to his scalp. He pushes the box against the door and slides quickly into bed.

'You OK? How's Nula?' His lips brush mine, then he lies back and yawns. 'Is she going to pull her weight?'

'Yes. Can I tell you something.?'

But he turns onto his side. 'Will it keep till tomorrow?' Within seconds he's dropped into sleep.

I turn into his narrow back and breathe in his familiar smell. I'll tell him in the morning. With his medical knowledge he'll know what to do. That's what I promise myself. I'll tell him when I get a chance. When there's time to talk about it properly. I have so little I can call my own; sometimes the smallest things give me a sense of power.

When I see them the next day Jamila walks lightly, as if she's been relieved of a burden; she dances over the frosty ground. Almost like a child.

'Anna, I've got to tell you first.' She's breathless with excitement. 'Mum says it's not a secret. It's not, is it, Mum?'

Nula, carrying Tiny, smiles at us both. 'It doesn't matter who you tell, love. But slow down… Tell Anna. And Tracey too, if you like. We'll let the others know in good time.' She means the men.

Jamila stretches up and whispers, 'God's given me a baby. Because of what happened. He wants me to be happy again. It's in here.' She points to her belly and laughs. 'When it's grown enough, he'll take it out and it can be my own baby. And when it's big it can play with Tiny.' She blows a raspberry on her brother's tummy. He giggles. 'Only you've got to be nice to her, Tiny. No bullying, OK?'

When she hugs me it almost hurts. I kiss her soft cheek.

'I'll race you to the field,' she says, laughing, and springs away from us.

When I was a child I ran everywhere. Away from my

parents when they argued. To the top of the local park, along the river bank at Kew racing the river. Looking at Jamila as she sprints off, I realise again how much I've changed; I used to be so strong, and now every movement is an effort.

'Thanks, Nula,' I say when Jamila is out of earshot.

'I didn't have much choice, did I?' She shrugs.

'Robbie's a nurse; he has medical skills. Will you let him help her?'

'No! No men! That's enough.' She strides away from me, determined. 'What needs to be done today? I'll do what I can.' And that's the end of the subject.

'If you go to the field, Daniel's there. He'll tell you.'

'But what will I do with Tiny?'

'I'll take Tiny inside. It's good for him to go to different people. Tracey loves children. She practically brought up her little brother after their mother died.'

Nula narrows her eyes.

'Ewan. He's Tracey's brother. Fifteen years younger.'

She hesitates, holding on to the baby straining in her arms. Then she sighs, kisses him and gives him to me. 'Make sure he's safe. None of the men, right? I don't want them near him.'

She walks away, pulling herself up to her full height. She doesn't look back.

When I take him up to the nursery, Tracey is already there, cleaning the highchair, and has set out what baby toys we have. She's so absorbed in what she's doing she jumps when I approach her.

'Oo, lass, I thought you were a ghost!' Her grin is lopsided. She usually hides her long teeth when she talks. Not now. She puts her arms out and her face lights up when I hand him over. He goes readily.

'He looks like his mam. Nobody to play with but me. Poor

la'al thing.' She presses her lips to the top of his head and breathes in. 'Babbies smell lovely, don't they? She loves her kids, doesn't she? I'll look after him, Anna. I won't let owt happen to him.'

She means it. She'd give her life for a child. I know that. She's never told me herself; George, her father, did. How she pulled her little brother from the flood when their mother was swept away. That choice. She's a strong woman. Intuitive. Kind.

'You know, Anna, I saw two magpies today. *One for sorrow, two for joy*!'

Before I leave the room she's singing quietly. A sound I've not heard for a long time. There's a brightness in her voice.

As I walk back to the field, I can see them all bent to the task. Nula is digging up some of the leeks we leave in the ground over winter. This year they've grown tall and fat, full of flavour; they're good this year. Jamila has started on one of the rows where the soil needs to be prepared to plant potatoes. Her mother stands up and shouts something and they both smile; but there's something wrong and I don't know what it is, a darkness that won't go away. I need to speak to Nula again.

The sun catches on the metal of the tools and on the river down in the valley below us. Rushing over the weir the sound of water is constant. A hush of noise that can mask a whisper.

'She's no idea, has she?' I say.

'What?' Nula's been working hard, out of breath. She stands up straight and smiles. 'Jamila knows she's going to have a baby. That's all she needs to know. Look how happy she is. I want to see her smiling like that for a change.'

Our voices are covered by the river, but Jamila sees me and waves.

'She needs to know what's going to happen to her body.'

'I don't want you interfering. I'm her mother, right?'

'She'll have to be told one day, unless –'

'I've agreed not to get rid of it.' Nula's voice is rising; she's angry. 'Jamila's never had a period. I was a late starter too. We were on the move. Surviving. Getting somewhere dry was what mattered. Not talking about the birds and the bees... I didn't even think she could *get* pregnant. Do you want me to tell my sixteen-year-old daughter she's going to have her rapist's baby?' Her dark eyes widen; her face is ugly with anger as she looks up at me. She walks away, stretching her back and arms. I don't have the strength in my legs to keep up with her. 'I don't want her to know *anything* about it, until the day it's born.'

I don't catch her up until we're nearly at the gate to the field, further away from the river, and I don't have an answer; but a thought solidifies as the words bubble up: *Ignorance is bliss.* A stock phrase from old NOAH promotion videos, emblazoned on posters. A random, irrelevant memory perhaps; I try to dismiss it, but the words echo at the back of my mind.

'If it was you, wouldn't *you* want to know? You can't wait till she's in labour.'

The words spit out like water on a hot iron. 'I'm grateful you took us in, OK? But what gives you the right to preach at me? I've had enough of people telling me what to do. She doesn't need to know until it's time, does she? You'll make sure nobody tells her.'

Before I can answer she goes to join Jamila, hoeing out weeds, and I'm left with a sense of foreboding. I can't do it on my own. I have to tell Robbie.

I've witnessed birth – it's not something you forget. We were part of the mass exodus leaving London, part of the endless crowd pulling wheelie suitcases, pushing bikes and shopping trolleys, carrying children. The ones who'd left it too late for trains or cars. It was when the crowd ahead slowed to rubberneck that we knew something was happening. Then we heard it – a woman crying and keening. On the grass verge of the motorway, I glimpsed her: half-standing, half-squatting, being supported by other women and a man, I guess he was the father. The crying turned into guttural moans with bouts of cursing. Robbie instinctively dropped my hand and ran to help, and I was carried along with everyone else, trying to keep my feet on the ground, not to let go of our belongings. The only way was to sit down, at the risk of being crushed; then everyone moved round me and I was a small island in the flood. It felt like a lifetime, but finally a cheer went up, and a wave of very British applause. Then, over the trundle of suitcases and the march of feet, we heard the unmistakeable, tiny cry of a newborn baby, quickly drowned out by the roar and bleating siren of a paramedic motorbike.

Jamila is hardly more than five foot, slim, underdeveloped. A child. It's difficult to believe she's pregnant until suddenly she throws down her hoe and runs to the edge of the field, retching and heaving. She stays there, squatting, then rubs at her mouth with the back of her hand and meets my eyes. She's scared. The knowledge of what birth entails and of her obliviousness, her mother's way of protecting her, makes me shiver.

'Sorry.' She's panting. 'I'm better now. I'll be OK.'

'I'll fetch you some water.' As I go back to the house I see Nula hugging her. She takes a cloth from her pocket and carefully wipes her mouth.

By the time I'm back, Jamila has started working, as if nothing has happened, but she downs the water in one.

'God moves in mysterious ways,' Nula says. 'You see, love, it's to make sure you slow down. So you don't harm the baby.'

'I don't want to slow down.' Jamila starts on the next row

and I walk behind picking up larger weeds to add to our compost heaps. It's the most we can do when the ground is so hard. After last night's frost the weather is clear. We'll have to wait for warmer days to plant potatoes. Spring is late this year. Even later than last year. We've constructed polytunnels to extend the season, to start crops off earlier. They gleam long and silver in the cold morning light. But, as the global climate heats up, our own warm seasons are shrinking, the weather unpredictable. Storms rise up out of nowhere; one at the wrong time can destroy a harvest.

'My back's aching. When can I stop? I'm bored, Mum,' Jamila says a few minutes later, then, realising she's contradicted herself, she laughs. They both stand up straight, hands on hips and turn to the gate. I didn't hear the bell, but with my hand cupped around my ear, I can make out Daniel's voice calling from the other end of the field. Baby Tiny is awake and needs to be fed. Without mobiles or pagers we communicate by older methods, and the thought comes to me, as it often does, that we were innocent in those days, before the water came: blindly confident that life would get better, that technology was there to make life easier and quicker. As if speed were the only thing that mattered. We ignored the signs until it was too late.

Jamila tuts and sighs dramatically. 'Mum! I've done enough! I'm tired.'

'I'll be half an hour. That's all,' Nula yells as the gate clicks shut behind her. And she's gone.

Jamila jabs her hoe into the half-frozen soil, pulling up clods of mud and weeds.

'Come on, la'al lass, that's no good.' Daniel has brought the wheelbarrow back to collect the weeds. He smiles and takes the hoe out of her hand. 'You're making a right pig's ear of it. You need to cut the roots off below the top of the soil, not dig the whole plant up.' His prematurely lined face is leathery and his nose pinched red. When he laughs his breath comes out in a long curl of steam.

'It's too hard. I can't do it.'

''Course you can. Big strong lass like you. Put a bit of welly into it.' Only Daniel could describe this slight girl like this. He never concedes anything negative, never admits defeat for himself or anyone else.

He rapidly hoes the row while she watches. She does look exhausted. The shadows under her eyes are grey and her skin has a dusty pallor, her nose shiny in the cold. Nobody gets away with slacking. Pregnancy isn't an illness, but she's a teenager and weak from lack of food. It won't be long before we'll have to tell the men. They'll react badly unless we prepare them. I know George has already spread rumours that they're NOAH spies. But George suspects everyone and everything. I bet he was a *Daily Mail* reader in the old days.

We've had health issues in the time I've been at the Mill, but we've never had to deal with a pregnancy. When Robbie's back from the market, or when we're on our own tonight I'll talk to him; he'll know what to do.

Jamila takes the hoe and starts again.

'Let her have a rest, Daniel. I think she's done enough for today.'

'Not like you to make excuses, Anna. Mellowing in your old age!'

'She's exhausted.'

Jamila is breathing heavily.

I've worked hard to earn his respect; he listens to me. I'm good at seeing weakness in others. It mirrors my own.

Daniel looks at her with narrowed eyes, then puts out his hand. 'Right. Off you go, Jamila.'

She drops the hoe and skips away, back to the house. I finish the row.

By the time Nula comes back, my body aches, every joint

burning. Daniel tells her to take over.

'You've earned a break, Anna.'

'I'll have a walk,' I say, 'then I'll help Tracey in the house.'

It's something I've taken to recently. Daniel encourages me to rest when I can. Since my illness, my body is too fragile for this degree of physical work, but who would ever want to give in? Giving in is giving up. I want to keep going, until I can't.

I leave my tools in the wheelbarrow, knock the worst of the mud off my boots, and take the narrow path up through the woods to the park at the top of the hill. Funny we call it the park. There's a rusty slide and an empty frame for swings, the parts taken for better use. You can't waste metal. Names stick.

When I get there and stop for a breather, Ewan is on the lookout in his red hat, tufts of blond hair sticking out, binoculars slung round his neck. Fowler, his dog, is sitting on the ground, ready to bark at strangers. Ewan gives me a nod and climbs down to speak to me, his strong legs making the ladder creak. He smiles broadly. He has his darker moods but most days he'll be the one to laugh. When I first came to the Mill, so much of what I loved was lost, but I couldn't help noticing those blue eyes, flecked with gold, that straight nose, the kind I've only seen in paintings. It's hard to believe he's Tracey's little brother. 'An afterthought', George calls him.

'How's the back? I was watching you down there. Tried more of that herbal stuff I got you?'

I shrug.

'You should take it easy. That la'al body can do her bit now. If she's staying; is she?'

I'm out of breath with the climb. I manage to smile. 'Yes, I think so. I'll see you for lunch, Ewan. We'll talk about it later.'

'Aye lass. You off to see your dad?'

I nod.

'Well, I'll sithee then.' He turns and adjusts his field glasses, stamps his feet to keep warm then begins the climb back up the ladder. I carry on up to the other side of the hill.

Being on lookout can be arduous. Standing on the platform between the oak, sycamore and lime trees, high on the hillside in all weathers, even if it's a relief to have time to yourself. Scanning the horizon from the line of the old A66 towards Keswick, over to the mass of Grasmoor End in one direction, towards the coast in the other until your vision blurs, expecting the worst, hoping your whistle doesn't pack in when you need it. Lonely or bored. Sometimes the sound of voices from another settlement, the flash of a window opening, the smell, on certain days from the smoke house down in the town where they preserve fish and meat. The malt smell from the old brewery.

When we first arrived, I could fight back if I had to; my hearing hadn't deteriorated. I take my turn, not that they expect me to. I won't give up easily.

All the time we've been at the Mill the water has been steadily rising, as the rain that rarely stops quietly hisses on its surface. I've often stood where Ewan is, wishing everything could have been different, that it hadn't come to this. The thought is automatic, associated with this walk up the path, mud crumbling under my feet. Tree roots and blackberry bushes hold the hillside together with long spiky stems that arch over and tangle to form dense thickets where rabbits hide. The curse of gardening. But rabbit stew is a favourite, so we allow some to live. A balance between pest and prey.

In the early days, when shops were well stocked and shelves full of tinned goods, packets of rice and pasta, there was plenty to eat. Fresh food soon went, eaten or rotten; but you could make a feast from a few tins, as George says, and if the labels were washed off by floodwater, you had some surprise meals. But once electricity went, freezers and fridges were only full of mould. It didn't take long for it all to go. Ransacked or left to quietly rot. No lorries coming up and down the motorways to restock. No shelf fillers working through the night.

A new silence, apart from people walking, dragging suitcases, pushing trolleys, wheeling baby buggies, the endless lines of refugees from the south, the occasional helicopter hovering overhead. The few who survived the flood organised themselves as well as they could, back to hunting and gathering, to subsistence farming. Seeds became a currency, looted from the cavernous garden centres full of the vegetable stink of dying plants; seeds endlessly recycled, saved and reused. A fragile, thin life when we've lost so much, and it's all our fault. But a life.

At the top of the hill, I turn round to see beyond our own valley, where the Buttermere fells rise up like a stone wall with a sprinkling of fine snow. They look near enough to touch; ten miles though, and hard walking when we came, the river in flood and the land drowning as the two narrow lakes became one. Now it looks peaceful. I shake my head to get rid of the memory.

Down through the trees I can make out the red of Ewan's hat against the moving background grey of water. Here the river flows north, tumbling white over the rocks and slate until it reaches our mill pond and becomes a still, dark eye reflecting the blue of the sky. Even on a warm summer's day, when clouds are piled into towering heaps, the mill pond is dark. Like ink or fresh tar. And there's the weir, holding the river back, a ridge of stone and rubble held by the forces of the structure and by plants lodging and growing, knitting it all back together after the floods. One day, after we arrived, I came up here with Robbie, picking blackberries in the autumn, feasting on them until we felt sick. We'd lost everything, but we'd arrived, we were safe. And Dad was here.

Three

The path leads between two wind-stunted crab apple trees, each with traces of miniature ruby fruit clinging to the branches, then past the rotting bandstand and the moss-covered bowling green, and over to the far side, facing west. You can't see it, but the sea is only seven miles away.

The sea! Growing up in London, I remember the excitement of a seaside holiday – playing on the beach all day, swimming in the cold water of the North Sea or the Atlantic. Fish and chips on the wall of a promenade. Ice cream. Lying on the beach after a swim, even in England, drying off in the heat or the sea breeze, listening to the boom of the surf on the layers of sand. The rush and hush of the water. The sound of a constant withdrawing as the waves sucked in pebbles, then hurled them down again with tons of sepia-coloured water, frothing with sand. Never stopping. Since the first sea. And now it's come closer to reclaim the land. A terrible roaring that won't stop. Water has lost its attractiveness; the sea is too close, an enemy creeping up along the river, drop by drop.

I think of school science, how each cubic centimetre of water equals one gram. All you have to do is multiply to understand the weight of water. The force of moving water, of the sea, of a river in spate.

Here. This is where the townspeople were buried. Feet pointing into the setting sun, as if they could get up out of their sandy beds and admire the view. It's high enough that if the water rises again, they'll stay put. Down in the bowl of the town and along the banks of the river, hundreds were swept away, both living and dead. Plucked out of their small, busy lives into the flooding river and down to the sea. As in so many towns and cities. Imagine a vengeful god, like a small child lifting a piece of flat slate to see the tracks and channels of an ant colony, then pouring on a bucket of water.

I remember those first weeks. When there was a shelf for our belongings. A roof. Walls. How I tried to cling on to Robbie, and wouldn't let him out of my sight. How long it took not to fall asleep afraid. Not to wake up afraid. Cold and hungry. When I saw Nula and her children, I understood: it's the same for all travellers who make the long journey through the camps and get this far: no matter how unique we think we are, we're all the same, we all feel the same. Focussed on our own survival.

Robbie and I haven't been here long, less than three years, but our previous life is already like a book. Sometimes, when I go into the library up on the first floor, I imagine I could find it there, if I looked hard enough. Foxed, water-damaged, the marbled endpapers giving off the smoky, soot smell of fires that have long been doused out. The life we used to have.

~ ~ ~

The summer before we left London was hotter than usual, the best for years, perhaps even for decades. Waves of relentless heat. A fine blue sky with an unblinking sun. Looking back now, it was like the final gasp.

We'd been together for two years. Robbie was my world, and I was his. Far into the future, we'd think about kids; we were only in our twenties; we weren't ready. All night we lay in each other's arms, the sheets kicked off. When it was too hot, I could feel his breath on the back of my neck, down between my shoulder blades. If I reached round I could touch the fine skin of his arms, and even in sleep his hands relaxed and caught hold of me, held me. His long legs tangled around mine. Our friends laughed and said we were too young to settle down, but when something's right you know it deep in your body, somewhere that doesn't have an anatomical name. We knew we were lucky. Some never find that quiet contentment. That hot summer was the beginning of long years together, we thought; a golden time that would never stop.

Every morning, I cycled down to Kew Gardens, the heat already blistering the tarmac, causing a haze to ripple the cars and buses crawling over Kew Bridge. The Thames gently flowing down to the sea so far away it was like a memory. All the elegant houses on the bank of the river that had been there for centuries, lit by the morning sun. I was innocent then. Excited at the prospect of spending my days among trees and plants, of being out in the gardens where the river ran past and there was shade from the sun. Each day was mapped out – bus-loads of school kids coming from all over the country to find out about the work of the Royal Botanic Gardens, how they were leading the way in the preservation of rare species. I loved the changing seasons, and I loved working with new groups of children. Their infectious enthusiasm. I never minded what the weather was like – rain, snow, fog or sun.

I feel happy surrounded by trees, and Kew felt like the safest place in the world. But, by mid-summer that year, trees were starting to lose their leaves. They crunched underfoot. It was only August. It never seemed to rain, and everywhere was covered in a fine dust. We were both worried about the climate, me more than Robbie. He would come home from his shift in the hospital, complaining of the heat, and jump straight in the shower to wash off the dust and cool down. Then we sat on our tiny balcony, eating pasta and drinking cold beer. When Dad came over for a meal every Thursday, we talked long into the evening, watching swifts flying high above our heads making their shrill squeaking cries, until the sun sank in a flush of red, and a few pale stars were visible over the London skyline. Even at night it was hot. We enjoyed it. We were happy.

But it wasn't right. We all knew that. Dad especially. He was an independent scientist, advising the government.

'All these committees and working parties,' he said. 'So much talking and endless emails. It's all party politics and keeping the public sweet for the next election. Nothing ever gets *done*.'

'Come on, Dad. Everyone knows it's happening. They can't ignore the evidence. They have to listen to *you*. You're one of the experts.'

'They never see the urgency. I'm hitting my head against a brick wall.'

After an hour of this, Robbie would head indoors to fetch another beer, then Dad would start on his other favourite topic – a place in West Cumbria on the edge of the Lake District where they were making a go of sustainable living. The Mill.

'We had a couple of holidays there when you were a kid, Anna.'

I didn't remember. I only remembered the seaside.

Once Dad got started it was difficult to stop him. I knew from the way Robbie was tapping his foot, then when he started sniffing and rubbing his nose, he was bored. Irritated. He claimed it was the dust.

'On an early tomorrow. I need my eight hours,' he'd say, yawning, leaving me to try to calm Dad down. Or to change the subject.

Later, when I joined Robbie in bed, he'd laugh and put his arms round me. 'Your father is crazy. Banging on about the Mill. Like it's some Blakean paradise. No way am I going to join a commune of smelly hippies.'

'He's trying to think of answers. That's all. If nothing happens soon, if the government doesn't do something…' I started. But I confess I didn't take it seriously either. Dad was in his late fifties, too old to start a new life in the countryside. And he loved London.

One evening, it was late August by then, the city was baking and a hosepipe ban had been in place for three weeks. Railway tracks were buckling, commuters stuck for hours on crowded trains. Thick dust on every surface. The smell of bad drains. Dad was getting started. Robbie had slipped away to bed as usual.

Dad took a long drink then placed the bottle on the table. He looked over the balcony at the young plane trees that had been planted when our flats were built, their remaining leaves dry and brittle.

'Anna, I spoke to your mother last week,' he said quietly.

'What?'

He sighed. 'I know.'

'But I thought… I didn't know you were in touch.' I'd not seen my mother since she left us. The occasional birthday card until I reached eighteen and sometimes a phone call at Christmas. We weren't close. She had her own life. Dad never met anyone else.

He shrugged and half smiled. 'Well, we are.'

'What do you mean?'

He took hold of my hand. Something he rarely did.

'I tried to get her to come with me.'

'What are you talking about?'

'The Mill, Anna, that's the place to go,' he said and squeezed my hand.

"Did she say yes?'

He shook his head. 'I had to try. I couldn't not try. No, she's staying in Paris… But I want you and Robbie to come. You have to.'

I laughed and pulled my hand away slowly. 'I'll think about it, but I'd need to find a job up there first.'

'This place is fucked. The city.' He drank down the rest of his beer and got up. 'Look at it. This is only the beginning… or the beginning of the end.'

He stood tall and straight, and rubbed his hand along his beard, pointing to the trees, the brown grass and the haze of pollution. 'Look at it. It's bad here. But it's going to get worse. You've seen the news. In other countries there are already water wars, fires out of control and crops failing. We're not exempt. One day soon it's going to be here and there's nothing we can do to stop it. It's already happening.'

I'd never seen him so serious. 'I'll think about it.'

'You've got to. Both of you.'

'I'll message you.'

'Speak to Rob. It's time to get out of here. I know what I'm talking about, love. You can't argue against the science. We're at the tipping point and God knows what's going to happen. This government is flailing around and before you know it someone with a clear plan will barge in and try to take control. Could be the NOAH lot for all we know, with their false promises of a better life, secure jobs.' When he laughed it had a hollow sound.

I kissed his cheek, feeling his beard scratch my lips. It was flecked with grey now, his hair thinning on top. I could smell the sun on his skin. He hugged me hard.

'We'll see you next Thursday.'

'I know you're an adult, you can make your own decisions. But you're my little girl.'

'Dad! Mum said I was built like a rugby player.'

'Well, that's your mother for you. You're my little girl.'

I hugged him again. 'You're getting soft!'

A week later he messaged to say he wouldn't be there for dinner; there were things he had to do. He tried hard to persuade me, but I said no. A fortnight later he'd gone. For a few short weeks we had messages from him, but then he said he was at the Mill and electricity was only for essential uses. So that was it. Robbie and me, soaking up the last rays of sun.

Then the weather turned. The rain began and everyone relaxed and smiled at strangers again. It was so wet you took an umbrella every time you left the house. The wettest autumn on record. Electric storms, high winds and hurricanes buffeted our small island, and the flood warnings started: yellow, orange and red triangles marched over the map of the country. Moss crept over walls and pavements, filling the gaps like spongy, green mortar, covering the trunks of trees, statues and lamp posts. In graveyards, it erased the names of the forgotten dead, and when the wind blew, lumps of it fell from gutters and roofs. The lions in Trafalgar Square grew a thick pelt of vivid green.

Soon, we were all experts in rain. Like all the Inuit words for snow – we had to invent a new language. The sound of it – dripping, roaring, splashing and falling. The look and smell of it. Rain falling on the roof tiles, gurgling down the drainpipes. I remember when the Antony Gormley figures on the coast at Crosby that had survived the ebb and flow of tides for decades finally disappeared under the rising sea. I'd never seen them in real life. Dad had often said he'd take me. It felt like an omen.

But, for a while, we felt safe. We had the Thames barrier and other flood defences and we lived well above the flood plain – cycling home from Kew was uphill all the way. And the weather would change. 'It always does,' said Robbie. But the rain continued, unrelenting, as if it were the end of the world. Which, looking back, perhaps it was. The end of our predictable world.

So close to the Thames, the trees at Kew were soon standing in water; it was impossible to carry on showing school groups around, and I was directed to help with the emergency measures. For a few short weeks, sandbags protected the gilt pagoda. But one day it slumped over, the foundations soft and damaged; it was all over social media. (In those days there was always someone with a smartphone ready.) Then the glass houses started filling with water, like enormous Victorian aquariums. The army was called in, and I had to work remotely, updating the education pages of the website. I imagined London, Bristol and Manchester becoming cities of canals and lagoons like Venice or Amsterdam; if they did, we'd make the best of it, I told Robbie. 'Whatever happens you'll not be out of a job. They'll need nurses.' And we waited.

The internet was full of 'end of the world' scaremongering, IKEA had a promotion on flat-packed boats (for use in emergencies) and *The Daily Mail* had a special on war-time recipes; but it was only when the government issued instructions on what to do in a flash flood that the panic buying started and the slow trickle of people leaving turned into an exodus. Street by street, houses and tower blocks were condemned and, as the Thames swelled, trains and coaches left the city in a mass evacuation like the Second World War. Talk of the Blitz spirit was common. Major roads out of London had exits guarded by the military: the Western gate, the Great West, Great Northern, Old Kent: single drivers had to take passengers. *Four to a car* was the slogan. It was rush hour all day. Then there was rationing and queues for everything – fuel, as well as food. It was the same further north – the whole country thrown into emergency measures.

Churches and temples (at least the ones on higher ground) were full, all religions praying together for the rain to stop. Food banks were set up for flooded-out families. Sales of boats went through the roof. When hashtag NOAH went viral and there was a fashion for long beards and robes, Robbie's younger brother, Simon, joined NOAH. *Turn to NOAH and forget all your troubles.*

'Cranks. Patriarchy and organised religion gone mad. If it gets more extreme, it'll be a danger to rational society.' Robbie laughed when he told me. 'I don't know how he could live on a boat. He hated canal holidays!'

But underneath it all, I knew he was worried about Simon; his brother's health was precarious. It was his frequent suicide attempts that had pushed Robbie into the mental health side of nursing. But nothing he said could stop him going.

Perhaps we were naïve, but in those days we had some faith in the government – they would do something to save us all, to save our towns and cities. It wasn't too late.

~ ~ ~

I remember the smoke of the fire rising high into the still air, the repetitive squeaking of the mill wheel turning. Thinking *we're here at last.* And, in spite of the exhaustion of the journey, a thrill rippling through me that I would see him again. But it's Daniel's face I recall now when I said who I was; the wordless way he pulled me in with both arms and hugged me told me everything.

My father was a strong man, invincible; when the water was too high he would have carried me on his shoulders if he could. He would have fought off wild animals. But that hot, summer's evening in London was the last time I saw him. I got here too late. Working at the Mill to finally realise his vision of a new world, he was killed by the smallest thing – a rusty nail. Without tetanus shots, antibiotics, there was nothing they could do.

Others have traditional, wooden crosses, standing out against the sun like stunted trees. A whole field of them, a growing forest making long shadows. Here's his grave marked by a pile of river stones. Dad didn't believe in God. Noah's flood. Ark-building. He believed in the land.

The graveyard shimmers and distorts but it's too cold for tears, and today the sun is shining.

'What you crying for? Chin up,' he'd say. 'You're here. You're safe. Keep going, love. I know you can do it.'

'But I miss you, Dad. I still miss you.'

The wind sighs up in the trees, rustles in the long stems of dead grasses.

There's a flash of brown and red, and a robin perches on the twig of a tree, so close I can see its tiny beak open as it begins its piercing song. Back down the hill behind me there's an echo. I know it's claiming its territorial rights, not singing for my pleasure, but it's beautiful, and for a moment I feel the song threading us together with a life we share, the bird and I. All of us who have survived. I wipe my cheeks and blow my nose. I leave my younger self at the graveside and go back down to do what needs to be done.

Four

In the kitchen, it's so warm my cheeks burn from the cold. Jamila is helping prepare lunch, the usual soup with variations, the steamy air scented with onions and sage, condensation dripping down the thin glass of the window onto the deep sill. With low ceilings, heat soon warms the room, as long as we're generous with the fire, or the cooker is on. It helps dry the washing, up on the pulley, not that clothes get washed that often. In summer, the thick stone walls keep the house cool. The long wooden table is set with spoons, knives and a loaf of hard, grainy bread twisted into a plait. Nula must be trying to impress us. There's a jam jar of small flowers: yellow cups frilled with green are winter aconites, and nodding between them the white ovals of snowdrops, each petal green-stippled.

I won't acknowledge it openly, but, according to the official calendar pinned up on the noticeboard it's Candlemas day, and I have a strong suspicion Nula has been telling her daughter snowdrops mean purity and a clean start after the winter. I remember learning all the festivals once, but no one here pays them much attention. Smiling to herself as she sets out plates and bowls, chipped from constant use, Jamila smooths her thin hand over her tiny bump. She wants to be noticed. It's time to tell the men. But I know they won't like it; a few more days won't hurt. I'll tell Robbie first.

The bell rings and everyone piles in, bringing gusts of icy air, and shouts to hurry up and shut the door. Daniel's children are first: Elsa runs in laughing, her fair hair flying behind her, and throws her coat and hat onto a chair. She rushes to find Agatha, a little jack russell, who starts yapping and jumping up at her. She's closely followed by her twin brother, Stefan. He stands, hands on his back, stretching to his full height, tall and skinny like Robbie. His nose is pink and his cheeks red and glowing, a bloom of acne along his jawline. He's cut from the same cloth as their father, but Daniel, shoulders rounded, his face lined and hair silvery-grey in the light filtering through the steamed up windows, suddenly looks old. A tough man, he never complains, but the damp weather makes us all creak and ache; I'm sure he feels the ice in his joints. Everyone coughs. Sometimes it's the smoke from the fire, or the dust that permeates every fibre of our clothes and lies on every surface no matter how often we make the effort to clean. Sometimes it's more. If someone has a bad fit of coughing, we look for the tell-tale darkness of blood. TB is on the increase. So far, we've been lucky.

Daniel's the only one standing, his eyes casting round the room; he's got something to say. He waits until we're all sitting down, with steam rising from our bowls, lumps of bread, a minute smear of goat's cheese, a platter of wrinkled, browning apples. A dish of our own hazelnuts.

'Right. I was thinking, now we've got a la'al lass, we need t' –'

'Let's eat first, eh, Dad. Everyone's starvin'. Nobody wants to eat cold soup.' Elsa catches my eye and raises an eyebrow. She's loyal and she loves her father, but like me chafes at long speeches, wants to get on and eat so she and Stefan can help George at the lookout. He's up on the hill now. At nearly eighty, he is too old for duties, but he can blow a whistle, and he's stubborn.

I put my spoon down. Robbie should be back now. Even though I know he can look after himself, if he's away too long I can't eat. The seed of fear grows and blocks my throat so I can't swallow.

Ewan nudges his older sister Tracey, and she passes him the plate of cheese. He's on the night shift again; you need to eat as much as you can if you're going to be up on that hill all night in the frost. He cuts off the mould to retrieve what's edible. Nothing lasts long here; apart from pickled veg and fruit, and what we can store in the ice house.

'Aye, all right, lass. After we've eaten.' Daniel sits down, letting out a sigh, and shovels his soup up. 'There's things we need to talk about.'

I'm letting my bread soften in the thick soup when Robbie comes in at last. He kisses the top of my head. I relax into his familiar smell, his warmth and solidity. We shift along the bench to let him sit down. I pass him a piece of bread, question him with a look, and he smiles at me. His beautiful smile.

Jamila is looking at her mother. 'It's fine, Jay. You can dip your bread in. Those are the old rules. It's different here.'

'Aye, and nobody wants a broken tooth neither,' says Tracey. She smiles broadly to show off the gaps in her snaggly teeth.

In spite of what we grow, we lack vitamins, and there's no fluoride in the water. The old days of toothache that George remembers are back. Even if you could find a dentist it would be difficult to carry out much work beyond extractions, with no materials and intermittent electricity.

'Well, Daniel?' I say, after most of us have finished. He's eating methodically, scraping each spoonful of sodden bread up, as if he's keeping time to a rhythm in his head. He puts down his spoon and clears his throat.

'All I was thinking is this. Now we've got a la'al lass again we need to make sure she gets some schooling. You could do it, Anna. You've got experience.'

It isn't what I was expecting, and Tracey raises an eyebrow: for both of us there's an irony in teaching English grammar and quadratic equations to a girl who's about to have a baby.

She needs a different kind of education. It's typical of Daniel to brush over the fears and suspicions these newcomers have created in our community and find something positive. He runs the farm as if he were born to it, but was a teacher himself and knows how physically draining the work is. It's unlikely he knows about the pregnancy, but it kills two birds with one stone: time for me to slow down, and for Jamila to save energy for herself and the baby.

There's only a certain amount of change everyone will accept in one go. No one wants a freeloader, least of all the men. When she starts to show, that's when it will get difficult. If George were here he'd have something to say.

'Go on.' Robbie smiles at me. 'You loved working with school kids at Kew, and when we were in the camps you set up…' He sees shades of grey, of small possibilities, while my world is black and white, before and after.

'But are girls allowed?' Nula looks fearful.

'I don't want to, Mum,' Jamila mutters. 'What's the point of school?' Her dark eyes are wide with irritation.

'It's not like there are going to be jobs at the end of it!' her mother says. 'I thought schools were banned.'

'Not here they're not,' says Daniel. 'You might think we're backward up here, but we think education is important. It's the basis of civilised –'

I break in to stop Daniel going off on one of his sermons, but I wish he had said something to me earlier. 'I'll teach you all kinds of things. It'll be *fun*.' I'm smiling at both of them, but Jamila frowns.

'There are loads of books upstairs,' Robbie says, always the peacemaker. 'And if you're lucky Anna will teach you to sing?'

'Ooh yes, lass,' Tracey says. 'You've mebbe not heard her but our Anna sings like an angel!'

'What about Elsa and Stefan? They're seventeen and *they* don't go to school.'

'Yes, but they did… and you're only sixteen, lass,' says Daniel, laughing.

She scowls. 'But I hate being indoors, Mum. Do I have to?'

Nula shrugs. 'They're looking after us. We have to do what's expected. It's better than all this physical work, love.'

'We'll start tomorrow morning,' I say. 'You can work outside in the afternoon.'

Tiny stops the discussion with a loud cry. Hungry again. Nula gets to her feet and Jamila has to drop the subject.

Daniel turns to her. 'Pass the watter, will you, lass.'

Her eyes are round with surprise. 'Does he want the water, Mum?' she whispers.

Nula nods as she picks Tiny up from the Moses basket and hefts him onto her hip.

'Oh, you've a lot to learn,' Daniel says, laughing. 'We'll teach you how to talk proper Cumbrian, la'al lass.'

Jamila frowns again, then when Daniel nudges her and winks, she smiles then starts laughing. The laughter ripples around the table.

Sometimes life is simple after all.

When we first arrived, I thought I'd crossed the border into a foreign country; I couldn't understand what they were saying. One day George called me a *la'al lass.*

'All it means is *little girl,*' Tracey told me. 'Folk say Cumbrians are blunt, but we're all friendly here.'

'No one's ever called me 'la'al' before,' I said, towering over her and smiling.

'Like your dad, bless him,' said Tracey. 'He was a good man… Such a loss for all of us.'

Not many make it this far north; people bring rumours with them, like the smell of burning caught in their hair and belongings, stories of survivors ending up in refugee camps for years or joining cranks like NOAH. Like Nula and Jamila, we were lucky.

Some who'd survived the river floods didn't exactly welcome us, George being one – more mouths to feed; we were *off comers* from the wetlands down south.

We've tried hard to fit in, to modify our accents, to tone down our *southern, London* ideas. Robbie more successfully than me. Dad was well-respected for his work and knowledge; he gets talked about. But, after three years, we're off comers: not from round here. No matter what we do and how hard we work, for Robbie and me, and for Nula and her family, there's a sliver of difference that could cut either way.

And we don't know who they really are.

The next day I'm waiting for Jamila, up in what we call the library. There are only two windows, but from each there's movement: as the river flows past, and clouds move in from the west. In the bare branches of horse chestnut trees at the end of our land, and through the alders nearer the water, sunlight makes a rippling pattern of shadow on the desk and along the bookshelves. We helped salvage what we could from the town library and abandoned houses. That distinctive smell of old, damp books makes this one of my favourite places at the Mill: in spite of the water, we have books. It doesn't matter if they're not ones I'd usually read; we have words and stories written down. In all the camps and along all the miles of flooded land, I carried a copy of *To Kill a Mockingbird* in my rucksack; I kept it dry for months, until it got lost and I had to start again. As long as there are books, there's hope.

Jamila's footsteps echo up the stone steps. I've laid out pencils as well as a notebook and some stories I think she might like. She flings open the door.

'Mum says I have to say sorry I'm late. But I'm not. I'm not sorry. I'm tired.'

Like everyone else, she was at breakfast, but didn't seem in a hurry, although we were to start at nine.

'It's hard to sleep with all the noise,' she says, yawning. She doesn't cover her mouth, then remembers. 'Sorry.'

'What noise?' I'm immediately alert to danger.

'*That* noise!' She's exasperated. 'Can't you hear it?'

I listen. There's nothing unusual. Only the rush of water catching in the mill wheel, the roar of the river over the dam. I laugh. 'I'm so used to it I don't hear it. It did keep me awake when I first came here. Now it's peaceful. White noise. The sound of the river.'

'It's annoying for me.'

'Soon you won't notice it.'

She sits next to me, shoulders rounded, slumped in her seat. 'What makes you able to be a teacher? I bet you don't know much more than me!'

Her lack of confidence in my skills irritates me, but Robbie told me to go easy on her. She needs to be looked after, not punished. She's suffered enough.

I pass her the notebook and let her choose a pencil. 'In the camps, I helped teach the little ones.'

'I'm not little. I'm sixteen. I don't need to go to school.' She jumps up again. 'This pencil's blunt. I need a pen.'

I search for the sharpener.

'This isn't a library. It's a barn.'

'We made it into a library.'

'What's that ladder for?'

'There's another room up there, but we don't use it. If more people come, Daniel says we'll make it into a bedroom.' I give her the sharpener. 'Here.'

She twists the pencil round so hard the point breaks and she has to start again. Then, as soon as it's sharp, she says she needs to go to the toilet.

'I'll be quick.'

Five minutes later, I call her. There's no answer so I go down to the latrine in the yard. She's washing her hands under the pump, then washing them again.

'Jamila! We've told you not to waste water. Or soap.'

The country is flooded, but water isn't clean; there's plastic, rubbish and all kinds of rotting things, and a limit to how much processed water we can store. We have tanks to collect rainwater for washing and showers, but for drinking it has to be boiled. Ewan sometimes gets soap at the market; it never lasts long.

'My hands are still dirty.'

Back in the library, she shuffles her chair in and out and straightens her book. 'I need a cushion. This chair's too low down.'

'I know you want to be outside, but you need to learn.'

In the camps, I helped teach the kids; there was always someone who would; I can't imagine what she's been doing for the last three years, but she knows how to avoid school work and how to distract a teacher. She's up on her feet again looking at an old photo of the mill.

'What's that picture, all those men standing around and digging? What are they doing?'

'Making the ice house.'

'A house made of ice. What for?'

'Sort of. Made of brick, going down, under the ground…'

'Why?'

'So the ice didn't melt for months. There were no fridges then, so they could store food and keep it fresh. We use it, when there's enough ice.'

'It's creepy. I bet all those people died. Maybe they fell in the river and got stuck in the ice…' She shivers. 'It's too dark at nighttime. Do you think there are ghosts here?'

'No.' I laugh. 'There's no such thing as ghosts!'

Thousands died in the Flood, so perhaps it was inevitable:

the spread of ghost stories; all the sightings of dead relatives. People using mediums to try to contact loved ones. Even Tracey, down to earth and practical, is convinced she's seen the ghost of a girl who died in the mill wheel; but I know what she wants, more than anything else, is to contact her dead mother. She saw her swept away by the river and could do nothing to help her. Guilt makes her work hard. A kind of atonement.

But superstition leads to eccentric religions like NOAH.

I pull myself up straight. 'Right. I know, let's do it like they did when I was at school, after the holidays. Write me something you like about being at the Mill compared to –'

'My belly's hurting. I feel sick. I think the baby wants me to have a rest.'

'OK that's *enough*! You're much better now, hardly sick at all, your mum says. I'll write the title and date, then you can start.'

February 6th The Mill

She furrows her brow and grips the pencil in her fist.

'Not like that, you crazy girl!' I try to make her laugh. 'Have you forgotten how to hold a pencil?'

The scowl deepens, then without warning she throws the pencil on the floor and drops to her knees on the square of carpet near the sofa, in front of the window.

I take a deep breath and, keeping my body as calm as I can, although it's not how I feel at all, slowly stand up. Daniel has given me some 'behaviour management' strategies. I'm grateful.

'A few sentences. That's all. Then you can choose a book to read. OK?'

But she's crying. Not pretending. I feel guilty I've pushed her. I put my arm around her. 'Two sentences to show me what you can do.'

Her brown eyes are liquid with tears, and I can hardly hear her voice over the river, when she says, 'I can't.'

'What do you mean? Have you forgotten everything?'

'Nobody showed me.' She catches my smile and almost laughs. 'No, Anna. It's true!'

'Not even your mum?'

'They wouldn't let her.'

'Who?'

'The men… But I can read some letters.' She brightens as she says this.

I write out the alphabet and she points to the letters she knows and reads them: A H N O. She goes back carefully, putting her finger under each letter. 'No, I don't know any more.'

'That's nearly *my* name,' I say. 'How about this?' I write J. 'I bet you know that one. It's for your name. J for Jamila.'

She shakes her head.

She can't have reached sixteen without knowing her own name. I wish I were better prepared. Grief and loss have affected us all, but how do you deal with a child's trauma? A pregnant one at that.

I try to be gentle. 'I can't believe you've forgotten! Let me show you how to hold your pencil.'

Finally, she makes an attempt at her name, forming the letters like a five-year-old.

'Pretty good.'

She smiles. If she relaxes and I can get her to trust me, she'll learn quickly.

'How come you know those letters?' I ask. 'The ones in the alphabet?'

She hesitates. Then she rolls up her sleeve. It's on the inside of her wrist, so small you could easily miss it. Or mistake it for a scar or bruise. Something flips inside me. Is this what I've been dreading for so long? What I felt was coming towards me in dreams? Life pulls the carpet out from under your feet and you're never ready.

On Jamila's thin wrist are the four letters: N O A H.

Five

When the floods started, NOAH was a group of new age hippies with a fashion for long hair and beards and #NOAH painted on the hull of their boats. But, in the time it took for the government to realise it was a national crisis and they'd left it too late again, with daily press briefings and lists of casualties, the whole country was on the move escaping the water, and NOAH had changed.

I can never forget the first time I understood how much.

We were among the last to leave, but at least we had escaped the flood. After days of travelling on foot we were hungry and tired. A walking mass of humanity climbing up and out of the shallow bowl of Greater London. All six lanes, the whole width of the motorway. An endless mob, splashing along the tarmac, children being dragged along, or pushed in buggies crying, or walking like their parents, silent and single-minded.

We had our rucksacks, hastily packed with what we thought were essentials. At the last minute I'd tipped out the savings jar and pushed notes and coins, which we so rarely used now everything was contactless, inside a pair of socks. Robbie laughed at me. But I wanted to be ready. Once we reached Oxford we'd have a bed: hotels, hostels, student accommodation, school and church halls; every space would be used. That's what everyone was saying.

Above us, the sky was a clean blue, the rain cleared away for once; and, if you looked up, you could see, high on the thermals, the great, outspread wings of gliding red kites. It was hard to imagine they had once been hunted to extinction but had been successfully reintroduced in the last century. Whenever we'd driven through the Stokenchurch Gap, the man-made cleft blasted through the ridge of the Chilterns to build the M40, heading towards Oxfordshire, I had a sense of expectation. The patchwork of fields and hamlets spread out in front of us, the flat vale stretching ahead as the motorway cut through the chalk of the Chilterns. The kites were part of it. So high. Their strange, almost otherworldliness. Their immense five- or six-foot wingspan, waiting to dive for prey or to scavenge for carrion.

We were almost there. Far from London and the water. But that's where it started, the rumours whispering back, mutters of sound getting closer and louder as words seeped back towards us. Murmurs of another flood. They said the valley was inundated and we couldn't go any further. Someone told us there were boats and dinghies, but not enough for the thousands of us arriving every hour.

'No need to worry,' Robbie said cheerfully to a family where the parents were pulling their children along, chiding them. 'If we don't get a boat today, they'll soon have measures in place for everyone. The government will issue tickets.'

I don't know what started the panic. As if a whistle had been blown, we all started quickening our pace. Then some broke into a run, elbowing others out of the way. There was swearing and shouting. We were pushed from behind.

'Slow down, Rob. I can't keep up.' My breath was ragged. Carrying my heavy rucksack I was ungainly. I was scared of what would happen if I fell.

He gripped my hand tighter and didn't speak. I felt like Alice pulled along by the Red Queen – racing to get ahead, stumbling and lurching from side to side.

Babies were crying. From somewhere there was a loud moaning.

'Don't look back. Don't let go,' he said.

The rattle of suitcases on the tarmac of the motorway, my rucksack jabbing into my back. The snap of something underfoot. Something breaking. Screams and shouts.

Then we were at the Stokenchurch Gap.

Ahead of us, as far as we could see, Oxfordshire was a vast lake.

Like dreams where I'm running over boggy ground to escape the tide coming in, I was running for my life. We all were. There were shouts and orders to stop but, propelled forwards by the crowds, we couldn't.

'Stay calm. Walk don't run.' An amplified voice, like the soothing voice of a Sat Nav rang out above everything else, but we couldn't stop.

Until the shooting started. From the air all around us: from helicopter gunships and from armed police and soldiers with automatic weapons.

'Stay calm. Walk don't run. You will all be dealt with in turn.' The disembodied voice rang out between the volleys of gunfire.

In the air at first.

Then it wasn't.

All around us they were falling, on top of those who had already fallen. In a rain of metal.

Robbie gave a shout and veered to the left, pulling me with him, leaning on one of the abandoned cars on the hard shoulder of the motorway. From his upper arm a dark stain blossomed through his jacket.

'Keep going, Anna. If you lose me, keep going.'

'I'm not leaving you here.'

'You might have to.' Struggling with the pain, his voice was flat and emotionless. 'I'll be OK. Keep going.'

'No. Of course I won't.'

Now it was my turn to lead. It was slippery and difficult to walk; the ground gave with every step. Then, at last, we had to stop. There was nothing in front of us but sodden land, then water. Heavy grey clouds rolled in formation from the west until the view of the valley was blocked by mist, and the rain came on again. A hard, cold shower. From the wounded lying on the wet, bloodied ground came cries and moans, like the groans of the dying after a historic battle, like Waterloo. I wanted to put my hands over my ears to shut out the sound of it. Children crying. From somewhere, a terrible screaming.

We were alive, those of us left standing, but Robbie was grey with pain, blood soaking through his jacket, dripping down over his hand as he pressed it to staunch the flow.

'I need a tourniquet,' he said. But we were penned in on every side.

Red kites began to fly low over the valley. Scavenging. Looking for carrion.

Pressed close to the edge of the swollen lake, all we could do was try to hold our ground, to balance. Visible in the distance, small boats and dinghies were moving away from what was now the shoreline, heading towards Oxford. Behind us, the crowds continued to bunch up, pushing into us from all sides, releasing a smell of damp, slept-in clothes, stale breath and worse; in front, making a solid line of defence, wearing helmets with the new purple and gold insignia, armed soldiers stood with riot shields.

'Stay calm. Walk. Don't run,' the female voice continued to loop from loudspeakers, while one of the soldiers yelled that everyone would have to wait for the next crossing. We were forced to squeeze in to allow soldiers to pass until we were so close together, I had to fight for space to breathe. I wasn't the only one terrified of suffocation. A wild-eyed man pushed at me until Robbie told him to *calm down, mate. You're not the only one.* Eventually, a sort of order was established and we were herded into holding areas.

Robbie was pale with pain. 'I need help,' he said. 'Can you see anything that looks like a medical centre?'

Pinned up were official notices with the symbol of peace, a white dove, some with instructions: *To speed up the process please have documents ready. Standard – £150 per person, reduced rates for under-fives. Cash only. No cards or contactless. Upgrades available for £250 per person.* Like priority boarding on a budget airline.

I spotted improvised signs, torn cardboard with biro scrawled over, like the kind drivers hold at airports – prices per person, per crossing. Either way, you needed money to secure a place.

I shook my head. 'Wait here. I'll have a look.'

'Let's go together.' Robbie squeezed my hand. 'When we can move.'

A woman with her hair caught up in a tight elastic band was shouting: 'You can't make us pay. This is England, Great Britain. We're refugees, for fuck's sake!' Her two children looked down, avoiding eye contact.

'Pay. Or go back where you came from.' The soldier's rifle shone blackly, like her eyes. Quiet. Self-righteous.

'I'm on my own with two kids to think of. This isn't right.' The woman rubbed her hand over her face, leaving a streak of mud.

The soldier shook her head. Shrugged.

'Who are you? Who's employing you?'

'We work for the government.'

'No, you don't. You're working for some private enterprise. No wonder you're after money. What are those letters on your uniform? NOAH? Is this some kind of joke?'

The woman turned to confirm she had an audience, then lunged at the soldier, but immediately crumpled to the ground, a look of disbelief on her face, almost before we heard the gunshot. There was a sharp intake of breath from the crowd, then silence as her children crowded round her, crying noiselessly, until they were escorted away by another uniformed woman.

'Stay calm. Walk. Don't run.' The Big Sister voice looped, like the Mind the Gap warning on the Tube. 'Stay calm. Walk. Don't run.'

After that, people were quieter and held on closely to their loved ones. When I squeezed Robbie's hand, he kissed me hard, there in the middle of the crowd, holding me with his good arm.

'You're still bleeding. We have to get you proper help. Let's go.'

After an hour of pushing and shuffling through the mass of people, we found it: precariously close to the water was a makeshift triage tent; we joined a queue. A nurse examined Robbie's shoulder. Nothing broken, a deep, flesh wound. It was cleaned then dressed with sterile strips; he was given antibiotics.

'You're one of the lucky ones; we're running low on drugs,' said the nurse. 'Make sure you finish the course. In a few weeks these'll be like gold dust, love.'

It was only when we were walking away that I realised not one of us had mentioned the gunshot wound. As if this were a new, acceptable normality.

People arrived continuously. Mostly young like us, exhausted and frightened. In a cordoned-off area, we were given basic supplies: water bottles, packs of hard bread and protein bars. This was the entrance to a holding camp. Most refugees from the floods walked around with an air of acceptance; but there was also growing anger. Everyone asked the same questions: how many were shot? How many dead? Rumours circulated like Chinese whispers: that people on the M40 behind us had got through safely, that no one else was even allowed through the Stokenchurch Gap. That they had to wait on the motorway among the dead and dying, under the shadow of red kites circling. Diving down for food. People trying to fight them off. Those huge beaks and talons.

It was impossible to get reliable information. Messages and emails bounced around, everyone trying to contact family, trying to get updates about the crisis. After the first day, most phones had run out of charge; the few who had the internet were questioned about what they knew. When I approached a soldier, he turned and chatted to a colleague. As if I were invisible. Then one afternoon all screens went blank. At the same time, as if the plug had been pulled.

There was a semblance of organisation, but we were there for three days, cold and wet and hungry. Each time a boat arrived there was a scramble for places; more injuries, fatalities. We learned to turn and look the other way. Soldiers in their improvised uniforms demanded bribes. I was glad I had the notes from the savings at the bottom of my rucksack. Money had its uses, at least for now. The triage nurse was right: we were lucky.

There were acts of kindness and altruism, but if someone attempted to board a full boat, the mob ruled. People were pushed off into the churning, stinking, muddy waters of Oxfordshire. Even children. They even pushed off the children.

That's when we knew how bad things had become.

But that was only the beginning. Yes, there were camps, but always transit, not more than a few nights. As we travelled, we got used to the private conversations out in the open, the arguments and the intimacy of family relationships laid bare; announcements and orders in the same honeyed tones and the heart-thudding bursts of machine-gun fire. The constant damp and hunger. We had to get further north, and the further north we went, they were everywhere: the sombre presence of what turned out to be NOAH soldiers, their boats on every waterway, the whir of their helicopters above every new expanse of flooded land.

Then the diseases started. I'll never forget the black shapes floating on the filthy water. More died from disease than ever drowned or starved. We were young, strong and healthy. No dependents. We had useful skills. At every checkpoint we showed our papers and were quickly processed, moved on to safety, to the next camp. Others weren't so lucky.

In each camp there was a limited supply of electricity, rigged up from generators that gave off foul, smoky fumes, vibration and noise. The power came on for an hour a day, in the evening to give some light. Before the internet was lost, we rushed to find sockets to charge our phones. It was a common sight: people arguing over whose turn it was, fights broken up by the soldiers, who appeared if there was trouble. Then, when the order came: *Lights out in five minutes,* we'd scurry to find our way back to our sleeping position. All lights out, the buzzing and rumble of the generators reduced to one. Darkness pouring down from the sky. Darkness covering the face of the deep.

In the morning, we dragged on damp clothes and ate whatever was offered. Long marches across ribbons of land, our feet never dry, searching for ground that was high enough to withstand the swollen, furious water. Gradually, the landscape changed as we trekked further north beyond Oxfordshire and through the Midlands.

When we finally reached Yorkshire, we had to avoid the Vale of York, now completely inundated. We spent two sodden nights camping out on a hillside in Leeds before it was cut off completely and became one of the islands. I think it was months before we arrived in the uplands of the North Yorkshire moors.

But my memory of that time is tainted by my illness. Robbie said I must have picked it up there, because the weeks after that are marked by a blur of fever, weakness and pain.

In every camp, word circulated: the soldiers were only a home-grown organisation and the government was in charge; they were a foreign-backed militia sent from Europe, or was it Africa? Or even China. Stories changed all the time. Someone said there would be foreign aid soon, it was on its way. In the end, we stopped asking. If we saw that uniform, the colour of spring crocuses, or those four letters, we kept our heads down. Kept quiet. Helped if needed, but focussed on our own survival. That's when I started some teaching; I had to do something.

I think that's when the dreams started, repeating like waves, rolling onto the shore, pounding everything in their way. Always beginning the same – an awareness of a wall of water coming towards us. Knowing in my guts that we had to run, but at the same time that the force and speed of the water made it inescapable. Running through sand where my feet sank. Climbing into the house, the house where I was brought up before Mum left us. But the house was never safe; the water was coming in so quickly, the only place to go was higher, up flights of stairs then, finally, into the attic with its old suitcases and unwanted clothes. I was balancing on a joist, the house filling with water, slowly tipping. Clawing my way out, breaking the skylight with my hands until air blew in, and I was on the roof. But the house was drowning in a roar of water and crying voices. Water closing over my head. Light fading. Silence. The light switched off.

But when I woke, crying, Robbie was there. As long as we were together it was possible to hold on to hope; but I remember how he changed. We both did. I remember the new smell, an outside, smoky smell. With something under it all, a smell that, when I think about it now or it filters into my dreams, I can imagine. A thin, metallic smell; if it were a sound it would be chalk shrieking on a blackboard, or someone running a knife along the side of a car: rawness, unhidden. The sharp smell of fear.

Six

Tracey shifts in her chair, shaking her head slowly. 'I was right. I knew it as soon as I saw them. I knew it. What did I say, Dad?'

'Just stop it now. You don't know owt about it. And you never said nowt to me.' George, normally so calm with her, sounds angry. 'I've told you – keep your ideas to yourself until you know the facts.'

She blushes and edges back in the chair.

Elsa comes in and, seeing Tracey is upset, pulls a chair next to her, smiles at her. Tracey is easily cowed by sharp words. She puts her hands in her lap and looks up at her father, the image of a good child. I feel sorry for her. 'But Dad,' she whispers, 'I was only saying… I didn't mean owt. They don't come from round here, you know.'

'Aye, lass, we all know that. From down south, like Anna. And that la'al body's doing her best for two children. If she'd stayed down there they'd have all drowned. You wouldn't want that, would you?'

I catch Daniel's eye and he smiles. Tracey means well. A natural with babies and small children, though she's never had her own. But she struggles to see beyond her own small picture of life; her dad has to keep her on track. Patience with his daughter is one of his good qualities, but everyone has heard George complain there's less food to go round now they're here.

'And there's the other thing too… I'm not to talk about that, but,' Tracey says, hand cupped around her mouth. 'That's right, Anna. That's what you said.'

'Oh, Tracey.' She's been sworn to secrecy about Jamila, but she's bursting to let it out. 'That's not what I said,' I say quietly.

'What are you two talking about?' Elsa says. 'Is there a secret? Something exciting? Tell me. Go on.' Her blonde hair tumbles around her face as she leans towards Tracey.

'Me and me big mouth again!' Tracey moves away and thrusts her bony hands under her thighs. 'I didn't mean to…'

'Lookit, lass, keep quiet and let Daniel tell us what's going on.' George glances round the kitchen nodding to himself, counting, then turns sharply. 'Everyone's here. Bloody hell! Have you forgotten, Daniel? Who's on guard?'

Elsa laughs. 'Calm down. My brother's up there now.'

'It's OK, George,' Daniel says. 'I know you think he's too young, but my Stefan's a strong lad. And there has to be a first time.'

'And tomorrow I'm going with him,' says Elsa. 'We're both seventeen, remember?' She bends down to stroke one of the dogs.

'Aye, all right then…' When George sits down, he holds on to his hip and lets out a groan. He's plagued by arthritis. This winter has been worse. His hip bothers him a lot. Not so long ago he'd be on a waiting list for a replacement. Pain is something we all have to live with.

'Right, we're waiting for the lads to get back then we can get on with it,' Daniel says. 'While lasses are out, we can talk.'

Nula and Jamila have taken Tiny for a walk to settle him.

The door opens bringing a gust of damp air; it's Robbie and Ewan, hair soaked, faces red and wet.

Ewan scowls then heads off to his room. 'Five minutes, eh. Got to change out of this lot.'

After the scudding clouds and sunshine yesterday, the rain's set in for the day. We need lights on that we can ill afford, and the room is cold, almost dank. Robbie pushes his hands through his hair to keep it out of his eyes, then sits next to me. I wish I'd told him about Jamila. What's wrong with me?

Ewan comes back, smiling, shakes himself then looks for something to dry his hair.

'Our Tracey says we're having a meeting. What's up?' he asks Daniel. He finds a towel and starts drying his hair.

'I've gathered you all here because Anna wants to say something. About the new lasses,' Daniel says, addressing the room.

I wipe my clammy hands on my jeans. 'I don't know where to start.'

Ewan rubs hard at his hair again and shakes his head. He catches my eye and smiles, then throws the towel on the back of the chair. 'Come on then. Not like you to be quiet,' he says. 'Spit it out.'

When I tell them what I've seen there's an intake of breath from Daniel, but before he has a chance to speak, Ewan laughs.

'So, she has a tattoo. It's a fashion thing. You know what lasses are like. Doesn't mean owt.' He never takes things seriously, plays the class clown.

'But you're forgetting how old she is,' I say. 'She's sixteen now, but how old was she when she got the tattoo?'

'No, lad,' Daniel says quietly. 'I know you're an adult, and you've seen a lot, but if you put two and two together –'

'– it meks five, by your reckoning.' Ewan stands up to his full height. Not tall, but he has the powerful, stocky build of men up here, like his father must have been before it loosened into fat and old age. Not skinny like his sister. Sometimes he's like a big, spoilt child, wants to have his own way, to be right. George tells him not to interrupt, but Ewan can twist him round his little finger.

'If you'll let me finish,' Daniel says. 'What I mean is that this puts things in a different light. We don't know a lot about Nula, do we? She came here asking for help and we took her in. 'Course we did. But we know plenty about NOAH; too bloody much.' His voice wavers and he turns to find a seat.

I move to put a hand on his arm.

'What they believe is wrong,' Robbie says, banging his hand on the table, 'on so many levels. How people can believe such rubbish I can never understand; but they do. That's what makes them dangerous.'

Ewan snorts. 'Them ones that came from Buttermere way were soon sent packing. Tripping over their fucking beards!'

'You know that's not true, Ewan.' Daniel's voice rises. 'We lost some good stuff. Machines. Supplies. And you weren't laughing at the time!'

'Aye, well I'm laughing now. It's a sad world if you can't laugh.'

'Ewan!' Tracey hisses at him. 'Sit down and behave yourself!'

'You need to listen to Daniel, Ewan,' I say, surprised to see my hands shaking. 'I don't know much, but when we came, we saw things we won't forget, didn't we, Robbie?' He nods and is about to say something, but I don't let him. 'It was early days, and no one knew what was going on but… it was the ones in uniform. Everything was so confused. We didn't know at the time that they were NOAH.'

Ewan flashes me a look. 'Aye, but them lasses don't look much like soldiers to me!'

'That tattoo means they've been involved,' I add. 'We have to question them.'

Daniel nods. 'To be truthful, for a long time I didn't think NOAH had got this far. Everyone said they were down London way. Then we had that last trouble from Buttermere, and we knew something was going on. People on the hunt for food, medicines, who knows what else. They disappeared again… But now they're in Keswick.'

'What?' I say.

Tracey lets out a 'No!'

'Rob and me. We've talked about it, but we didn't want to start everyone off.'

Rob doesn't meet my eye.

Daniel sighs. 'You all heard about last summer's Convention, didn't you?'

Tracey laughs. 'But them religious folk have been coming to Keswick for ever.'

'Aye, good ordinary Christian folk, eh?' says George. 'Nowt extreme about them.'

'Our dad's right,' Ewan says. 'Convention's been going on for best part of two hundred years. They come from all over in summer for a bit of a pray and a get together. Each to their own. Harmless.'

Robbie bangs his hand on the table again. 'If you think that, you're fucking naïve. The Convention is expanding, taking over old buildings. The pencil factory. School halls. Churches… it's not the usual crowd. It's different. More organised.'

'Well, some folks turn to religious when they get scared. It's normal. There's plenty of things to worry about nowadays,' says Ewan, 'but they're not going to bother us here.'

'You think so? Only thirteen miles,' says Robbie. 'The old railway line…'

'Aye, but on foot, through floods, that's at least a day away,' says Ewan.

'Our Ewan's right.' George turns to Tracey. 'Don't worry, lass. He told me about all them shops selling long robes. Fancy hairdressers for fellas who've got nowt better to do.'

'Men with scented bloody beards! I've said that a hundred times; that'll nivver last in Cumbria!' says Ewan, laughing.

George frowns at his son. 'I've telled you, Ewan! Just listen, will you?'

'I thought it would die down after last year's Convention,' Robbie says.

'Rob's right. They're making up laws, checking everyone's wearing the right clothes. Some say women aren't allowed to cut their hair and have to keep their heads covered. Men with regulation beards.' Daniel hesitates. 'I'll tell them, Rob. They need to know… You maybe didn't hear about the old fella from a farm outside Keswick, used to deliver milk. He refused to grow his beard. Even when they threatened him. Beaten so badly he can't look after himself. His son has to feed him.'

'Nivver! No one ivver tells us owt!' Tracey's voice rises to a shriek.

So I'm not the only one keeping secrets. Robbie said nothing to me about NOAH getting so extreme.

'Aye that's Keswick, but. Not here,' Ewan says. 'You get that lot trying to sell you scented pomade and most folk would laugh in their faces… what you could see of them! That lot's fucking brainwashed.'

'But, as I'm trying to tell you, it's not only cosmetics.' Daniel is exasperated at Ewan's flippancy. 'Like Rob said, it looks systematic. Like they've got a plan.'

'People are vulnerable. They want certainty. Someone in charge. They listen to people who sound like they know what they're talking about, then all kinds of idiots and extremists take over,' Robbie says. 'Remember the US under Trump.'

'But this isn't America, is it?' says Ewan.

Daniel's fingers are drumming on the edge of the table. 'This is getting us nowhere.'

'Nula and Jamila will be back from their walk soon,' I say. 'We need to decide what we're going to do.'

Robbie nods.

'Right. From what Anna says, I think we need to get ready, get as much information as we can,' says Daniel. 'We need to ask some questions.'

'I say leave be,' says Ewan. 'You can't take them seriously. Them NOAHs. It's a load of religious rubbish. Even if some of them like to throw their weight around and take folk's stuff. Sticking their notices up all over.'

Daniel sits back, thinking. 'But didn't you say you'd seen new faces round the market, lad?'

'Mebbe I did, but you can't stop folk moving around,' Ewan mutters.

'Your Ewan thinks I'm overreacting, George.'

'That's not what I meant.' Ewan drops down into one of the chairs.

'I want to keep us safe. That's all I want,' says Daniel.

Then it's as clear to me as if I'm looking down into the deep bed of one of the lakes.

'Nula and her family came out of nowhere. My gut instinct is they're ordinary refugees, but who's to say they're not NOAH spies.'

'Anna's right. It's more than religion. Or fashion,' says Rob. He gives Ewan a hard look. 'We'd be stupid not to investigate. Before it grows into something we can't handle.'

'Right. We need to keep a close eye on the new lasses,' Daniel says.

George shakes his head. 'You'd never think to look at them –'

'Let's play it gently,' I interrupt. 'I think I can get more out of Jamila if you let me carry on with our lessons, and give me some time to talk to Nula. What do you say, Daniel?'

Ewan smiles. 'Could be nowt, so why don't we ask them, direct like?'

'And scare them? Then who knows what they'll do?' Daniel says.

Tracey slaps her brother's arm. 'Sometimes you've no sense. Just when we've got it nice here.'

'Aye… Mebbe they've got friends waitin' over yonder to come and take our patch.'

'Anna's got a way with words. Let her have a go first.' Tracey sits back down, breathing heavily.

'You can ask round the market tomorrow, Ewan, when you're doing the food swap,' I say. 'There are some pickles and cheeses. And the milk. See what you can find out.'

'But don't go barging in,' says his father.

'I agree. Keep it low key,' Robbie says. 'Someone's bound to know something. I'll see what I can get out of the patients.' He pulls me in towards him and squeezes my shoulder. 'Come with us, Anna. It's about time you did. You're a good listener. We can all compare notes afterwards.'

'I'm no use pushing a barrow,' I say. 'You'll have to do the heavy work.'

Ewan shrugs. 'Aye, of course, lass. But there's nowt new around market. Some marra trying to flog his old rubbish. Same as always; stories and rumours. It's hard to find out the truth. You have to take it with a pinch of salt… Aye, alright, Dad.' George is shaking his head. 'Come and help us, Anna. You can barter for a change. Our Tracey says there's some stuff left.'

'Well, see what you can do, eh?' says Daniel to finish. 'I'm getting hungry. I don't know about you lot.'

'Here they are,' says Tracey, as the dogs start barking and all eyes turn to the window. 'Lasses are soaked to the skin, both of them. But at least babbie's asleep. We can have our dinners in peace.' She smiles at me and adds, 'You know what to do, Anna.'

Over the meal Ewan tries to make Jamila laugh, but the atmosphere is tense. She's worn out with walking. Her eyes are closing. We need to let the men know that she's expecting, but I must speak to Nula.

Seven

The first one I see is pinned to the trunk of a sycamore tree as we walk to the market the next day. That gothic font, the gold and purple border, faded and crumpled in the rain. A wave of the old nausea. It's a long time since I've seen NOAH propaganda. I hold tighter to the barrow. I nudge Robbie and he steps over and tears it down.

'That's old stuff,' Ewan snorts. 'Couple of years ago they tried to get a foothold here. Wankers… Come on, Fowler.' He pulls hard on the dog's lead. He's in one of his darker moods today. 'I said come on!'

Robbie scans the notice and squeezes my hand. 'Same old crap: *Turn to NOAH and forget all your troubles… The trip of a lifetime on the Ark itself!*'

I remember Dad fuming at their naïvety, almost spitting with rage at how they were giving people false hope, the ones without jobs, the ones who'd been flooded out. I can't believe I didn't take it seriously. I was even more naïve, or a poor judge of human behaviour.

Robbie crushes the paper in his hand then goes back for the drawing pins.

'Might as well, eh?' says Ewan. 'They're not going to have much use for them now.'

A thick smell of wood smoke permeates the market. Stalls are huddled against the walls of the castle for protection against the icy wind. When the Flood came, what was already crumbling fell into the river, leaving it more and more open to the sky and weather. People have come from miles around, from hill forts and small settlements to the town, only there's no 'town' as such, only small communities clinging on. A crowd has gathered around one stall where there's a smell of frying meat – smoked bacon and lamb meat balls.

Yesterday's rain has turned to sleet and, by the look of dark, sulphurous clouds rumbling in from the sea, it won't be long before it snows again. It's like a car boot sale; everyone looks miserable but is intent on selling their stuff, no matter what – rusty tools, broken electric goods, bits of furniture, old clothes darned and patched, woollen jumpers unravelled and made up into balls of wool for knitting, and a few with plastic recycled into new things. One stall has a couple of bedraggled chickens, their feet tied together, eggs and boxes of muddy, unidentifiable vegetables. All are spread out on trestle tables protected by make-shift awnings to keep off the worst of the weather.

As well as information, I'm looking for fresh fruit – our apples store well and we use damaged ones to make vinegar, but we lost most of our plums and damsons last year because of the rain. They split, then fell and rotted. I can't remember the last time I had an orange. It must be years.

Seeing so many people in one place is unnerving; and what strikes me is that it's not only us – everyone, or nearly everyone (it's hard to tell because they're so well wrapped up against the weather) is underweight, undernourished. Like Lowry's stick men and women in this cold place. If someone's a healthy weight then we'd be suspicious: why is their diet so much better? There are a few who pile on the fat, no matter what they eat, but the floods have solved the obesity crisis. Poor skin, teeth. Very few over seventy.

Our barrow is full of goat's cheese wrapped in old cotton from recycled clothes, some packets of flour, milk and our own pickle and jam. We used to throw jars in the recycling bin and feel we were saving the world; now we hang on to everything that has a use.

As Robbie brings the barrow to a standstill, a few flakes of snow are beginning to fall. It's incongruous, and I find myself laughing: 'Makes me think of German Christmas markets: crêpes, sausages, mulled wine. Those twirling brass angels. Silver and gold baubles. Glitter in snow globes.'

Robbie frowns at me, then rubs his hands together to get the circulation going again. I know he thinks I'm too flippant.

Soon heavy snow is falling on the stalls, on people trying to make something out of very little. It settles and chills and soaks everything.

Ewan heads off. 'Meet you in half an hour, eh? I'll sithee.'

'Have you got time to show me round then?' I ask Robbie.

'There's no one waiting at the moment. But I'll have to keep an eye out.' The shed where he runs his surgery is at the far end of the market – an old bus shelter with add ons. There's always someone with a cut, or a sore throat.

A skinny woman, with what looks like the contents of her kitchen cupboards spread out on a piece of rough carpet, crouches under a tattered shower curtain. Her hair springs out from her wool hat in iron grey wisps. She calls us over.

'Hiya, lass! Need any bowls? Pans? Got some knives and forks. Solid silver.'

I smile but shake my head.

'How about your fella?'

'Nothing today, thank you,' I say. 'We're looking to get rid of these.' I take the cover off the barrow: the green, ruby-red and yellow of the chutneys and pickled vegetables glow in the winter light.

'All them colours on a cold day! What can I give you for one of them'uns?' She points to a small cheese. 'I've not had owt decent to eat since day before yesterday. Go on, look at all this lovely china, hardly used. You won't find no cracks or chips.'

Robbie pulls at my arm and frowns. On the way here he warned me about her: Karen Sowerby. One of the Sowerbys, a local ring who ransack houses then try to offload the stuff at the market. She's here twice a week, all weathers, her dog lying under the stall, and in Workington other days. Only in her fifties, she has the wrinkled face of a woman decades older.

But what does it take to spend a few minutes, to talk to someone? Life's hard enough as it is. We all have to survive somehow.

'I could use a few of those jam jars,' I say. Robbie gives up and starts to push the barrow away. 'Hang on, Rob. I need to get…' I have to half-run to catch him up. Difficult when the ground's getting more slippery and my legs are never as strong as I expect them to be.

'We don't want to be involved with that lot. Were you listening when I told you where she gets it from?'

'But she must be freezing.' I pull a small cheese out of the barrow and put the cover back on. 'Her sons take advantage of her. Ewan told me how they talk to her.'

I go back and give her the cheese. She packs a handful of jars in a mould-stained pillowcase and hands them to me. Her hands are so thin you can see every tendon, every bone. I see her saying, 'Thanks, lass.' But the air is torn apart by the scream of a jet and I can't make out what she says next. Everyone looks up at the sky as the aircraft is swallowed up by the leaden clouds.

'What the hell?' I say. Planes are a thing of the past.

Karen Sowerby shakes her head. 'Ee that flayt me to death. Heart's going like the clappers!'

'You're not the only one!' I say. 'I've not seen a plane for years.'

She shrugs. 'There's allus some bugger showing off. One of them NOAHs or that new lot. You know… them EUROS.' She laughs, showing black gaps between her teeth. 'Well, thanks, lass. I'll enjoy this cheese.' Then turns quickly to a customer rifling through a box of mixed cutlery. As I walk away I hear her say, 'Solid silver, marra. I can do you a deal on them'uns.'

Robbie is standing in front of a vegetable stall, bartering with the market trader for carrots and leeks. He nods to me. Robbie has this capacity to switch the way he talks, to modify his accent. Unlike me. I don't have the ear for it.

'That didn't hurt, did it?' I kiss his cheek loudly and he pulls away.

'It's not what we're here for. You can't afford to be sentimental.'

'Well, she appreciated it. Till that plane went over.'

He lowers his voice. 'Look, that guy in the blue puffer jacket, with the green scarf? If Sowerby was really in need she'd go to him. Next time you can donate something to him. He runs a food bank like in the old days. Bit of a Robin Hood. Not everyone knows about him, so keep it to yourself. OK?' Before I can speak, he's walking away. 'Let's go. Too bloody cold to stand around.'

'Wait, Rob. That plane...' I have to push myself hard to keep up with him. 'Robbie, she said it was NOAH or... I can't remember what she called them... oh yes, EUROS. Like the currency.'

He stops dead. 'Is that what she said?'

'What does she mean?'

He gives a small shake of his head and sniffs. 'Not here. Let's talk later,' he says under his breath, then in a conversational voice, 'I can see someone at the clinic. I've got to go. You be all right? Ewan can't be far away.'

'Of course. It's level here. I can manage the barrow. Rob, tell me about –'

'Later, OK?'

I know when he says that, there's something he's not telling me. But I'm getting too cold here to think about it. Need to focus on the job in hand.

For the next hour I push the barrow and manage to trade some of the milk and flour, a few of the jars. It's slow work. My hands feel as if they're frozen round the handles of the barrow. I decide to look for Ewan.

I hear him before I see him, his voice is so distinctive, with his full-throated laugh, but I'm distracted by a smell I wasn't expecting. Under the falling snow the silver-marked skin of mackerel and herring gleam, the herring almost iridescent. I could cook mackerel with cider vinegar, a few soft, greying potatoes. A half-decent meal for a change. My mouth starts watering. The stall-holder has red skin, and hands like claws, the rest of him smothered in hat, hood, scarf and a thick sheepskin coat. All you can see are his eyes.

Collar up, hair flattened by the snow, Ewan's taken off his hat. His hands are deep in his pockets and he's kicking a stone, absently talking to the stall-holder. He does it so easily and naturally. He makes people feel relaxed; I can hear them laughing from here. His mood has obviously improved. He must be telling one of his stories. He'll know more than Robbie and me; he's the real local; he'll clock anything new or different.

'No one told me there'd be fish!' I say.

'Aye, and they're fresh, like,' says the man. 'Not like them smoked ones… fresh today.'

'Gives us an appetite. Not had fish frae sea in a long time.' Ewan laughs and kicks the stone into a pile of snow. 'I get the odd trout or salmon frae river, but there's not many with all the other crap in there. And it's getting worse.'

We're grateful for the mornings when Ewan brings in a salmon, and turn a blind eye to his methods. The line with baited hooks, secured at one end to catch them overnight. The gaff hanging with the other tools. We compromise. Or starve. Even Daniel.

'How about some of this?' When I show the stall-holder our haul he takes an approving in-breath.

'Goat's cheese, is it?'

'Aye,' says Ewan.

'Owt else?'

'Apple pickle, runner beans, rhubarb jam,' I list, pointing to them. 'And flour.'

'Flour, eh?'

'Aye, good stuff an' all, not manky stuff full of weevils like some you get! And how about…' Ewan reaches into the bottom of the barrow and pulls out a large bottle of cider and a handful of packets. 'And a few ciggies.'

'I'll have the lot then.'

'What?' I say.

'Mouths to feed,' says the man.

I nudge Ewan. 'The ice store,' I say, under my breath. We can take as much fish as he's willing to give. It will keep fresh for weeks. Or take it to the smoke house.

'Well, that's grand, then,' says Ewan.

The man wraps the fish in sheets of yellowed paper, a stack of old posters telling you to *Go forth increase and…*

'Sorry about paper… It's clean enough,' he says.

Ewan's face gives nothing away. Paper has a value but it's getting harder to find. Every scrap. Everything has a price.

'Anyroad, best be off. You here next week, marra? Name's Ewan, by the way.' He holds out his hand and the man grasps it in his reddened paw.

'Jes, short for Jeston… I'll be round and about, lad.'

He's come from the sea, and the sea means danger. I can sense Ewan hesitating before he says, 'New to town, like?'

'Nae. Allus around.' He's from Maryport, he tells us. Got himself a small fishing boat.

'Maryport. I thought so,' says Ewan. He laughs.

Too much small talk. I dive in: 'I'm Anna.' I hold out my hand, but his hands stay in his pockets. 'Seen any newcomers?'

'What's it to you, lass?' As if he's said what's it *worth* to you. I've asked too much.

'Got to look after each other, like, haven't we?' Ewan makes light of my confusion and both men laugh. Heat rises to my face and I have to look away.

'Same old,' says Jeston. 'Nowt changes.'

'Well, sithee then, Jes.' Ewan takes hold of the handles of the barrow and pushes it away towards the other side of the market.

'Anna, let me do the talking. You don't get all the ins and outs of market. Information's too precious to barge into. Too dangerous. You're here to listen and look.'

I'm angry with him. And with myself.

'But did you notice the paper?'

''Course I did but I wasn't going to say owt. For fuck's sake think before you speak.'

'I thought we were keeping all our cider… And where'd you get the fags?'

'I done a few deals. There's plenty of stuff if you ask the right people. Things are looking up, and folk don't want fucking chutney!'

'Well, go and do your own spying,' I hiss. 'If I'm so useless. I'll stay with the barrow.'

He shrugs and goes, Fowler his dog trailing after him.

I push my aching hands into my pockets and sit on a plank balanced on a stack of bricks, sheltered by an awning. Nothing will stop the snow from blowing in. My hands are throbbing and my back feels like it's being clawed. I try rubbing my hands together to warm them. I'm light-headed so I shut my eyes; then I'm aware of someone blocking the blitz of snow. Robbie pushes a mug into my hands.

'There you go. All done for today.'

Around mine, his hands are warm from holding the mug. A hot brew of herbs. Tears block my throat.

'The market's not a place for sitting around. Only if you have to!' He chinks mugs with me. 'You OK, love? Maybe it was wrong to bring you.'

'What have you found out?'

He warms his hands, curling his long fingers around his own mug. 'Nothing out of the –' His whole body stiffens.

'What?'

'Not now. Wait till we move. Behind Karen Sowerby.' He shivers. 'How about you and Ewan?'

'He's so full of himself. He's getting on my nerves; I'll tell you back at the house.'

'Anything else?'

'The one with the fish. He took all the milk and cheese.'

Robbie blows on his drink then looks towards Jeston, the fish man. 'Him? Big family near Maryport – kids with colds or stomach upsets.' His breath steams in the icy air. His lips are shining from the hot drink. 'He's safe.'

'How do you know for sure? If he's from the sea…?'

'Gut instinct. How he is with his kids. You can tell. OK. Look now.'

Behind Karen Sowerby, bundled up like everyone else, are three men. There's something about the way they're standing. Close together, hands in pockets. And they're not buying or selling. I smile, and the shortest in the middle nods at me. The two taller ones flanking him say something and he laughs. Even at this distance, I can see his pock-marked skin, and small eyes. I've been registered in some way, noted. But there's no time to think. Ewan's back. All his anger gone.

'How about this, but?' He feels around in his pocket and with a flourish brings out a flat glass bottle, like a whisky flask. 'Want a swig, lass?'

'You know I'm not big on drinking, Ewan.'

'You'll learn, lass,' he says, drinking some down. He coughs and his eyes water. 'Strong stuff that, but warming... Change your mind?'

'Where'd you get it from?' We make beer and cider when we can and it's never enough, but it's not often you get spirits. 'Who did you trade with?'

'Off that marra yonder.' He points towards a man in a khaki hat with ear flaps, nose blue with the wind. He winks at us and puts his thumb up with a questioning look. Ewan confirms with the same gesture. 'Good stuff. The best.'

Robbie is happy to take some. 'Who is he? What did you give him?'

'Nowt of value. He gets the whisky. He collects old phones, tries to get them going. We traded.'

'But what can he do with old phones?'

'Lookit. There's nowt going on. He's a collector, and there's some folks think once 'lectric is up and running...'

He glances over to the stall selling old electric things. 'You've got to look to the future. Got to think it's going to get better.' His face is bright when he smiles.

'It could be a cover, mate.'

'How d'you know *he's* not a NOAH spy?' I say.

'Oh, stop twining, Anna lass.' He gives me a play-punch on the arm. 'Mebbe they're all in it together. Mebbe he's reporting back through secret microphones, not just having a bit of crack with that biddy, Karen with her old pots and that!' When Ewan laughs I smell the whisky, warming and earthy.

'Now you're skitting us, Ewan. It's serious. Those three standing around, near Sowerby's? Tell us what you know about them.' Robbie is impatient.

Ewan looks over 'All right, marra?' The three smile and wave. 'Taller ones are from out of town, used to work with me on a farm out Broughton way. Silage in the summer, ploughing in spring. Serious bastards, not much between the ears but they're all right. Middle one had a job with the council, pen pusher, but knows how to enjoy himself.' He laughs. 'Aye, I miss them nights down the pub… I'm glad brewery's started up again. Won't be long. Mebbe once distillery gets going…'

'We've got new arrivals at the Mill and I saw what was on that paper the fish man gave us,' I say.

'You're getting in a right state about them NOAHs. *Go forth increase and multiply. Britannia rules the waves.* That's old news. It's daft to think about repopulating the town when it's a struggle to feed ourselves.' He puts a hand on my shoulder. I shake it off. 'Everything's OK. Right? Life's too short for worrying. I've asked everyone I know. What d'you think I've been doing while you've been trading cheeses?' His voice is serious. 'There's no one I don't know up here. You can rely on that. Same as allus. Like I said. Time to ga yam. Here, Rob. Want some more?'

Warmed by the whisky, Robbie takes the barrow and leads off, talking to Ewan. I try to keep up but there's more snow now and the ground shifts under my feet. It's Ewan who notices I'm trailing behind and comes back for me.

'Here, lass, I got you some more of them herbal pills you like.' He winks and presses a paper bag into my hand. 'For your aches and pains.'

'Thanks. I'll try it once we're back. I'll be glad to get home, out of the cold.'

'Strong stuff so don't overdo it!'

'As if I would!'

Ewan is the one who found me crying out on the hillside and realised how much pain I was in. He gets me something for it when he can. Living in constant pain is draining; sometimes you have to compromise. I'll try to make them last this time.

I don't feel I've been much use, and there's nothing to report back apart from the paper. Which amounts to nothing – old fading paper. I need to find out as much as I can from Jamila.

We approach a man, face hidden by a beard, who's playing the penny whistle. When he sees us he starts up with 'Winter Wonderland'. Ewan puts a wrap of ciggies in his pot and bends down to pat the man's terrier, has a quick word with him. Looks at me to show me his generosity.

'I've an idea.' Robbie doubles back to speak to the man then lopes back to us, grinning. 'For Music Night tomorrow I've asked him. Name's Mike. Could do with a change from Daniel and his fiddle.'

'Aye, grand idea,' says Ewan, bringing out the whisky. 'Some of this, marra?'

'But is he ok?' I ask.

'Yes, he's on our side,' says Robbie. 'You can trust him.'

Robbie hums as he pushes the barrow back and I join in singing. Ewan does a jig and falls in a pile of snow. Fowler starts barking, pulling at his lead. On this cold hillside our voices ring out, with the river tumbling down to the sea. My voice soaring above theirs like a bird taking flight.

Eight

Ewan's dog is squatting on my chest, its breath in my face. Meaty and rancid. The smell of burned ash. Ewan is on the walls, over the ceiling. Crawling as if he's climbing up a vertical rock face. Ash falls from his pockets and from his hands. The air is cloudy with it. He's breathing it out, blowing it out, and ash falls like grey snow. The whole room is filling with it and I can't breathe. The dog bares its teeth and growls into my face. Its breath makes the ash swirl like sand falling down in an egg timer, slowly revolving. The words on my lips: 'I am soft sift in an hourglass.'

'What's wrong? Tell me what's wrong?' Ewan says, but his voice is wrong.

It's Robbie.

The ash clears. There is no ash. I'm lying with my hair dripping with sweat, my body running with it.

'You were having a nightmare. Talking in your sleep. You scared me, Anna.'

'Ewan was in it.'

He smiles and puts his hands around mine. 'You need to relax. You're doing too much. You're going to make yourself ill with all this.'

'But Ewan…'

'He can look after himself. Don't worry about him.'

'There's something not right. I've never thought about it before but there's something, I'm sure.'

'You're doing it again.'

'I'm not.'

'Anna, stop. It was a dream. We're all on edge. You're too

sensitive sometimes. I know it's a hangover from your illness but you have to stop. I'll be back in a minute. Try to relax. Deep breaths. Take some of your herbal stuff if that helps.'

He goes out of the bedroom, pulling the door not quite shut behind him. I do as I'm told. A breath in for the count of three then a longer one out.

But I'm tumbling back into the dream.

The dust or ash has cleared. I'm up in the woods, near the lookout. Ewan is there and there's a ringing in my ears. Church bells at first. Then, more like a phone ringing and no one answering it. A sense of urgency and helplessness. Then the ringing sound is only in my ears: tinnitus. Since I was ill it sometimes happens. There's a clink on the hard slate of the floor. Robbie puts down the mug.

'You fell asleep again.' He kisses me.

The last dream image is Ewan's hand dropping something. It falls into deep snow, sinks down and under the surface. We're both reaching for it and I'm falling too. Falling awake.

~ ~ ~

Water frothing over the stones of the weir. Cutting through the layers of rock laid down slowly over millennia, the river falls away with a constant rushing sound, racing, hurrying along the seven miles to Workington and the sea. Whatever happens to us, the water will keep flowing down to the sea until the sea rises and (our worst, unspoken fear) washes back up the river.

On the opposite bank, a heron is standing on one leg, so still you'd easily miss it, camouflaged against the grey slate.

'Hey, Jamila. There's the heron.'

'What?' She sits up and follows where I'm pointing. The tip of her nose is red, and her hands are mottled and dark purple.

'On the other side of the river.'

I take an old cardigan from the back of a chair and offer it to her, but she shakes her head.

'I'm not cold.' She shivers. 'What's it doing?'

'Looking for food. Fish.'

She slumps back into her chair. 'Is it only going to be me? All the time?'

'I wish there were more children here for you.'

'I'm not a *child.* I'm going to have a baby. Remember?' She shivers again and puts the cardigan on. It's an old one of Tracey's and hangs on her loosely, like a child dressing up.

Flakes of snow are swirling in the wind. This is one of the hardest winters we've had. Tonight, when it's my turn to milk the goats, it will take an age to warm my hands up. But I still enjoy their sweet smell, and the spurt of milk into the metal bucket is soothing. If the wind picks up, the snow will start to drift, but it's powdery; flakes fall into the river and are washed away. Like us, I think moodily; each one individual, there briefly, then gone for ever.

'Poor bird. Must be freezing out there.' Jamila sighs. 'It's cool. Can I draw it? That bird?'

It's the first time she's shown enthusiasm for schoolwork. 'OK. Then some writing.'

'Fine.' She's sulky again. 'But you have to help me.'

While she's drawing, she's calm and more settled. This is my last chance to talk to her before we have to confront her mother. It's not only George and Ewan who are getting impatient. Daniel has decided we're having a meeting tomorrow with everyone. He says I'm taking too long. He's taken it out of my hands. I have to give in to him as leader.

'Do you think she's lonely?'

'Who?'

'The heron.'

'They're solitary. They like being on their own.'

'I don't…' Jamila stops herself and finishes the sentence under her breath. 'I *hate* being on my own.' Her fingers are tight around the pencil, gripping it until her knuckles turn pale.

'What's wrong with being on your own? No one gets time to be lonely here, it's so busy! Tonight there'll be music. Something to look forward to.'

She doesn't answer, doesn't look up. Then she does, and the heron flaps its ungainly wings and flies away, legs trailing behind it. It climbs through the falling snow, high into the trees and, almost in slow motion, follows the river and away.

'Now I can't…' She drops her pencil and pushes the others away, coughing. Only she's not coughing, she's crying. Heavy tears drop onto the paper. 'Anna, I'm scared. I don't want to have this baby. Mum says it hurts. A lot.'

I touch her gently on the hand.

'I'm scared of… the men. They did bad things. When I'm on my own I keep thinking about it. It's like…'

'You don't have to tell me,' I say.

'But I want to. It's like a horrible secret. A disgusting nightmare. Every time I shut my eyes. On my own. When it's dark.'

'Is it about the people who did that to your wrist? The NOAHs?'

'Mum says don't talk about it. Forget about them. She said God gave me the baby.'

'You can tell me if you want to.' When I touch her slight shoulders I can feel every bone, like her mother, only these bones have never been broken and had to grow back together again.

'Mum says God wants me to be happy.'

She grasps my hand and holds it tight. In her dark eyes there's a reflection of the library window, its four panes divided by a cross.

'But I *know,* Anna.'

'Know what?'

'They did it to all the girls. After the hymns and prayers, after the music. When we were in our cabins. At night. They came and they did it… but I never got pregnant then. It was later… when we got away. They came after us. Lots of them. And that's how there's a baby.'

I remember Nula's description: how there was nothing she could do while they took turns raping her daughter. How she screamed for them to stop.

I hold her and stroke her back.

She sniffs and sobs.

'In the night, when Mum's asleep and it's dark. That's when I see it. Like it's happening again. I get into her bed and I can't stop crying. She hugs me but the dreams won't go away.'

'You talk to her about it?'

'She says forget all about it. *She* has. But she's an adult…' She cries again, unable to speak. 'I remember it all the time.'

'Jamila, we're all here to look after you. You won't be on your own. When you see your baby, like Tiny only much smaller, when you hold her (or him) in your arms, you'll be so happy you will forget everything else.'

She sniffs and rubs her face against the long sleeves of the cardigan. The heron lands back in the same spot, folding up its clumsy wings.

'There it is…' She kneels so that she can see out of the window. 'OK. I'm going to finish my picture now. I'm going to draw all the birds. And the animals.'

For the next half hour while she sketches, sniffling and sometimes sighing, I search the shelves for a bird book. Some are so water-damaged the pages are stuck together, the print illegible. They'll have to go for kindling. It hurts to burn books, but wood is in short supply and each month we have to travel further away from the Mill and safety to find timber for the fire. We're rewilding as much as we can and have a planting programme to replace what we use. We only light a fire on the coldest of days. We don't want to lose the windbreak or the cover it gives us against attack. A balance between defending ourselves and keeping warm; between growing crops and protecting our environment.

I imagine Jamila and other girls living in their cabins deep in a forest, like Center Parcs. Or Hansel and Gretel. Her story makes me shiver. Those crude posters *Go forth increase and multiply* in yellow and purple. This rape was more than a weapon used against women in time of conflict; it was organised, systematic. I've been hesitating too long, trying not to upset this vulnerable family. The others are right: I need to confront Nula and, for the sake of the whole community, she needs to be honest with us.

'Oh! What was that?'

She squeals and makes me jump. She's terrified. I stand up, expecting the worst, but she's holding her belly.

'I felt something. Bubbly. Like wind.' She grips my arms and buries herself into me. 'I felt the baby. It's wriggling!'

'But that's exciting!' I say calmly. 'Let's go and tell your mum.'

'It's real now, isn't it? A real baby inside here.' She points to her belly.

'Your own. And your mum's first grandchild.'

'But it won't be mine.'

'Of course it will.'

'You don't understand, Anna.'

I'm holding her gently but she could break, she's so fragile. Her heart is pounding and her breath coming quickly. 'We'll look after you. We'll keep you safe.'

'They'll come.'

'You mean the men? I don't think that's what they want.' I picture Nula's bones, broken and healed. Men out for only one thing.

Since the Flood, so much has changed that we could never have imagined, but Jamila is a frightened child. She needs reassurance.

'Let's go and find your mum. I know it's hard, but you have to think about the good things. Can you hear that?' A thread of music has drifted up through our conversation.

The baby forgotten, she runs to where Daniel is tuning up his fiddle, as if the music has cast a spell and transformed her. She's dancing. Like a spring of water bubbling out of dry ground. Tracey and I clap along as she moves, faster and faster, her face glowing, smiling.

Then the door opens and it's her mother, back from milking the goats. Nula clangs the bucket down. 'Jay, stop that.'

The violin breaks off in the middle of a phrase. A sudden quiet.

'Stop it, Jamila. It's too dangerous. It makes me feel sick to see you doing that. Stop it, now.' Nula's eyes are even darker when she's angry. 'Have you been to collect the eggs yet?'

Mid-flow Jamila freezes and her arms fall flat at her sides. Then she throws herself into a chair. 'I was having fun. For once. You won't let me do anything!' she shouts. Then adds in a whisper only her mother and I can hear: 'The baby was dancing too. I felt her moving.' She bursts into tears.

'Oh, love. I'm sorry.'

Jamila pushes her mother away and runs outside. Framed by the window, she starts kicking the snow, the cardigan dangling from her narrow shoulders like a cape.

Daniel shakes his head then tucks his violin under his chin again and plays quietly, trying out new tunes, tapping with his foot. George joins him on his piano accordion.

Nula starts sieving the milk, pouring it into the bottles we use and reuse.

'Let me,' I say.

She shrugs, her back to me. 'It's OK. I can do it myself.'

Outside, Jamila is collecting snow in her bare hands, hurling it at the door of the workshop.

'I've told her.' Nula speaks so only I can hear. 'She won't listen to me.'

'But dancing can't hurt. She's young and fit.'

'You know nothing about it. I don't want her to dance.'

All I can do is leave them to sort it out. Now there's a grey pall over a day when we usually have something to look forward to, when, for a short time, we forget how fragile our safety is.

But light, warmth and music change everything. By the evening, Nula and Jamila seem to be reconciled, although neither of them dances. Mike, the bearded man from the market, who plays the penny whistle, arrives. He's in his twenties like Robbie and me, and lives in the town, Ewan says. The whistle is bright, and he plays so fast my feet are soon tapping in rhythm. I'm sitting at the side watching the dancers when Nula brings me a mug of mulled cider, concern in her face, in her voice.

'I didn't realise it was so hard for you to…'

'I can sing. That's something I *can* do,' I say, and laugh.

'I've heard you. You have a strong voice. It's lovely to listen to. I wish you'd sing more often.' She hesitates. Like everyone else she wants to know why. I hate having to share my physical weakness. But above almost everything I prize honesty.

'What happened? I'm sorry, that's the sort of thing I tell Jamila not to ask.'

She sits next to me and we listen to Daniel playing his violin. On the deep window sills and on the shelf next to the fire, candle flames waver and make shadows dance on the walls. She glances at me, then away.

'On the journey here, I was ill. A kind of rheumatic fever, Robbie thinks. I can't remember much about it. Ever since, my joints have been inflamed, painful.' I blurt it out. Quickly. No hesitation. It's the only way I can bear to tell my story. 'But I made it here. I was lucky.'

'I'm sorry.'

'Everyone's lost something. Someone. You have to keep going. And I have Robbie. I'd be lost without him.' He's dancing with Elsa and Tracey, kicking out his long legs, all three singing along to Beatles songs. 'How about Jamila's dad? What happened?'

She shakes her head. 'It wasn't that kind of relationship. I never think of him.' She goes to the window and opens it then stands, breathing in the cold air. When she moves back towards me, the candles flicker and smoke.

'What is it?' I say.

'Nothing. Sorry.' There's an edge to her voice. A fragility. Her eyes slide sideways away from mine. She's holding back. Wavering. About to say something else. But the deafening squawk of George's piano accordion fills the room, and Ewan comes over to bring us back to the group.

'Hey, we've got a proper band now! That Mike's dead good, eh? Anna, give us a song, lass!' His eyes are very bright, each pupil a dark hole. Beads of sweat on his upper lip. 'Are you going to dance then, Nula? Your Jamila's like a la'al ballet dancer. She says you're even better.' Ewan reaches out his hand to pull her towards the open space where Elsa and the children are dancing. 'Come on!'

'I don't dance, thanks. And I've told Jamila not to. Where is she?'

'Come on, I bet you're dying to have a go.' Robbie is out of breath and laughing.

'No. Thanks.' She turns away, and drinks her cider.

Robbie's not one to give up easily. 'Go on. Look at Elsa, she hasn't stopped all night, given herself a coughing fit with all that exercise! I can see your feet are itching to get out onto the dance floor.'

The look she gives him is fierce; it stops him in his tracks. He shrugs as if to say *what the hell*, then looks so deflated I almost laugh. He only wants the best for everyone. Like a physical injury slowly healing and no longer so raw and open, the pain of all our losses is there in the room, but something has changed in me. I know it for sure when Robbie grabs my hand.

'Right, your turn. Let's have a song.' He's radiating heat and as usual his hands are hot and dry. 'Something quiet. I need a break!'

Ewan grabs my other hand and pulls me up. Beer and something else on his breath, he's full of rough energy, it's bouncing off him. Blond hair darkening with sweat, sticking to his forehead. Eyes shining in the candlelight.

'Aye, I've had enough of our dad and his squeeze box for one night. Can't hear mesel' think. Mebbe that'll get Nula on to dance floor.'

I have a word with Daniel and he nods, then everyone moves back to give me space.

The room is so hot, condensation is dripping down all the windows and I feel stifled. I hold on to the old roll top desk for balance, my heart beating unevenly in my chest, and it's as I take in a breath to start, I'm suddenly outside myself, watching my hand pressing down onto the worn wood. I hear the words of 'Fields of Gold' pouring out of me, a song that's not much older than me, yet feels as if it's an ancient folk song. And something is happening in the room. It feels as if I'm creating something for the first time, something personal for each one of us. Those who know the tune hum, those who know the words join in. Then it's Ewan's voice I hear, harmonising in a rich baritone, making the music deep and whole. Healing. Mournful, but hopeful.

A half-smile crosses Nula's face and she looks at Ewan, as if for the first time. Admiration. Perhaps more. These things happen in an instant. The quickening of life. Yes, there's something. Even if they're not fully aware of it, and Nula so broken by her experiences of men. I can feel it like a surge of electricity.

It's also a glimpse of our lives as they used to be only a handful of years ago, when it wasn't survival but living. Choosing. Celebrating and enjoying. Not fearful of what will happen, or what someone might say. Simple pleasure in relationships.

How we all live is so different, but we're together in this. I don't know how likely it is, but we have to believe the water will gradually withdraw; we'll build our community and welcome new members. We have to believe in a new and better life.

The frown that so often mars Nula's beautiful face melts away. She glances at Ewan. They both look away, then back at each other. They smile. And there is something so joyous in witnessing this subtle recognition, I feel myself smile too.

George wipes away a tear. The song is sad but there's an edge of optimism too, and Robbie starts the clapping; it's when he smiles at me and something inside me twists that I know how far I've come. I've sometimes thought I could never feel desire again, that the blind, biological push had drowned. But it's there, gasping for air, and I'm almost unbalanced by it; blood rushes to my face and the room spins.

'Whoa, look out, Anna. You need to sit down.' Tracey brings me a chair. 'You've gone right pale and pasty.'

I never used to, but since my illness I get faint very easily.

'Or maybe some air? It's close in here, isn't it?' says Daniel.

'Aye, come on, lass, give us your hand,' Robbie says, in

broad Cumbrian, and leads me out to the garden, putting a coat around my shoulders.

Voices and music fade to a faint murmur. It's bitterly cold. Without streetlights, the sky is pinpointed by thousands of stars, the moon a slim fingernail, and the only sound is the river; not many venture out at night. In the cold, the stars seem to be vibrating; Dad told me people used to believe that if we could listen to the right frequency the old music of the spheres would be audible. I can almost hear it.

Each year, winter is longer and colder, and in the summer there's scorching heat and drought, downpours of rain that flatten our precious harvest. But we go on. We won't give up.

'You sang that beautifully, it wasn't only George getting teary!' He pulls me in close and when our lips touch there's nothing else I want more than this, here, now.

Nine

The next day, Stefan is slicing greens he and his father, Daniel, foraged yesterday, to add to the ubiquitous cabbage. We're going to have some of the fish tonight – Stefan has a plan to cook it the way he remembers their mother used to prepare it, with layers of carrot and rosemary.

While I chop potatoes, Jamila stirs the pan.

'What does three mean?' she says, turning to me. 'When they blow the whistle three times?'

'Someone's coming… Why? Did you hear something?'

Out of the window, the garden is empty. There's no one there.

'Didn't you?'

I shake my head, wipe my hands roughly on my legs. We aren't expecting anyone. We rarely are. I act without thinking. 'Go to your mum. I think she's up with Elsa. Keep Tiny quiet. Quick.' She's swaying from one foot to the other, hesitating. 'Now.'

'Can I go with her?' Stefan says. Even now, when we could be in danger, I can't help noticing how the light from the window picks out the vibrant green of his eyes under his blond fringe.

'No. Stay here. Keep slicing. Whoever it is, we have to eat.'

I open the front door, my heart in my mouth.

A short man. Familiar. I don't know him, but I've seen him before.

'Hiya, lass. Local census.'

'Oh, it's you again, mate. What is it this time?' Daniel, coming in through the back door from the Mill, stamps his feet and shakes snow off his shoulders. He eyes the man. In the warmth of the kitchen, his wet clothes start to steam.

'Routine call, Mr Lister. Nowt to worry about. Updating the census. Checking who's living here.'

'On whose authority?' Daniel steps towards him, but the stranger ignores him, opens a cupboard and looks in, then lets it close with a bang. He picks up the spoon Jamila was stirring the soup with and dips it into the pan bubbling on the stove. He blows on it then tastes it.

'Mm, not bad… could do with more salt, lass… Got a big potful. Expecting a crowd?'

'Same as always.' Daniel leans in and bangs the lid on. 'Hungry work. I asked you a question, you know.'

The man backs off. 'Has to be done every three months now.' He takes a crumpled paper out of his trouser pocket. 'I've got the official list.' He clears his throat. 'Go on then. Who's living here? Tell me everyone's name.'

'Me and my twins, then there's George Huddart and his two –'

'Names?'

'Mine are Elsa and Stefan. That's him making dinner. You know the surname. And there's Tracey Huddart here, and her brother, Ewan.'

Tracey looks up from putting out the cutlery, and gives a shy smile the man doesn't return.

'And this lass?' pointing at me.

'If you let me finish… this is Anna. Her boyfriend, Robbie, is hereabouts. Both up from London three years back.'

'Oh aye, he's the doctor, like? Tall and skinny like your lad?'

'There are eight of us.' Daniel ignores him but it worries me. The way he says *doctor*.

The man picks up one of the plastic plates. 'Your twins using babbie stuff?'

'We use what we can. Not everyone has a Wedgwood dinner service.'

The man ignores Daniel's attempt to joke.

'And babbie toys.' He picks up a set of teething rings. 'What you got them for?'

There's the briefest pause, then Tracey says, 'It's me. I've been sorting them out for market. There's allus a few lasses need new things for la'al uns.'

He sniffs. Irritated. 'Aye… well I hope you get sommat good for them.' He moves towards the back door, then stops. Half turns, like a cliché from an old war film. That's when I know he's going to say something.

'Oh, by the way there's a report of you lot asking questions around town, asking about strangers. What's that about? Why are you so interested? Have you seen someone new?'

That's when I recognise him. From the market. One of the three men standing together in a menacing, Cold War way, observing everyone. The short one in the middle with pock-marked skin. My stomach starts churning. Have they been watching the Mill? Have they seen Nula and her children?

'You have to keep an eye out,' Daniel says. 'You hear things. We were checking up. You know how it is.'

'Oh aye. You can't be too careful with strangers hanging around, can you?' He affects a lightness that is not meant. Then he points to the wall. 'Good you've got calendar up, Mr Lister, but where's your portrait? Did you not get one?'

Daniel narrows his eyes. 'What are you on about?'

I know what happened to it. Ripped to pieces and thrown in the fire.

'Oh, I'm sorry, Mr Lister. They must have missed you. You're so far out of the way down here.' The man rifles in the pockets of his overcoat and pulls out a rolled-up poster. 'There you go. We all need someone watching over us nowadays…'

Daniel takes it, frowning.

'One last thing...' the man goes on. 'Martlemass this year. Mek sure millwheel doesn't budge. Nothing to move at Martlemass. The date's on the calendar. I'd put a ring round it if I was you, Mr Lister. They let you off with it last year, but it won't be so easy for you this time. Rules are rules, you know. We've got to sing from the same hymn sheet, eh? Enjoy your dinners.'

He bangs the door behind him.

'Daniel! What was that about? What's going on?' It's hard to get my words out.

He unrolls the poster. A stylised image of a bearded, long-haired man, smiling benignly, against a calm, blue ocean, full of swimming fish. *Britannia rules the waves again.*

'Fucking NOAH propaganda. I know where that can go!'

'No. Hang on to it.' I point to a mirror on the wall. 'You could stick it on the back... After what you said about NOAH; if he comes again...'

Reluctantly, Daniel pins the poster on the back of the mirror and turns it round to face the wall. 'Right! Enough of this nonsense. Martlemass! Never heard of it! They're inventing new saints and festivals by the day!' he snorts, then turns on his heel. 'Tracey, that was quick thinking, lass! Go and find Nula.'

She blushes and mumbles, 'I'll get her.'

Daniel puts his hand on his son's shoulder. 'Well done, Stefan. That's a pile and a half of greens! What can I do to help with dinner?'

'When Jamila comes back she can help.'

'Daniel, can I ask you something?' I say.

'Come on, lass, that fire looks good. Let's get warmed up.'

He sits down, stretches out his legs and yawns. 'What a wanker!' Then, automatically, he starts tapping out a rhythm with his fingers on the arm of the sofa.

'Did you notice when he talked about Robbie, the way he

said "doctor"? It made me uneasy.'

'That's how his kind operate. Hinting. Insinuating. But there's not a lot he can do.'

'What do you mean?

'Ex-council. Jobsworth. They're looking for people with medical skills. But he can't make Rob work for them, can he?'

I put my hands out to feel the warmth of the fire. 'What was he here for then?'

'No idea. Snooping. Giving out NOAH crap.' He smiles. 'You were right to hide Nula and the children. Whatever we find out, it's innocent until proved guilty in my book. We need to give them a chance… Ah, here they are!'

Jamila, straight back to stirring the pan, gazes adoringly at Stefan. Overnight she has developed a huge crush on him. He's acutely aware of it, and self-consciously pushes back the blond hair that flops over his forehead.

'Who was it? What did he want, Daniel?' Nula's voice is low and urgent. 'Did he…?'

'It's OK, lass. Nosing around as usual. I don't think he'll be coming back in a hurry.'

She sighs 'But did he ask about me and the kids?'

Daniel shakes his head and smiles. 'Anna will tell you. I'm going to see what needs doing.'

I mention the census, but not the plates and toys. The way he picked them up as if they were dirty or offensive. She's already scared; she doesn't need more to worry about. But I tell her how he sounded when he mentioned Robbie.

There's a pause before she asks, 'What kind of doctor?'

'A trained nurse. Psychiatric. He does what he can, but he's not a doctor.'

'Everything's different now.' She shakes her head slowly. 'And he's got valuable skills.'

'Sometimes I wish he would put himself first. It was Ewan's idea. He brought a kid with a swollen thumb. It was infected and needed to be lanced, and when the father said, "Can you sort it out, doc?" it appealed to his pride; he couldn't say no. He loves nursing, but there's a niggling regret he didn't push himself harder to get to medical school. He had to look out for his brother, Simon. He struggled with his mental health. Robbie couldn't forgive himself when Simon joined NOAH.'

She smiles. 'So he's set up his own clinic!'

'Once people heard, they brought their kids, parents, everyone. They give him all kinds of random things – food, alcohol. Even jewellery, which he refuses. People do anything for their children. You know that, of course.'

'We all do what we can for the people we love. You'd do the same for Robbie, wouldn't you?'

I nod and smile, but she doesn't return my smile.

'Anna, what he's doing is dangerous.'

For once, the intensity of her dark eyes irritates me, as if beauty trumps practicality.

'That's nonsense. He's helping people,' I snap. 'How can that be wrong? Do you want us to go right back to the dark ages – herbal remedies, bread poultices and superstition?'

'Of course not. That isn't what I meant.' She hesitates and lowers her voice. 'But he needs to be careful. Especially now.'

'You'll have to spell it out for me. I don't know what you mean. It's mostly first aid. It's not as if he's got medical supplies that people are desperate to get their hands on. He's making do like everyone else.'

'OK then. Let me put it like this; if it looks like he has surgical skills, NOAH might want him.'

'But they must have their own doctors?'

'Yes, but no one wants to work for them. They need more.'

'It would take a lot to persuade him to work for extremists! He'd never agree to it.'

'NOAH don't need to persuade you. They don't interview you or offer you a job. They don't operate like that, Anna. You've seen what they do. Please warn him.'

Ten

Snow must have fallen all last night; when we dug a path to get to the goats for milking it was dark, but now it's bright in the house, even though there's no sign of the sun. Light is glancing off the snow, clouds heavy with the threat of more to come. My stomach is rumbling. Breakfast was a thin affair – toast tainted by the taste of mould and ersatz coffee from roasted dandelion roots; another recipe George found in his grandmother's wartime cookery book. Knowing the meeting was happening, I couldn't eat.

With Daniel's agreement, I ask the twins to cover my guard duty. Their first time together. At seventeen, they're too young to have a vote, and they've been pestering their father for months.

'It's OK, Anna,' Stefan says.

'It's cool.' Elsa sneezes. 'I've got *another* cold, but who wants to listen to Dad and his boring meetings?' She laughs and pulls a face at her brother as they put on matching moss-green beanies. 'Last one to the lookout's a loser.' Then she's out of the door, feet kicking up clouds of snow.

Stefan dives after her, grasping for her scarf, but as usual she's far ahead before he can catch her.

Daniel's written the agenda up on the board, ever the teacher, the leader; we rely on his organisational skills and the way he holds us all together. If he wasn't here, I sometimes wonder who'd step in, but I never let myself linger on the thought.

New members

Role

A O B

George is Chair. He clears his throat.

'Let's mek a start,' he says. 'What's number one, our Tracey? Read it for us, will you?'

She tells him in a whisper. He can never find his reading glasses.

'Right, lass… So, our new members. How are you lasses settling in?' It's the first time Jamila and Nula have been at a meeting. Jamila is sitting near the fire, playing with one of the cats, dangling a piece of yellow wool for it to jump at. Having a cat keeps the mice down.

'Good, thanks,' says Nula. 'We're grateful to you for –'

'It's OK.' Jamila smiles at me with more confidence. 'But I wish there were more kids. It's boring, just me and Anna. No offence.' She drops the wool and pulls the cat up onto her knee and starts to stroke it.

'Did Elsa and Stefan go to school?' asks Nula.

'We gave them what education we could,' says Daniel. 'Everywhere was flooded, buildings unsafe, not enough teachers. We did what we could, what was possible.'

'There's that new one,' Ewan says. 'I heard at market it's open now. Folks are sending their kids there – at least they're out from under their feet. Not everyone likes to teach their kids at home!' Sometimes he's quick to fly off the handle, but now he has that air of supreme physical confidence. He's smiling, glancing at Nula. 'What do you think, Nula?' he adds in a softer voice.

Robbie's arm is along the back of my chair. I can feel the tension in his muscles. He sniffs. 'Another fucking religious school. Indoctrination happening right under –'

'Robbie!' Tracey digs him in the ribs. 'You can't swear! We've got la'al ones in the room.'

'We've not had a school for over five years,' Daniel says, slowly. 'We need proper schools but…'

‘But what are they teaching them?’ Robbie squeezes my shoulder.

‘I can find out if they’re taking new kids,’ Ewan says. ‘More fun than being stuck here, eh, Jay?’

‘Yes please, Ewan. I want to go to a proper school.’

Daniel shakes his head. ‘Rob’s right. We need to find out first. There could be all kinds of –’

‘I don’t want her to go. She needs to stay here, OK?’ Nula says, abruptly, and the smile dies on Ewan’s face. ‘And the other thing… Oh, Tiny, stop it. He always starts when I want to say something. Jamila needs more food. She’s a growing girl. We’re both hungry all the time here. And heating. A few more logs on the fire.’

She looks pinched and cold, hugging the baby close to her for warmth. He struggles to his feet, bouncing on her lap. Oblivious to her irritation.

George laughs. ‘Soft southerners! Look, lass, we had plenty before you two came. We’re sharing everything. You should be grateful. There’s plenty of woollens to wear if you’re feeling the cold.’

Daniel frowns.

‘Aye, Daniel, I know. But we’re stretching to feed two more already, then there’s babbie to think about. He’s Tiny now, but he’s not going to stop growing, is he? We don’t want to turn folks away, but it’s got to be fair.’

‘Of course, that’s how we try to be at the Mill,’ Daniel says. ‘It’s fundamental. Sharing resources equally. Everyone doing what they can.’

‘Well, how come you’re cossetting la’al lass?’ George says triumphantly, his chin jutting out.

‘You’re right, our Dad. When Anna came she was a good worker. What’s wrong with her?’ Ewan laughs and points his thumb at Jamila. ‘Proper soft southerner, eh?’

‘She’s a child, George. A child.’ Daniel smiles at Jamila.

'Children need to eat well to grow strong. We all know that.'

Jamila hides her face in her hands. 'Mum! Tell him!' She turns to me. 'Anna?'

Managing Jamila's fears and balancing the baby, who has started whining, Nula is quick to come to the boil. 'Tiny, *stop* it, will you!'

'Let me take him.' I reach for his wriggling body.

'No, let me.' Tracey gets in first and tugs him onto her knee. 'What are you twining about, lad? Now you're with Auntie Tracey, you've got to be good. We all need to hear what Anna's going to say.' She nudges me. 'Go on, Anna lass, you've got to tell them now. Or do you want me to?'

Jamila slumps further down into her chair, her shoulders rounded, trying to disappear. The only sound is Nula's foot tapping on the stone floor. Tracey raises her eyebrows, urging me to speak, then kisses Tiny on the head, making faces at him until he smiles.

'Come on. What's the secret? You lasses all know something we don't, so I think you need to share it,' Daniel says.

I can feel Robbie's arm tightening. I've never kept something like this from him. It's a betrayal.

'That's right, Dan. We can't have secrets,' says George. 'That's what we said. It's in the rules.'

'Anna, what's wrong?' Robbie whispers, moving his arm away so he can look at me properly.

Heat rises to my face. Why did I think I could sort it out myself? I decided not to tell the men for the good of all of us. But why didn't I tell Robbie? I remember when we were on the road, those endless months travelling through the Flood camps. Before I was ill. We were somewhere in the Midlands, south of Yorkshire. There were notices warning of the penalties for stealing food, but I wonder now if he could even read. To creep into the stores and steal fruit. I remember the look on his face – disbelief, shame. He must have been so hungry to do it. A small, hungry boy. Light brown hair, bleached by the sun and grown long, curling around his ears and over the collar of his jacket. They found him with his mouth full of apple, apples in his pocket, for his sister. He didn't deserve it, but there was nothing his parents could do. For a whole afternoon they made him stand on his own on a chair in front of our section of the camp. Not far from the perimeter of the camp, as if to highlight the gravity of his sin, was an apple tree laden with fruit, in a flooded, inaccessible field. I remember how his face glowed with humiliation. How his eyes filled with tears, not only for himself, but for his whole family. The deep shame of it.

At least he was a child; it could have been worse. But I'm an adult and I've made a stupid mistake.

'It's not what you think…' I say. My words stumble out.

'Them bloody NOAHs. That's what it is. I thought so.' George rubs at his nose with the back of his hand.

'No, that's not it.'

'Come on, tell us,' Ewan says. 'And shut up, Dad. You're jumping to conclusions. Let her speak.'

Daniel stands. 'You need to pipe down. All of you. What's the problem, Anna?'

Robbie would have known how to tell them without getting their backs up. But, before I can take a breath, Tracey is on her feet, jolting Tiny, who cries in fright. With him bawling in her ear, she has to shout to hear herself.

'That'un, she's going to have a babbie. La'al Jamila.'

Jamila looks up, her face frozen, hands shaking. 'But it's a special baby,' she whispers. 'It's from God. You can't take it away from me!'

In the quiet that follows her outburst, the room is claustrophobic. Our shadows waver on the walls as a draught down the chimney disturbs the fire.

Ewan's the first to break the silence. 'She's too young! You're her mam. Are you sure?'

Nula nods, her bottom lip trembling.

With the low ceiling, Ewan fills the space, towering over us. His hands grasp the back of the chair where Tracey has sat to pacify Tiny. 'When's it due?'

'Another few months. We don't know for sure. When it's warmer. Spring,' I say.

'Bloody hell! Another mouth to feed.' George shakes his head. 'This throws a spanner in the works. But how come you…? What kind of mother…?'

Robbie rests his hand on the old man's shoulder. 'Now, George. This isn't helping. You know what the world's like now. Some men take what they can get, use their strength, don't have respect for –'

I know what he's thinking: why didn't I talk to him before it came to this? Why didn't I trust him? Why didn't I ask for his medical opinion?

'It wasn't like that,' Nula shouts, close to tears and cutting him off mid-flow. 'Jamila's been chosen by God to have a baby.'

'Well, she doesn't have to have it *here*!' George thumps the table. 'We already know what risk a new babbie brings… Who.'

'Oh not again, Dad!' Ewan slaps him on the back. 'Why's everyone allus on about NOAHs? NOAH this. NOAH that. You'd think everything that happens is because of them NOAHs. When was the last time you saw one round here? Not for months.'

Daniel is a short man, but when he speaks we all listen. 'You're not thinking straight, half of you. I don't know about babies coming from God. I don't believe in all that. Never have. But I believe what I've seen… and there've been disappearances. Folk here one day, then gone the next. I know people move on looking for something better, but sometimes they're not given a choice. We've all seen their posters. Someone's putting them up, even if it's not bloody Noah himself! That spying idiot who came the other day…' He snorts. 'So I don't give a damn if this baby's a gift from God or what, but if those NOAHs get wind of this… Two babies is two too many to feel safe. We need to come to a decision, and I know what *I* think.'

In Tracey's arms, Tiny is laughing, bouncing on his bandy legs. Jamila's face is wet with tears. Nula offers her a scrap of cloth.

'I'm sorry, Nula. It had to come out sometime. We need to make a decision that's fair for everyone.' My heart's racing. I should have told Daniel earlier, paved the way for this moment.

George sits up straight. 'Well, in that case, as Chair, I propose we let them go. I'm too old to deal with NOAHs. I don't want to take the risk. Remember that lot with all their fancy walls and security a few years back over Papcastle way? Did nowt for them in the long run. Nobody there now to tell the tale. It's ruined. Abandoned.' He looks meaningfully at Nula. 'Folks said it was NOAHs, but I don't know. Sorry, Nula lass, I've got to think about my own. We need to let them go, Daniel.'

No one else speaks, then it's Ewan. 'You're all makin' a mountain out of a molehill.'

'Once the meeting's finished, I need to examine Jamila, if that's OK with you, Nula.' Robbie's voice is level, calming. 'But first we need to put it to the vote.'

There are slow nods around the room. Nula reaches down for her daughter's hand.

'Please let us stay.' Jamila's dark eyes are round and brimming with tears. Her voice a whisper.

'There's nowhere to go.' Nula's voice is low and quiet, boiling anger replaced by fear and exhaustion. Close to tears too. 'If you throw us out in this we'll die. All three of us. The baby too.' She points to the window where snow is falling and feathering the sill.

'Please, Anna. Please, Robbie.' It's unbearable to hear the pleading in Jamila's voice. 'Let us stay. At least till the baby comes. Then we'll go. Won't we, Mum?'

'We can't throw them out.' Tracey, who rarely goes against her father, stands up, holding Tiny. 'Even if they don't meet them NOAHs, they'll freeze to death!'

'Tracey's right. It would be inhuman,' Robbie says. 'Against everything we stand for.'

'But how do we know they're telling the truth?' George is bristling with anger.

'Listen to yourself, George!' Robbie is rubbing his nose, finding it hard to control his anger.

'Oh Dad, have a bit sympathy,' Ewan shouts. 'You lot allus go on about NOAHs, but what's a couple of lasses going to do to us?' He winks at Jamila. 'We said we want to keep the community going. And if we want that, we need more of the next generation.'

I could hug him; I knew he was on our side. For a moment I see the softening in Nula's face again.

'They could be spies, lad. You don't know nowt. You're allus too cocky. You don't know nowt.' George spits as he shouts.

It's then we hear it. Ewan grabs his coat and runs to the door. In the uproar of all the raised voices it could have been going on for minutes, a quarter of an hour. It's the sound of the whistle.

PART TWO

Ten

Up ahead, Ewan's red hat bobs through the trees and Robbie strides close behind him. Daniel and I follow, but I soon fall behind. We have rakes, shovels, anything we can grab. Daniel takes his black labrador, Victor. We've done it before, but the last thing we want to do is fight; we'll give them food, supplies to keep them going. We don't care who they are. But we vowed we'd never fight.

The whistle sounds – three short, three long, three short blasts, then a gap, over and over again. S O S. Then the gap lengthens.

Daniel looks back and we exchange a glance. We're both straining our ears, willing it to start again, or for the All Clear to sound. There's nothing. Only a ringing silence; a swirl of wind blows clouds of snow off the trees, dusting our faces. Neither of us speak; there's no need to voice our thoughts.

The twins' footprints are already covered. We're almost wading through the snow, deeper than I've ever known it, sliding and tripping over stems of bramble, exposed roots, each step takes a superhuman effort. In front, Daniel gestures for me to go back. But I want to be there. I feel responsible. His children are so young, only seventeen, and it was my turn to be on watch. I pause to catch my breath, my heart bursting with the effort. Down in the valley, the Mill looks like a Dutch landscape, the faces of the goats peering out over the doorway of their hut. A slim feather of smoke rises almost perpendicular, then is blown sideways as another gust of wind comes down from the north. I listen hard for the whistle. There's only my own breath, my pulse in my ears, and then my feet crunching through the snow again, climbing, my legs burning with the effort.

It all happens in a moment. A shot rings out and echoes against the hill, startling the rooks that rise cawing in a black swirl. Ahead, Daniel disappears out of sight over the ridge. I'm alone.

Then his voice comes, clear over the snow: 'Go back down, Anna!' but it's too late; I come over the top of the hill and see them at the base of the lookout, squatting down. No sign of the twins. As I get closer there's a shape on the ground and a disturbance in the snow leading away from the lookout post.

'You don't need to see this. Go back, Anna,' says Daniel. His voice is controlled desperation.

I shake my head. 'I don't need protecting. I've seen more than you know.'

Stefan is lying face down. Blood spreads and pools under him. Like a swimmer in the snow.

Robbie takes his pulse. Shakes his head slightly then draws in a quick breath. 'He's alive. Quick. Help me turn him over so he can breathe.'

'How serious is it?'

Against the white of the snow Stefan's green knitted hat falls off, releasing long blonde hair. Only it's not Stefan. It's his sister.

'Oh god no! Not my la'al lass!' Daniel is panting with the climb, gasping. 'Where's Stefan? Where's the lad? What have they done with him?'

'What the hell?' Ewan is shaking; he can hardly speak. 'They've took the lad. What's going on? They were wearing the same hats.'

'Look at her. She's not moving. She can never keep still.' Like a piece of paper thrown in a fire, Daniel crumples down into the snow next to her.

Robbie puts his hand out towards him but Daniel shakes him off.

Ewan helps Robbie lift her up, then Daniel cradles his daughter in both arms, her weight making him sink deep into the snow. He kisses her cheek over and over again, then looks around, eyes wild, scanning the hillside. 'Where are they, the bastards?'

Ewan starts to stride off. 'I'm going after them.'

'Not worth it, Ewan,' Robbie says, trying to restrain him. 'They'll be far away by now.'

'Or waiting to make another attack,' I say.

We're all breathing heavily, talking in low voices.

'Doubt it. Difficult to hide up here without giving themselves away,' Robbie says.

'So we do nothing? Is that what you're saying?' Daniel says. 'We let them come and take their pick of our kids?'

'They were armed. We've got nothing. And we need to get the lass home now. It could be broken.' Robbie points to where Elsa is bleeding from a deep gash on her calf. The bullet has grazed her, but her foot is also badly twisted. She is shuddering from the shock.

'Ewan, you got here before me,' Daniel says. 'What did you see?'

'Same as you.' Sweat is dripping off Ewan's brow as he touches Elsa's face and gently brushes the hair out of her eyes. She moans. He's been like an older brother to the twins. They look up to him.

'Poor la'al lass,' Daniel says, choking back tears. 'Let's get you home. But my Stefan!' He stumbles, and Ewan keeps him upright by bracing against him.

'It's terrible. But why try to kill the girl then take the boy?' I say. 'I don't understand. Are you sure you didn't see anything, Ewan?'

He shakes his head. 'Nowt.'

'Why didn't we hear them shouting then, when we were coming up the hill?' Daniel is so angry he sounds almost accusing.

Robbie shakes his head. 'It all happened so quickly.'

'It was a surprise attack. Stefan could have been unconscious by the time we even left the house,' I say. 'It must have been Elsa blowing the whistle. She wouldn't let him go willingly. Look.' It's not far from where Elsa was lying. I pick up the whistle and blow the All Clear.

'I can't believe they shot her.' In Daniel's arms she's breathing quickly. 'A child. My child.'

'Some buggers are ruthless,' Ewan says. 'Maybe they shot her to shut her up. I'm sorry, Daniel, but that's the truth.'

'This would never have happened if I hadn't let those newcomers stay in the first place. It's all my fault.' Daniel's voice is a growl of anger. 'Maybe George *is* right – those lasses are part of a plan to take over our patch, to break up the Mill. We need to throw them out. Today.'

He doesn't mean this. It's out of character.

'You were doing your best, what anybody with a heart would do, Daniel –' I start.

'But now my Elsa's hurt. And they've taken my lad.' When he breaks down, sobbing, it cuts through me.

'Ewan, help Daniel take her down. Let's have another look, Rob,' I say.

'Come on, marra. We need to get her back.' Ewan touches Daniel's shoulder and they set off.

The ground is smeared with blood. Dragged over the fresh snow and down the other side of the hill past the graveyard. Stefan must have slid and slithered as he struggled to escape.

'We've no chance of catching them. Look, Anna.' Further ahead, Robbie points out hoof prints in the churned up snow, two sets that lead off westwards. We strain our eyes, scanning the white land of copses and fields rolling away into the distance. Nothing.

'Horses.' Robbie shakes his head and kicks at the snow. 'And whoever they are, they're armed. We'll have to double the watch.'

We turn to catch the others up. It's then that he says it.

'Why didn't you tell me? You've no idea the strain pregnancy puts on such a young girl. She needs medical help. Advice…' His voice is icy. '*We* don't keep secrets from each other. What's wrong with you?'

'I don't know. I was trying to protect her.'

'From *me*? I don't understand.'

I scramble after him, limping badly. I've pushed myself beyond my limits.

'Robbie, Nula told me something. The clinic. You have to be careful.'

'Too late for that. I'll do what has to be done.'

He strides away from me. Doesn't look back.

It's easy to spot Ewan in his red hat, Daniel carrying his injured daughter. We soon catch them up. Drops of dark blood mark the way.

When we tell them what we've seen, Daniel stops and frowns. 'There's only one lot I've heard about who keep horses.'

'Let's get her back first, Daniel.' Robbie speaks gently. 'Then we can make a plan.'

Daniel nods slowly. 'Aye, lad. I suppose you're right.'

There's nothing else to be said. We all thought we knew what NOAH wanted; but now Stefan's gone, everything has changed.

We make our way through the woods back down to the Mill, in silence, Ewan pushing aside the jumble of overhanging branches. Every time one of them loses his footing and stumbles, Elsa moans.

We each have our own thoughts. Each glancing back. The sense of a dark burden, shadows following us. Powdery snow blows off the trees and bushes in a swirl of white as if you could see the biting wind, then drops again. Down at the Mill, the plume of smoke rises, as if nothing has changed; a blackbird chitters its warning cry, scudding over the snow-covered path. Near the river a brown rat, long tail held above the stones and ice, darts in front of us. I remember Stefan's green eyes smiling at Jamila when she first arrived. She adores him; I don't want to see her face when we tell her. In this closed, frightening world every feeling is intensified.

'Come on, Robbie,' I say. 'Let's go ahead and tell the others.'

My legs are weak, but adrenaline makes me move quickly. I try to put Robbie's words to the back of my mind – now there's something hard and bitter between us that wasn't there before. I need to make amends.

George is at the window; the others will be crowded into the kitchen, ready to move, to run. In spite of the All Clear, there's fear on their faces.

Tracey throws her arms around me and I realise how cold I am, soaked and frozen. 'We didn't know what to think. I was so scared I'd lost you, Anna.'

'Where's our Ewan? Is he hurt?' George's white-bristled chin wobbles. He's survived this long with both his children, he's thinking his luck must have run out at last. 'Tell us, Anna.' His voice is old and reedy. 'What's happened, Robbie?'

They all start talking at once. It's the heat and the smell of stale food, but also shock and guilt too. I'm falling into dark, everything vibrating. The floor is coming up towards me.

'Ewan's…' My own voice falters. My teeth are chattering. I can't stop shaking.

"You're crowding her.' Nula says, though I can't see her;

she's a silhouette against the light.

'Ewan's fine,' Robbie says. 'And the others. It's Elsa.'

'Anna needs to sit down.' Nula takes over. I try to imagine being a mother, on duty, putting others' needs first. She holds my hand. 'I'll put the kettle on. Oh, your poor hands. They're freezing.'

From his cot in the corner of the room there's a squawk: Tiny's awake.

'It's OK, Mum. I'll get him.' Jamila sniffs back tears and stands, allowing her shirt to balloon over her belly.

'Don't fuss,' I say, trying to take off my wet coat. 'Please don't fuss.'

Tracey reaches up to help me.

'What's that on your jacket? Oh my god it's blood, isn't it? There's blood on your coat! See!' Tracey turns to the others. 'It *was* a shot. I told you it was a gun. I knew when I saw Daniel put that poster on the back of the mirror something bad would happen.'

'Enough of that nonsense, our Tracey.'

The room's spinning. George puts a chair behind me and gently pushes me into it. 'Tell us, lass. What happened?'

'Elsa's hurt,' Robbie says. 'Ewan's helping her dad bring her back. They'll be here soon.'

Jamila jumps up from next to the fire, her voice cutting through my haze. 'Stefan's all right, isn't he, Anna?'

I shake my head. 'He's gone, love. They've taken him.'

Jamila drops to her knees silently, almost in slow motion, next to her mother.

'Here they are!' Tracey runs to the door.

When we hear them stamping snow off their boots, Jamila buries her face in her mother's hair. Then the door swings open and Daniel staggers in. 'Help us bring her in, someone.' He puts Elsa gently on the sofa then stands, leaning on the back of a chair. Shoulders slumped, wheezing.

Robbie fetches blankets and towels.

'I'll sponge your coat, Ewan.' Tracey's voice is thick with tears.

George puts an awkward hand on his son's shoulder then hugs him roughly.

'It's fine. Nowt broken.' Ewan pushes him away. 'Dry your eyes, Tracey. Coat can wait. Someone needs to be at the lookout. You and me, Rob?'

It's the first time I've ever heard him sound worried; I've often wondered if anything could upset him. He smiles a thin smile. 'Any road, I vote they stay. Anna, you can vote for me, eh? Rob, you see to lass, then come up to the lookout.'

When the door slams behind him, all you can hear is the wind moaning in the chimney, the fire crackling. Jamila's quiet crying.

Twelve

While Robbie examines her, Daniel holds her hand, but it's Nula who keeps her still while Robbie splints and winds a bandage around her leg. Elsa moans, tears running down her face, trying to fight her off. Without painkillers it's not a task we want to prolong. Daniel has to turn his head away.

Afterwards, Nula is near to tears herself. She sits on the edge of the sofa and smooths Elsa's hair, then wipes the sweat off her face with a warm towel. 'It's all right, love. You're safe.'

'Let me help. I feel better now,' I say. 'I want to help.'

Elsa is shuddering, her teeth chattering. 'Where's Stefan? Is my brother back?'

At the sound of his name Jamila starts to cry again; she's about to blurt something out, but her mother shakes her head and she stops herself.

Robbie says something quietly to Nula. They must be arranging a time for him to examine Jamila and discuss the pregnancy. He keeps his eyes lowered.

When Elsa is calmer, I help Daniel carry her up to her room. Tracey has made her bed warm and lit the fire. At the sight of her brother's empty bed tears well up in Elsa's eyes. She cries soundlessly while we help her into bed, then lies, hardly moving, her eyes shut, exhausted.

'I can't find Stefan. Have you seen him, Dad?' she says as her father makes sure she's tucked in. 'I can't find him anywhere.'

Daniel kisses her then shakes his head.

'He's not far away,' I say. 'He'll be here soon.'

'I want to stay with her. Can I?' Jamila says.

'But let me break the news to her,' Daniel tells Jamila, 'when she's ready. Do you understand? I don't want anyone else telling her.'

Jamila is breathing quickly, her skin is grey. 'Elsa's going to be OK, isn't she?'

I hug her. 'She needs to sleep, then she'll get better. Wrap yourself in a blanket. We don't want you getting cold too.' Under my fingers, she trembles like a small creature. I attempt a smile. 'If she wakes up, get us straight away. Remember now.'

Back downstairs, the atmosphere has changed. In Tracey's arms Tiny is asleep. George is slumped in an armchair, staring into the fire, all the aggression knocked out of him. 'You can put him down now, lass,' he says to her. 'He's well away.'

Reluctantly, Tracey stands and lays the baby down in the Moses basket. He makes small mewling noises and she strokes him until he settles.

Nula is knitting what looks like a yellow baby blanket. Until now, she must have been doing this in her room.

"Jamila is staying with her,' I tell her.

She rolls up the knitting and pushes the needles into the ball of wool, then walks to the window. 'I'm sorry this has happened.'

George glances at Nula half-silhouetted against the cold white light. 'They need to go. Or they'll be attracting all sorts. We can't take the risk.'

Nula ignores him and stands, opening and closing her fists, stretching her fingers.

'Daniel, I'm so sorry. I'll go up and sit with Elsa too. I know you want to talk and I'll understand if you decide to let us go. But I swear to you, I didn't bring them here.'

She shuts the door quietly behind her and we listen to the creak of the stairs, then her footsteps on the landing.

Before George can speak again, Tracey starts: 'Dad! You can't push them out in this. Did you see Elsa's face? Did you see what they done to her? I don't know what they're after, but folks that shoot a lass then dump her back to freeze, don't care about owt! We can't –'

'But this wouldn't have happened if *they* hadn't turned up.' George indicates Nula and Jamila upstairs. 'Right! That's the agenda sorted. Actions from the meeting. I propose they go. Who's going to second me?' His wild eyes search the room. He clears his throat of the residue of tears, anger. 'It could have been any of us up there getting shot at. But why didn't they tek lass?'

I speak over him. 'George, *they* didn't ask NOAHs to come here. It's not their fault. I think it's a coincidence.'

'Well I don't agree. What do you think, Daniel, eh?'

Daniel grits his teeth. 'I was in two minds, but now I think it must be NOAHs.' He pauses. 'And they've got horses.' He leans against the door frame. 'They know where we are and they've taken my Stefan. We need a plan.'

George interrupts. 'Aye. But we don't want NOAHs coming back. I vote the lasses go. We have to think of oursells. Us lot, the ones who were already living here.'

'Ewan said let them stay. If Ewan said it then…' Tracey says quietly, sitting on a low stool next to the baby, making sure he doesn't waken.

'No, Tracey. He's too forgiving of a pretty lass, is Ewan.'

Tracey's face is blotchy and red. 'But you always say Ewan knows what's right and what's wrong. And Jamila's going to have a babbie, Dad!'

I step in to stop the argument from getting worse. 'No one else knows they're here. They've never been out to the market, only along the river bank. We can hide them here. They could stay till the weather's warmer.'

George shakes his head. 'Someone's bound to see them.'

‘Not like we get many people passing!’ I say.

‘You’re varra friendly with them, Anna, lass. You’re not from round here neither.’

‘Don’t be daft, Dad. Anna’s been here years. Don’t start with all that nonsense again.’

‘There’ll be rumours, then who knows…’

‘You need to stop panicking, George,’ Daniel says quietly. ‘I know you want the best for everyone here, but what does it say about us if we push them out?’ His voice is a whisper and we all lean in to hear him; the sound of the wind is almost as loud. ‘Would you do it to your own daughter? To your Tracey?’

‘Of course I wouldn’t.’ George scratches his head. ‘Our Tracey; well, she’s nivver had to look after herself, has she? That’s different.’

‘No it’s not. I’m more capable than you think.’ Tracey gets to her feet. ‘And I think you’re wrong, so I’m not going to sit here and do what you say. If Nula goes, then I’m going too.’

‘Don’t talk soft. Why would you do that?’ George stands too, his knees creaking. ‘Isn’t it time we put it to the vote?’

Tracey is trembling, her face flushed. She sits abruptly and takes hold of Tiny’s bare feet, enclosing them in her hands. His eyes flutter as if he’s dreaming, but he doesn’t wake up.

‘Lookit, George, when we started we agreed no violence. That’s what we said. Remember? And sending lasses out in the cold and to god knows what…’ On the back of the chair Daniel’s knuckles are white. ‘You’ve seen what they did to my lass. Only a girl. They’ve got my lad to do their fighting or whatever it is. I don’t know what NOAHs want. I thought it was women. Girls. That’s what people are saying. But they’re fanatics. If it comes to a vote, George, I think you’re outnumbered.’ He sits down and puts his head in his hands.

George grunts and sits down, huffing.

I think of Nula looking out of the window at the frozen,

white landscape. There was something about the hard line of her mouth, her balled fists… I wonder if I'm wrong. If we can trust her after all. Whether I've been taken in, and whether her sad story and Jamila's pregnancy is true. What if they are a ploy to let the NOAHs in? A Trojan horse?

'Stop a minute,' I say. 'We need Nula here. We need to find out what she knows.'

Thirteen

When Nula comes into the room her eyes catch mine. There's pride and stubbornness. And something more. A spark of fire between us.

'Before you start, Anna, I can guess what you're thinking: the old man could be right and the NOAHs have planted us here to get your supplies, your land, the Mill. You're not sure you can trust us.' She comes to stand next to me.

'I don't…'

'I can see it in your face, I can hear it in your voice.' When she puts her hand on my arm I think it's to reassure me, but she's leaning her whole weight on me, searching for stability. 'You've been good to us; when I thought we were finished, you took us in.' She takes a deep breath and moves away. 'Anna's right. We escaped from them and I didn't think they'd find us up here, so far away. I thought we were safe.'

'And you think we're going to believe that? After what's happened? What made them come so far out of the way?' George sprays saliva as he speaks.

'Let her speak,' says Daniel.

I'm beginning to understand, and hazard a guess. 'Go on, Nula. Show them.'

Nula breathes in deeply, holds up her wrist for everyone to see.

Everyone stops talking and looks at the four damning letters etched on the inside of her wrist.

It's not only Jamila. Her mother too.

'She's in with them!' says George. 'That's what it means. It's not fashion.'

Nula is shaking her head. 'When I had it done I was proud. I thought I'd joined something new and exciting, an organisation that was going to help in the emergency, the temperatures rising all the time. Then the rain and flooding.'

'Ha! There you go, what did I say?' George is triumphant.

'No. I couldn't have got it more wrong.' She scratches at her wrist. 'It's a mark of servitude.'

Tracey puts her arms around her, and Nula's brown eyes fill.

'We escaped. But we've got something they want…'

'There you are. I was right,' George says again.

'No, that's not it, George.' Nula speaks to him gently, then to all of us with sudden authority. 'I told Jay the baby's from God. But we all know that's nonsense.'

'Well, whose is it then?' says Daniel. Straight to the point as usual.

'It's a baby of NOAH,' she says simply.

'And who's he?' George laughs. 'One of them fellas on horses? Them thugs?'

'What are you talking about, lass?' Daniel's voice is quiet, controlled. 'We need to know the truth. What we're up against.'

'NOAH leaders don't do their own dirty work. Those were soldiers.' She spits the words out, as if she has something vile in her mouth. 'I had Tiny. We got away… from the Hulks. Then Jamila fell pregnant.'

'She's bloody mad!' George laughs. 'How can you believe owt she says? Bloody mad woman. Hulks! What's she on about? All I know is we were safe from NOAHs before, and since *she's* come we've had nowt but trouble.'

'George, shut up for once. You're not thinking.' Daniel talks so quietly the wind is taken out of George's sails and his mouth opens then closes like a trout. 'What I want to know is what made them come here, now. It's too much of a coincidence. Tell us. How did they know you're here?'

'Aye, it doesn't make sense. All I know is Elsa's hurt and her brother's gone,' says Tracey abruptly. 'They want *something*, them NOAHs, but.'

'I'm sorry, Daniel. I never wanted to hurt anyone,' says Nula. 'We've stayed close to the Mill since we got here. I don't know what made them come now.'

'How about that census fella? What did he come here for?'

Daniel nods. 'You could be right, Tracey.' He rubs his cheek. 'I'm minded to trust you, Nula, but I don't know.'

In the fireplace, the flames are licking at a thick log of wood, orange embers glowing brightly then crumbling to ash.

For a short time Daniel is quiet, looking into the fire, thinking. He turns to me. 'Anna, you've spent more time with Nula and Jamila. What d'you think?'

Nula's face is a darkness I can't read, but words hum in the bones of my skull. *After you've sifted all the dross away, look for the bright truth. People tell you whatever they think you want to hear to get their own way. But look in the shadows, part the vegetation and undergrowth and you'll find it. If you look. The bright needle of truth pointing due north.*

I don't know how long I've been staring into the fire, its flames wavering and changing, but at the heart there's a comb of gold. Nula puts her hand on mine. It's burning. Those broken bones, healed and knotted together, like a damaged tree, growing and healing over; protecting her children.

'We've all lived through times we never expected,' I say to her quietly. Something she said registers with me, words that came out naturally in her story but that don't make sense. *The Hulks?* George is right. What does she mean? I'm aware of the others waiting for me to speak. 'I want to trust you, but something isn't right.

'I'll never forget how you took Robbie and me in and made us feel part of the community, George.' I smile at him and touch his old, trembling hands. 'Something terrible has happened to them, and we need to take care of them. It seems obvious to me. But we need to protect ourselves from NOAH. I think we might have to arm ourselves.'

'Yis, aye, lass. But what have we got?' George's face is flushed. 'Nobody here's got a gun. I wouldn't even know what to do with one.'

'Thanks, Anna.' Daniel's voice is warm. 'George, I've told you... Sit down and listen for once.'

George sits, and Tracey puts her hand on his shoulders. 'Come on, Dad. You'll make yourself ill if you carry on like this.'

'Right.' Daniel pulls himself up like a teacher taking control of a disruptive class. 'That leaves us with two questions: Why didn't they take our Elsa? And how did they know Nula was here?'

'Elsa's no good to them. It's Jamila they want; she's carrying a NOAH baby.' Nula looks as if she's going to throw up. 'And they want Tiny too.' She takes a deep breath then walks over to the cot where he's sleeping and kneels down, stroking his face.

'I don't want to risk everything we've built up, for a mad woman who thinks she's got pregnant by some fella out the Bible!' George snorts and stands up. 'If them lot come back, hand lasses over.'

'Pipe down, George.' Daniel gestures for him to sit back down. 'Why didn't they come back? They had horses, weapons, it would've been easy. And,' he adds almost under his breath, 'what use is Stefan to them? He's only a young lad.'

Nula seems to be hesitating, wavering like a flame in a draught. 'Must I?' she says to me. 'Raking it all up makes me feel so helpless. I wanted to forget everything.' She's close to tears.

'Go on, Nula,' Daniel says. 'We're listening.'

Nula sits down, and for a few moments I think she's not going to speak. She folds her arms around her body.

Then she starts.

'You're safe here, in your cosy community. You've no idea what's going on in those places…'

'I've seen what happens. I think we've all seen plenty, Nula.' My fists are clenched. Sitting away from the warmth of the fireplace, the temperature plummets. 'Girls and women forced to… I don't need to spell it out, do I?'

She continues, almost ignoring us. 'Yes, it's always women, isn't it? Throughout history. Every conflict. But NOAH is worse.' Nula's shoulders drop, then she shakes her head as if dismissing a disturbing image. 'At first they wanted the tall ones, dark-haired. But now they're getting desperate. When it comes down to it, they'll go for whoever's available. I think that's why they took Stefan.'

'What do you mean?' Daniel says. 'Tell it straight.'

'NOAH has no interest in girls. Girls are easy to find. It's young men they need… For INCREASE, their programme.'

'Programme?' As I ask this so many memories come together I have goose pimples on my arms.

'Anna, love, you have no idea, have you? NOAHs don't live like this.' She gets to her feet and sweeps her arm around the kitchen, pointing to our smoky candles, the frozen mill wheel motionless in the background. Our breath steaming. 'They don't live from hand to mouth. They have everything. Huge storage warehouses, the old Amazon ones repurposed. On board they have everything the rest of us have lost.'

Everyone starts to talk at once. It's Tracey who speaks over us all: 'Shut up the lot of you. Let the lass speak. Bloody hell. Give her a chance, will you? Come on, Nula. You sit here next to Tiny.'

~ ~ ~

'We were ordinary. Like everyone else,' Nula begins. 'I was the youngest. Two older sisters – a lawyer and a radiographer. Church every Sunday. I was brilliant at maths and I could've gone to university too, to study engineering, but I'd been dancing since I was four years old. I wanted to have fun.'

She sighs heavily.

'Pregnancy sorted that one out. When Jamila was born, her father left; he didn't want to know. For years it was hard: the floods were starting, Europe, the NHS destroyed and the government running out of ideas. I had nothing to lose. I heard about a friend of a friend. She was a dancer too. She'd done well; so when I saw the posters…'

'We all remember them,' I say. 'On billboards, outside schools, on the sides of buses. On TV ads. They were everywhere, weren't they?' I bite my tongue. I never thought anyone intelligent would take them seriously. Crude day-of-reckoning slogans. Religious images of a smiling Noah leading happy people and their children into the ark.

Daniel shakes his head slowly. 'How could you fall for them?'

'I know: all over our estate, round the church. At first I was cynical but then everyone was saying the government was crap and at least someone was *doing* something. They had a religious agenda, but they promised everything – a way out of poverty and hunger and, if you made it to the higher levels, career progression. They'd look after you. There was only Jamila and me. I could see the future opening up. So I joined.'

'But when you saw what they were like…?' I say.

'It was the chance I'd been waiting for: working on a cruise ship – plenty of entertainers get by on worse – our own cabin, no meals to cook. Specialist training, free medi-care and physio. School for Jamila, as well as entertainment and competitions. OK, once we left port there were the daily prayers, rules; but when there are three thousand people living closely together…' She laughs bitterly. 'The purple and gold was more a brand. I didn't see it as a uniform. I was too busy and too excited to think about it. And, you know it gets to you – I'm ashamed to say it now but I didn't even feel sorry for the refugees – that's how well NOAH sold us their way of life. We were *grateful.* We'd been saved for a greater good. Daily updates about the Exodus only confirmed it. Cities sank, but I didn't look back. We ignored the people clinging on to trees, the cries for help. It made us more *grateful.* We felt it was right. We were saved.

After a few weeks my section was offered an audition for the best jobs – more than a dream, it was the celebrity I'd longed for. We practised for days, gave our best performance. But, when the music finished and the houselights went up, there they were – the Captain and his officers. The 'chosen ones'. The elite. All in NOAH uniform. We were taken to a deck I didn't even know existed, entered by a security door. The INCREASE suite.' She rubs her shoulder and lowers her voice. 'For us, they weren't cabins. They were prison cells.'

There's something so bizarre about her story I shake my head, but Nula ignores me.

'That's when I realised what NOAH meant.' Nula pushes back her sleeve and holds out her arm again. The four letters stand out black against her brown skin. 'National Organisation for Advancing Humanity. *Go forth increase and multiply*, as it says in the Good Book.'

She laughs bitterly. 'Dance, fill the wine glasses and submit. It was easier not to protest. For men it was worse – I often thought of the First World War – frightened boys, kids as young as fourteen taken away from their families.'

'Like my Stefan.'

'But some men would…' I say.

'Aye, lads aren't going to say no to a bit of… regular like, are they?' George looks around the room for confirmation. No one responds.

'Some. Yes, George.' Nula smiles kindly at him. 'A few loved the celebrity cult, the pop star status. The chosen ones, the seed-carriers. We were *allowed* to watch them in the gym. It was a privilege to have sex with them. Even with Noah himself, we were told. Not that I ever saw him.'

'If he exists.' Daniel says. 'Like the Wizard of Oz.'

'But they're as much slaves as we were. If they don't perform, or try to rebel, there are no second chances. They join the Uncleans, the underclass. Taken to the Hulks.'

'Hulks?' The word Nula had let slip. 'What do you mean?' Daniel leans forwards.

'Prison ships: old, rusting sweat shops – where you work until you can't – where you disappear. Men and women. The ones who won't conform, or who have children who don't meet the standards. Or who can't give birth any more – that's where they end up. Or worse.'

'So my Stefan?'

'Kept in solitary, if he meets the standards. Then taken to the INCREASE suite when they find a suitable match. I'm sorry, Daniel.'

Daniel thumps the table, making Tiny startle in his sleep.

'Once we were part of the programme, we lost all our privileges. Jamila and I were put in a lower deck, under the waterline, in a dormitory with all the other 'dancers'. Our lives became intolerable. She was only fourteen when I heard about the junior INCREASE initiative. Fourteen years old! She was excited, of course. She thought she was going to be a dancer like me; every time she heard music, she was off, spinning and twirling like a little sparkler in the dark. By then I was seven months pregnant, forced to take auxiliary roles.' Nula rubs at her wet cheeks.

'Here, lass.' George gives her one of his large handkerchiefs.

'I couldn't keep her safe. I couldn't protect her. That's when I knew I would do anything to get her away. The good people were terrified to step out of line, of course, but they did it anyway. There was a man who listened to me. When I last saw him, he was alive. He helped us. God bless him.'

Her tears fall silently.

'I can keep a part of myself hidden but I'm so scared for Jamila. She never had an ordinary life like me – every night she has nightmares, cries out in her sleep. NOAH wants my children. Please help us.'

She stops speaking and the room is eerily silent. When I drag my eyes away from her face, the light is cold and grey. Sleety snow falling again.

Fourteen

Then we hear the whistle, the ordinary signal for changing guard; two hours has passed so quickly. George heads for the door. 'I'll go and tek over… You all know what *I* said, but it don't mean owt now, I reckon.' He clears his throat and for a moment stands awkwardly in the doorway. 'These lasses have gone through enough.'

'I'll come with you.' Daniel fetches his coat, then takes my arm and pulls me into the corridor. 'I want the rest of us to be safe.' His voice is low. 'But especially you, Anna. We need you here.' I'm trying to say sorry for keeping the pregnancy a secret, but he hugs me. 'You were doing what you thought best. Look after Elsa.'

He whistles for the dogs then opens the door. The icy air rushes in like an enemy waiting to ambush us and my heart leaps. Daniel's been like a father, but he's rarely hugged me before. He crams his wool hat on, and as if he can read my mind, hugs me again. 'In case I don't see you for a bit.'

'Don't talk daft,' I say, shivering.

'Go back in and help them decide what to do, lass. Come on, George. Ewan and Robbie are up there freezing their arses off waiting for us.'

'Aye, lad. Don't rush us. I'm coming.' George looks every one of his eighty years. He's strong, but if anything happens to Tracey or Ewan I don't know what he'd do.

I picture Elsa sprawled in the snow, blood pooling. The echo of the shot bouncing off the fells. I hobble to the kitchen. 'Take these,' I say, and give Daniel the knives we keep for gutting fish, jointing meat.

'It's the last thing I want to do. But you're right, lass.' Daniel sighs deeply. 'I'll make sure George gets there, and I'll check the early warning system. Then I'll be straight back down.'

'Go safely,' I say to them both.

Daniel shrugs. 'We'll do our best, won't we, George?'

'Wear this instead. That one stands out a mile.' I throw Daniel a grey hat from the basket by the door.

Tracey is next to me. 'Don't try to sort things out yourself. Let Daniel take the lead.' Her voice breaks with tears. 'Dad, don't do owt stupid. I want you back here tonight.'

She goes to check on Elsa, then I start preparing a meal. Whatever happens, someone has to make food; we have to keep eating. I focus on what I can see of the path up to the lookout. I miss Stefan. He loves cooking more than his sister, keeping up a flow of chatter and songs. Without him the kitchen is too quiet.

Robbie's taking his time. My heart thuds like a dog leaping at a closed door.

'Why're Ewan and Robbie not back yet?' I say. 'They should be back by now.'

Nula wipes her eyes dry then puts her hand on mine. 'Let me help, Anna.' She picks up a knife and starts peeling onions, discarding ones that are too far gone and green with mould. 'They'll be back soon.'

'Nula, thank you for telling us. I'm sorry for –' I start, then the hinges of the gate squeak and my whole body jumps. Nula instinctively backs away from the window. It's Ewan. And Robbie. I want to run and kiss him, but Tracey gets to Ewan first and there isn't room for all of us in the hallway.

'Here he is! I was worried sick.' Tracey helps him take off his wet coat, brushes her brother's cold cheeks with her hands and tries to hug him. 'Come on, the kettle's boiled. Did you see owt?'

Ewan pushes her away, but gently. Her fussing would annoy anyone. 'Nowt different. It's getting dark now and plenty of cloud. Them NOAHs'll not be back till they can see where they're going. And who knows, mebbe they've got what they wanted. How's la'al Elsa?' he says, his voice breaking.

Jamila has climbed into the bed with her, Tracey tells him; they're keeping each other warm. I imagine their hair on the pillows, blonde and dark mixed together.

'I'll see how they are while you talk,' Nula says to me, unable to bring herself to look at Ewan or Robbie.

'Your dad's changed his mind about sending them away, Ewan, but we need your vote. I know what Robbie will say.'

'He's a stubborn bugger, our dad.' Ewan laughs quietly. 'What made him change his mind?'

When I give a brief resume of Nula's story, Robbie pulls me in close. 'I'm not surprised by anything religious extremists come up with,' he says. 'Look how my brother signed his life away; they prey on the vulnerable. But this changes everything.'

Ewan scratches his head and looks out of the window. 'You nivver know what folks'll do…' There's something about his reaction that's not right. And the words jump into my mind then disappear as soon as I read them, as if they're written with smoke: *he knows something*. The dream I had, the ringing in my ears, something dropping into the snow – the disturbing feeling of the dream comes back to me.

Night is closing in, with the snow falling like heavy, white wings. I remember when this was the kind of snow children loved, the kind to make snowmen and snow angels. For snowball fights. There's an expectant quiet in the room as if we're all holding our breath.

'We've got to look after each other. Who could send lasses out in this?' Ewan is angry. Restless. 'I'm going to take the dog out for a walk. Sithee in a bit. Come here, Fowler.'

The decision is made.

When he's gone, Robbie holds me at arm's length. 'Don't keep things from me again, Anna. Promise?'

I nod. 'I love you so much, Robbie. I'm sorry.'

He puts his arms around me again and says quietly, 'At least it's all out in the open now.' He kisses me. 'I love you too.' Then he pulls away from me and, in a louder voice, says, 'Right, I need to check over Jamila again and make sure she's eating enough. As much rest as we can allow. And check on Elsa.'

All night, snow falls; shutting us in and dampening down sounds from outside. At every slight noise – the wind in the chimney, the creaking of the house settling – we jump. When snow falls from the overhanging roof with a thump, I wake with a start. Through the darkest hours we women take turns to sit with Elsa and keep watch; the men organise themselves to be on guard up at the lookout. Jobs split along the old gender lines. It's a luxury we can't afford, but all night we keep the fire in her bedroom burning. Every two hours Daniel comes in and sits with her, refusing to sleep. When it's my turn, Jamila is reluctant to leave her too, but she's exhausted.

'You've done more than enough. Time for some sleep, Jamila.'

Her brown eyes look huge in her narrow face and she shakes her head, but I remind her about the baby. I take her to the family room and she slides into bed with Nula and Tiny. Soon she's sound asleep.

I'm nodding off and pinching myself to stay awake, when Elsa moans and starts mumbling. 'My brother's lying in the snow. Help us someone!'

I'm not sure if she's awake or dreaming. Where she's been injured, blood has seeped through the dressing. Her fair hair is wild. She tries to get out of bed, her clothes drenched in sweat.

'Where's Stefan? Why's he not in bed?'

'He had to go out,' I say. 'He'll be back soon. Don't worry about him. Get back into bed, love. Lie down.' Her head is burning.

There are no paracetamol; we haven't had any for at least a year. They were used up the last time we had an illness. Sometimes, the herbal remedies work. I sponge her with lukewarm water to reduce her temperature.

'Drink this, Elsa.' I hold the glass of water to her lips but she pushes me away.

'Stefan! Blow the whistle again!' She's in pain, thrashing her head from side to side. 'Don't touch me. Take your hands off me. I don't like that. Don't *touch* me.' Her hands move, slapping and clawing at me. 'Leave my brother alone. Stop. Please stop.' She lunges at me and scratches my face.

'Elsa, love. It's Anna. You're safe.'

Her eyes blink open. 'Anna! Watch out. They'll get you too.' Then, falling back, she slumps against the pillows and is gone again. In sleep, her body twists and turns, winding the covers around herself like a spider with a fly.

When Tracey comes to relieve me, she brings warmth and her own smell of clean air into the sick room.

'Your face!' she says. 'Here, let me bathe it for you.'

'I'll sort it out. It doesn't hurt.'

She puts her hand on the girl's burning forehead.

The thought won't lie still: it was my turn on watch. 'It should've been me, not her.'

Tracey's only in her early forties, but her hands are prematurely brown and aged; when she pats mine the simple physical contact brings a lump to my throat.

'It's my fault, Tracey.'

'It could have been any of us up there when them NOAHs

came. No point blaming yourself.' Her hand is warm and reassuring. 'You've been up most of the night. Get something to eat, and rest.'

'What use am I? I can't do anything.'

'You're not physically strong, but that doesn't mean owt,' she says. 'You've other strengths. We need you here.' Her voice is lost to the wind in the chimney. 'Go on, lass. Sleep.'

It's a relief to lie down. I dream I'm falling into an inky black place – like the mill pond – cold water closing over my head, sinking down without a struggle.

I'm in the same position when something wakes me, hours later, and I see a pale, yellow sun breaking through leaden clouds. There's an insistent knocking on my bedroom door.

'Come in. It's not locked.' My voice is hoarse and croaky.

Jamila almost falls into the room, her hands flapping. Agitated. 'Anna, can you hear them?'

I go to the window; there's no one there. 'It's OK, love.'

'Can I get in with you? I'm scared.'

'A nightmare?'

She nods. Her body feels frail. Under her pyjamas and oversized jumper, the swelling of her small belly is visible. She presses her thin, bony legs next to me, her slim fingers clasping mine.

'Can't you hear them?'

The bells in All Saints Church up on the hill in the town centre are ringing – an old sound, from before the Flood, one that has become so infrequent it's almost unfamiliar.

I put my arms round her; she's trembling so violently her teeth are chattering. 'You don't need to be scared. It's not the tocsin, that's only for warnings. Those bells are telling people to come to church, ordinary Christians. Nothing to be frightened about. It's Sunday.'

'You don't understand! I need to find my mum.'

'She's downstairs making breakfast. I can smell –'

She pushes against me. 'You don't know anything. I need to talk to my mum.'

'I'll come with you.' But, by the time I lever myself out of bed properly, she's gone. I pass Tracey on the landing, taking a blanket for Elsa.

'Better?' she asks.

'I'm OK,' I say. 'Elsa?'

'Lass has a temperature but she's calm.'

'Who's at the lookout?'

'Dad. Ewan.' She sniffs back tears. 'Our Ewan won't take a rest.'

Nula is cooking eggs. She flips them over and presses them down hard with the spatula.

'They've started here, haven't they? It's them.'

I must be looking blank because she shakes her head slowly.

'Anna, who do you think is ringing church bells?'

Jamila hops from one foot to the other. Fierce and mistrustful. 'I hate those bells. Mum, are they coming to take us back?'

'Come here, love.' Nula pulls her thick cardigan around both of them.

'They rang them in the churches in the villages and towns. When we escaped, that's when we heard them. We knew how close they were.'

The eggs start to catch on the pan. I lean over and take them off, nearly burning myself. At the back of my mind, memory ticks and counts down – Nula's story.

I get plates and cut bread, then we scrape off the burnt egg and try to eat.

When the bells stop, the silence is unnerving. We don't speak as we clear everything away. We're about to go to start our tasks when Jamila gasps.

'What's that, Mum? Did you hear something? Listen!'

I hold my breath to listen, but since my illness my hearing isn't as acute as it used to be. I shake my head.

'Yes, I can hear something.' Nula clutches for Jamila. 'Oh god. They've come back. Come here, Jamila. But keep down.'

I strain my ears. There *is* something. Like a dry leaf rustling. A scratching against the door.

'Quick. The cellar.' I'm running towards the door before I've even thought about it. 'I'll go.'

In a bustle of footsteps, slithering on the stone floor, Nula grabs Tiny out of his Moses basket, gathering up white bedding that trails after her. The baby doesn't have time to cry.

So many times, I've thought of this moment, but I'm not ready. Perhaps no one ever is. The last seconds of my life.

My feet are river stones held down by the weight of water. I take a breath, ready to plunge in and wrench open the door.

I nearly trip over him.

'Anna. I can't...' His hand falls back, the knuckles skinned and bleeding.

It's Stefan.

Fifteen

'At the very least he's going to lose some toes...' Rob shakes his head. 'But his heart rate... Fuck religion!'

Daniel has waited to finish his shift at the lookout. He runs in, red-faced and out of breath. 'My la'al lad. I thought I'd never see him again.' He stifles a sob with the back of his hand over his mouth.

Robbie puts his hand on Daniel's shoulder, but he shrugs it off. 'You need to prepare yourself, Daniel.'

'He's a strong lad.'

'Of course he is, but you have to be careful with hypothermia. We have to bring his temperature up gradually.'

'Dad!' Stefan's eyes flicker open, then close. A smile faint through the pain. 'Dad... is Elsa...?' He's slurring his speech. Drowsy.

'She's here, lad. She got back.'

'Always faster than me...'

Helpless, Daniel follows as Rob takes the boy and carries him to his room, next to Elsa's. When they come back, Daniel's shaking his head. I hear him say, 'I don't know, Robbie; who *do* they want?'

Who do they want? My heart lurches. I thought NOAH wanted young men.

'Robbie, why did they let him go?'

'He needs warm drinks, lukewarm. We'll talk later, Anna.'

My heart rattles, pounds out of rhythm. I know he's busy with two patients now, as well as Jamila to think about. Instructing Tracey. But sometimes his super efficiency feels cold. He's deliberately not answering me.

In the evening, I speak to Nula in the orchard. I'm collecting kindling. She's finding larger branches. The moon is nearly full again, lighting the stark trees black against the snow. The wind has dropped and the air is still. It's usually quiet at night. In the distance the bells are ringing again. I remember the silence when we first arrived, when the curfew started at dusk. Even now people don't often leave their homes at night.

'Wednesday. Daniel said it used to be the night they practised. In the old time. Before.'

'But for what?' she says. 'Is it going to be every Sunday now? Every day?'

'Nula, I'm scared too.'

She puts down her bundle and hugs me. 'I'm sorry. We'll deal with them if they dare turn up again. Bastards.' Her eyes catch the light. 'Can I tell you something?'

I nod.

She breathes in, holding her breath before she lets it out and speaks.

'Remember I told you how we escaped?'

'Yes, I remember.'

'He was a good man, Anna. For him, medicine was for health. For healing. He'd taken the Hippocratic Oath. Not for what NOAH wants.' I feel her eyes on me. 'I'm not going to say anything else. I think you understand, don't you? I think you know why they let Stefan go.'

I hold onto the trunk of a tree, feel it move in the wind that surges up through the valley. The movement goes through me and I'm there. In that other place. Hands helping. Kindness. Dedicated hands and fingers, caring for the sick, the dying. For women giving birth. And I understand what she is trying to tell me, without putting it into words. NOAH needs doctors for their programme. And if they can't get doctors, they'll take anyone with medical skills.

Daniel is outside playing his fiddle for Elsa. The sound floats over the hillside and seems to echo in my ears. Elsa's sitting up, smiling, but she's flushed and sweating. She's looking forward to seeing her brother when she's better. It's good to see her smiling again. Robbie's sure it's not TB or one of the viruses. Tracey is changing the dressing on her leg.

'Her temperature's up again.' Tracey sighs. 'That cut's taking a long time to get better. Come and have a look.'

Where the bullet has strafed her leg, the deep gash is swollen and surrounded by red, beginning to spread across her shin.

'She needs antibiotics, Anna,' she says quietly so Elsa can't hear.

I breathe in sharply. Dad.

At the time he was injured there were no antibiotics. Such a small thing. A rusty nail when he was helping to restore the Mill; medical support at the beginning was primitive and has never got much better. Illness is terrifying now. Both Elsa and her brother.

'There was a fella used to be able to get them. No one's seen him around for a good while but when our Ewan's back I could ask him.' Tracey shakes her head. 'There was nowt we could do for your dad, lass.'

I don't know how she does it, but she knows what I'm thinking. She smiles at me. 'You've gone quiet again,' she says.

'Ah, Tracey.' I lean down to hug her hard. 'What would I do without you? I'm so glad you're here. You need a break now; let me finish that. I'll ask Robbie,' I add, taking the bandage from her. 'Paracetamol maybe… but he can hardly ever lay his hands on antibiotics. I'm not sure about Ewan… some of his contacts are… Well you know what he's like!'

'Jamila!'

Jamila runs in and sits on the bed, distracting Elsa from the pain of the dressing being changed. Her eyes meet mine with a question and I nod. She leans over and kisses Elsa

'Oof. You're freezing,' Elsa says, laughing. 'Where've you been?'

Jamila laughs too. 'Can I get in with you, Elsa?'

For a young girl coping with her own pregnancy, she's making such an effort to be cheerful I feel a lump in my throat.

Elsa lifts back the covers and her dog jumps down onto the floor. 'Come on the other side. Don't look at this gross cut.'

'It looks sore.'

'I told you not to!'

'Does it hurt a lot?' Jamila wrinkles up her nose.

I secure the bandage.

'A bit. But Robbie's going to get something for it. That's what you said, Anna. Right?'

She overheard us. I wish she hadn't. 'He'll try his best. But you need to rest till it gets better.'

'You know, I had such a weird dream,' Elsa says. 'Stefan was in it. He said he had to go somewhere but he couldn't walk properly and Dad was crying and playing his fiddle. I was crying when I woke up. It was crazy. Stefan will laugh when I tell him! He's OK, isn't he?'

When Jamila puts her slim arms right around Elsa, her long dark hair falls forwards to hide her face. 'He's ill but he's getting better.'

Elsa pulls away, smiling. 'You're getting so big now. Can I feel the baby?'

'Put your hand there. No, lower. Yes. She's awake.'

'How do you know it's a girl?'

'Mum says we have to challenge the patriarchy. Everyone says 'he' if you don't know, or 'it'. So we say 'she'.'

'She's kicking like mad.'

'Tracey, come and feel.'

Tracey puts her mottled, brown hand on Jamila's belly.

'Aye, lass. She's going to be tough. Like her mum.'

It's cold tonight, but at least there's not going to be another hard frost. I pull the covers tighter over myself to get warm. The cold makes my legs ache so much and there's nothing I can do to make it better; Ewan says he can't get more of my medicine. Robbie tried to get antibiotics for Elsa today but came back empty-handed.

He's showering. I can hear him humming. Then he stops, and I know he's thinking about Elsa. About the possibility that Stefan won't get better. He wants to help everyone.

He's been so busy, we've hardly spoken for days. All we do is eat, sleep and wait.

He comes out, body shining, and picks up a towel, then smiles down at me. His hair sticks up all over his head, like a mad professor. He's not cut it for a while. He rubs at it then yawns. No matter what happens, as long as he's here, that's all that matters.

'You're frowning. You OK, love?' He dries himself. 'I'm sorry. You know I want to help them get better. Fuck. What a world we're living in. There's nothing I can do to save Stefan's toes; he'll have a limp, but he's doing well.' He finds a shirt. 'Elsa would be up and out of bed by now if we'd had the right medication. And I know someone's got access to it.'

I fold back the duvet so he can get in. 'Something else, Robbie. It's been bothering me ever since they came, but I couldn't work out what it was till now.'

'What?'

'I trust Nula. But there's a huge chunk missing from her story.'

'Like what?'

'Like how did they manage to get here?' I sit up. 'When we left London, we were together. Two adults with only ourselves to think about. No kids.' I remember the constant gnawing hunger, the cold. The pressure to move on, move on, to find safety. The boy who stole apples. Children abandoned and lost. A child, once, with huge eyes that looked right through me, staring, unfocused, in the arms of his older brother, nearly the same size. The terrible hopelessness. Asking for food for his brother, not himself, lying about already having eaten. 'We don't even know where Nula came from.'

Rob pushes the chest-of-drawers up against the door as usual. Switches off the torch and slides into bed with that faint smell of lavender from the soap that triggers memories of summer warmth, and how much I miss the constant buzzing of bees. For someone skinny who's had a cold shower, his body is already warm. We both get under the covers. He wraps himself around me and kisses the back of my neck, then down my spine.

'I think there's something she's not telling us,' I say.

He stops and moves away. Cold air shivers into the gap.

'What?' I turn towards him. The dark is thick between us.

'I'm not sure.' His voice is low.

'What d'you mean?'

'There's something…'

The dark between us solidifies even more.

'…something I never told you. I didn't think we'd need to – I mean, I didn't think *you'd* need to know. You had enough going on already.'

'Robbie, you're scaring me.'

He pulls me in close again. 'Either they were incredibly lucky. And that's practically impossible.' He pauses.'Or they had help.'

His voice trails off and there's only the white noise of the river tumbling over the weir. Cold water pouring down to the sea.

I start shivering.

He kisses me. 'I heard it at the market.'

He's whispering in my ear and something dark twists like an eel deep in my guts.

'There were these two women waiting at the surgery.' He doesn't laugh as he used to at the absurdity of calling the shed where he carries out basic nursing and first aid, a surgery. 'I've seen one of them before, from a farm out west. The other was her cousin, she said. Same features. They were chatting about the "system"; at first I thought it was a farming thing. But then they were saying, "Are you sure he is?" and "Yes, he's safe". I was busy with a patient. They didn't know I could hear them.'

'When was this?'

'It doesn't matter. Let me finish.' He hesitates, and shifts to get more comfortable. 'You know Mike with the terrier? With the penny whistle?'

'He came for music night?'

'Yes. Him… Hang on, I can hear someone.'

A door closes. For a minute, he's silent.

'Well, there's this "system". Like the Underground railroad in the States. To get people out.'

He stops again and I let out my breath.

'But why? What do you mean?'

'We all know NOAH's getting stronger. Every day it's harder to know who to trust. Spies everywhere.'

There's a cold emptiness in my chest, as if someone has hollowed out my heart.

'If you want to get somewhere. If you're desperate, there is a way.' He pauses. 'I think that's how they got here.'

I see Underground railroad images – desperate people running across open, flooded country, chased by dogs. Dark roads. Railway lines like the old post office system that used to run under London. People hiding in the tube stations in the Blitz. Lines going underwater as the river rises up to engulf them.

He holds me tighter. 'If anything happens. Here, at the Mill.'

I'm shivering as if I'll never be warm again. Ice in my chest. He means if something happens to him.

'How long have you known this?'

I picture a growing resistance undoing the ties of NOAH, their straitjackets and bindings, their tethers and ropes. Fighting back against the restrictions and regulations; who could imagine a fiery dawn rising in the east, over the land? A new dawn of freedom and hope.

'The old gun shop next to the bridge. That's where he lives. Mike the musician too. They're part of the "system". They help people in different ways. I've had connections with the ones who supply food, medicine. Taking from NOAH. I don't know if that's how she got here. I'm not going to ask. The fewer people know the better.' He kisses me. 'But if you ever need to. OK? Promise?'

'Yes.'

'This is what you have to say...' He tells me a series of questions and answers. He makes me repeat them several times. 'Got that?'

'Yes,' I say, my voice squeezed out reluctantly. Then I have an image of Robbie. Not escaping. Helping. Not only medical skills. Helping escapees from NOAH. 'But why have you never told me about this before?'

He kisses me then says, 'We'll never talk about this again. OK?'

'Robbie, how involved are you? Are you part of it?'

But he doesn't answer. He's already asleep.

Sixteen

The long winter drags itself into March without a sign of spring; buds on the trees stay tightly closed and even the robins are silent, snow falling on snow like the old Christmas carol. We're fugitives in our own home, exhausted and on edge.

For the next few days Elsa stays in her room, unable to get out of bed without someone to help her. Her condition deteriorates. She is running a temperature, her nose shiny, her breath rasping. She's paler too, with a pinched look. Sometimes she coughs so much she has to fight for breath. Nula and Jamila only come downstairs to eat. Tracey and I do what we can – managing the farm, tending to the animals and making meals – women cooped up in the homestead while the men are on watch, like frontier time in the Wild West. We avoid the market and have to scratch around for every meal. Occasionally, Ewan brings back a rabbit, but our fish has long gone. Conversation is limited to the exchange of news, as we hunch over our bowls, starting at every noise. Even Tiny's smiles and gurgling can't compensate. Underneath everything that happens, behind every conversation, we're waiting.

Tonight, when Robbie comes back from the lookout, he looks drained; he's frozen. In bed, we curl tight around each other and I do my best to thaw him out.

'Warmer now?' I ask when he stops shaking.

'Yes. Your turn now. Where does it hurt?'

'Shoulders, lower back. Everywhere.' He holds me, massaging my back and limbs, and as the pain fades, I begin to relax. But even the best massage can't make it go completely.

Why couldn't Ewan get me something? He's managed before. Being in constant pain makes me angry with him, at the way he mopes around.

'You're so tense, love. Come on, try to relax.'

'It's Ewan. I can't believe how pathetic he's being. We're all suffering. He lets Tracey fuss over him then if she tries to hug him, he pushes her away. No one else is making such a drama out of it.'

'But remember he was the first one to see the aftermath of the raid.'

I don't answer.

'You need to relax or you'll not sleep.'

'Tracey spoils him. She needs to let him grow up. He's not a child.'

He sighs. 'Survivor's guilt. He's more sensitive than he looks. It will take time.' Robbie looks on everything with his nurse's point of view. 'You're being harsh. What's got into you?'

'You can stop.' I move away. 'It's not working. Let's go to sleep.'

'Ah, I know what it is – where's your pain stuff?'

'Ewan can't get any. He says it's too dangerous asking, now they're so close. Showing weakness.' I shift right away and curl up tight. 'You can't help everyone, you know.'

'I wish I could.' He kisses the back of my neck at the hairline. 'Whatever happens, remember I love you, Anna. Remember that.'

I sigh irritably. 'I know you do. And I love you too.'

Pain takes over everything. But eventually I fall asleep. I feel as if I'm dreaming all night. Vivid, disturbing dreams of endlessly climbing stairs in a flooding house, climbing up to the attic, but the water keeps rising and gradually the house tips and sinks and there's nothing I can do. It's too late. I wake up exhausted and aching. Angry with Ewan.

I'm eating a quick breakfast before going out to milk the goats, enjoying a stolen moment of peace – the snow's cold light on the tree buds, a lone robin calling – when footsteps clatter on the wooden staircase and Jamila bursts in.

'Mum said to come quickly. You have to come now.' She breaks down, sobbing. 'She keeps talking rubbish and she's coughing so much. It's horrible! You've got to do something!'

By the time I get there, Nula comes to the door of Elsa's room, shaking her head, close to tears. In Tracey's arms, Tiny is arching his back, fighting to get down.

'You need to stay away,' Nula tells Jamila.

She goes downstairs again, complaining. 'Why can't I give her a hug? Why not? She's my friend. Why can't we get a doctor?'

'What is it?' I ask Nula. The sinking terror that it could be TB or one of the viruses that have plagued us since the flood, since sanitation has become so primitive.

'She's trying to say something, Anna. She's delirious.' Nula wipes her own face with exhaustion. 'She's much worse.'

I put my hand on Tracey's arm.

'You need to get Robbie.'

'What's wrong?'

'Just go. Run.'

Nula takes Tiny from her and he laughs, his whole body leaping towards his mother.

Elsa is sitting up, holding her hands in front of her, shaking them and crying. Her blonde hair is almost black, flattened against her thin face, her eyes like pools of dark tarn water.

When she's able to get her breath, I wipe her forehead to cool her down.

'Don't speak, love,' I say.

But she's desperate to say something. Stammers the same words over and over again.

'I can't feel my fingers, Anna. Look, I can't move them. Why can't I feel them? What's the matter with my fingers?' Then she starts coughing. 'Oh! It hurts so much!'

'I was trying to calm her. That's when she started saying it.' Nula's voice is shaking and so soft I can hardly hear her.

'About her hands?'

'Yes, I could make that out but then she gets confused.'

Elsa lies back, her fair hair plastered across her forehead. The room has the sour smell of sickness – Nula found flowers growing near to the house, sheltered from the snow, and has put them in a jam jar. Their rank, vegetable smell mixes with the smell of sweat. And something else I remember but can't name. A foetid, animal smell.

'I'll get more water,' says Nula.

Robbie runs in, takes one look and turns, biting his lip. He pulls open the blind. Then pauses. He stands back, so calm at first I think there's been an improvement, but when I go to him he almost shakes me off. Something is seriously wrong. 'I thought it was a chest infection! Fuck!'

Ewan finds me when I'm milking the goats. The smell of warm milk. The animals' steamy breath in the cold morning. He brings his own outdoors smell – smoky with a chemical tang, ash smudged on his face.

'What is it, Anna?'

'Sepsis. She needs antibiotics.'

He shakes his head. He looks so sad my anger with him dissolves and I want to put my arms round him. 'It's not your fault. You've done your best. But please, Ewan; I know you said it's too dangerous now, but Robbie says it's her only chance.'

He kicks at the ground. 'I should've looked after them. The twins.'

'We all got there as quickly as we could.'

'But the lad got hyperthermia, and now she's getting worse.' He kicks the ground again. 'It's my fault.'

'Elsa needs antibiotics and pain relief.'

He shakes his head. Since the NOAH raid, his confidence is shattered.

'You've found someone before.'

He takes a deep breath. 'Aye, you're right. I'll see what I can do.'

'But don't do anything daft, Ewan.'

He responds to the pleading in my voice. 'Come here. I can look after myself. Don't fret.' He puts his arms around me in a bear hug. 'I'll see what I can do.'

He's gone all day. With more of us to look after, more on guard duty, it's a long day. As well as all the work on the Mill to be done to get a meal. To keep warm.

It's only as the light is going that he reappears, a small package in his hand. 'Here – that's all I could get today but they've promised me a good supply.' He's haggard and cold. He pulls at the chain around his neck; his mother's wedding ring that used to hang from the chain has gone.

He slumps into a chair by the fire.

His father comes in. 'Get a move on, lad. You're due up there.'

'He needs to eat first,' says Daniel, 'or he'll not make it through another night.'

Ewan gets up quickly. 'It's no bother. I'll take some bread. I can eat on the way.' He walks lightly as he heads for the door.

'It's OK, lad. Rob's already up there. Take your time.' Daniel claps him on the shoulder. 'You've done good today. You might have saved my daughter's life.'

'Anna!' Elsa smiles for the first time in days. 'Where've you been? I've not seen you for ages.'

She's been so feverish she doesn't know we've all been taking turns to sit with her, night and day. I gently lift one of her hands and she winces. The fingers are swollen and discoloured.

'I wish you could make it go away.'

'What?'

'That dog. The black one. It's in the room all the time. Can't you take it away and feed it. It keeps biting my fingers and toes. It must be hungry.'

The jack russell, Elsa's favourite dog, is curled up on the mat next to her bed.

'Agatha's here, love. She wouldn't bite you. The others are outside. Fowler's at the lookout with Ewan. Victor is with Daniel. I can take her out if she's annoying you.'

Tears start in her eyes, course down her face, wetting her hair. She brushes them away with the backs of her hands. 'Not Agatha. She's my friend.'

It hurts her to move her hands.

'My brother was lying in the snow and he was so cold. Then they took him away. Will you help me, Anna? You're the kind one. Everyone's kind, but not *him*. Don't let him come back.'

'Who, Elsa?'

'Don't let him in, will you? You've got to promise you won't let him.' She leans towards me. 'I've got to whisper it. Or *he* might hear.'

I stroke her arm and put my arm around her shoulders. 'What happened? Who are you talking about?'

'Shh! He wants to hurt me. He set his dog on me. It's here in the room. It won't lie down. It wants me too.'

'What happened at the lookout?'

She tries to sit up in bed and I help her.

'But don't tell *him*, will you? Promise, Anna. Hope to die.'

She clings to me, so close I feel her burning body through

the thick pyjamas. I hold the glass of water for her and she drinks it noisily, thirstily. 'More please. You never give me enough. You're all trying to stop me from drinking. Why won't you give me some more?' I refill the glass and she drinks it, then I help her to lie down.

I shouldn't be questioning her when she's so ill. That's what Robbie would say. Too much excitement when she's beginning to recover, but I think this is important.

'Tell me what happened to Stefan. What happened to your brother?'

She sits upright, wringing her hands.

'They came on horses. Big horses. I was scared of their hooves. They kept saying I was Jamila. I said no so many times. They gave him something. They pointed a gun at me.'

'Could you recognise him again?'

Her face is a blank and I think she's forgotten, then she's back there again, reliving it. Her legs running, her fists flailing. 'What are you doing? Take your hands off my brother. Leave him alone.'

Panting, her breath comes in and out quickly and lightly, her eyes bright.

'Who, Elsa? Who was it?'

Then, as she falls back on the pillow exhausted, she says one word so quietly I can't hear her. 'Who was it? Say it again. I couldn't hear you.'

She breathes out the word again then shuts her eyes.

It sounds like *you*. Only when I'm walking away do I realise what she's said.

Seventeen

When Robbie comes to check Elsa, I go to the lookout; I need to thank Ewan for getting the antibiotics. But more than anything, I want to investigate, to find out. Before I tell Daniel.

I hear him before I see him. Talking in a low voice, squatting down and stroking Fowler.

I clamber up the steps towards him.

'Thank you,' I say. Then more quietly: 'I know what you did.'

'What d'you mean?' he says, pushing his hands into the pockets of his jacket as he stands. His look is so angry I take a step back. When I tell him I've noticed he no longer has his mother's ring, he relaxes.

'I hope it helps her.'

'Robbie says she needs a much longer course.'

He hangs his head. 'I'm keeping away from that lot,' he mumbles. 'Don't ask me again, Anna.'

His lip is quivering. I pull myself up and touch his arm, but he shakes me off. My leg won't hold my weight. It gives, and I overbalance, catching on to the wooden post to stop myself falling. Ewan grabs my arm and, in slow motion, I'm pulled up again. When everything rights itself I see he's dropped something in the snow. I reach for it but his hand comes out first to grab it.

Then there's a sound I've not heard in years, not since the Flood – the ringtone of a mobile phone. The old Nokia ringtone.

He swears under his breath, then climbs down the ladder.

But, by the time he picks it up, it's stopped and there's the bleep of a message arriving. His eyes meet mine with a flash of guilt and fear, hidden by a slow smile, that smile that serves him well. He looks at the screen, reads a message, then pushes the mobile back into his pocket.

'What the –'

'Before you talk, let me explain. That marra that collects phones, he can get them going again, he's been fixing them, trying to get them to hold a charge.'

'But there's no network; how could he?' Something in his look scares me. 'Ewan, who's ringing you? *Why* are they ringing you?'

He pats his pocket and turns away. 'Sometimes it's better to keep your nose out of other people's business. I nivver said I was perfect, did I? You've got to compromise a bit to keep in with them. To get what you want. I got meds for Elsa, didn't I? I'm doing what I can.'

The world is tilting and I hold the worn rail to keep my balance. 'What kind of compromises? Who are you "keeping in with"?'

His voice is dark when he says, 'Keep your nose out. Right?' Then he looks at his watch and his tone brightens: 'Anyroad, blow the whistle. It's time for our dad to come up.'

'What's going on? You can't keep secrets. It's dangerous.'

'You know nowt about it. And you don't want to, neither. I got the pills, didn't I?' he says again. 'Go on. Blow the whistle.' His fingers press hard into my arm. 'An' I'll get some more, right, but keep it to yourself, eh?'

When I put the whistle to my lips my teeth are chattering so much, all that comes out is a feeble, thin sound.

'Give it here,' he says and pulls it out of my hand. He blows it hard. 'Right. Time to ga. And don't say nowt, eh? Come on, Fowler lad. I need to get back.' His knuckles are white on the dog's lead. He walks away quickly, leaving me to struggle behind him down the hill to the Mill.

We pass Robbie coming up with George; Ewan barely greets them, nods briefly, head down. Keeps going.

'Be careful, Robbie,' I say. 'Please.'

'When am I ever not careful?' Robbie laughs it off and hugs me tight. 'I can take care of myself!'

I want to protect him, but Ewan's grip lingers on my arm, the ringtone going round and round in my head. He's scared me, but more than that I'm terrified of what is going to happen to all of us. I need to find Daniel.

I hurry back as fast as I can in time to catch sight of Ewan going straight into his room, bolting the door. Half an hour later he appears, smiling, his hands steady. I've sometimes wondered if he keeps alcohol in his room, something that lightens his mood. He's so full of jokes, I almost think I imagined that old ringtone chiming out over the hillside. But I know what I heard.

Daniel is sitting with Elsa. She's fast asleep. Since her illness and Stefan's attempted abduction, I could weep inside at how he has slowly withered, the fight gone out of him. Even with medication, her recovery is painfully slow. Her favourite dog, on the mat next to Elsa's bed, whines in her sleep. Daniel won't leave her side. I stand in the doorway as he strokes her hair away from her forehead, singing to her under his breath, his face grey and lined. Sometimes he's been motionless; doesn't tap his feet or drum his fingers, but holds his head in his hands as if all his internal music has been scoured away. I remember how my own dad would read me stories for hours when I was ill. But Elsa is beyond this.

'Daniel!' I say.

He turns slowly and sighs.

When I tell him about Ewan, he jumps up as if he's had an electric shock.

'What the fuck!'

'You know how he's involved in all sorts of things – it's the only way we could get the antibiotics.'

'Where is he?'

'He was so angry, he scared me. He's calmed down since he got back but I don't know what he might do.'

'Where did he go? Why didn't you get me?'

'He went out again. He'll be at the lookout later but I don't know where he is now.'

'If that bastard has something to do with hurting my kids I want to be the one who finds out. He's a fucking liability! We need to search his room.'

Before I can speak, he's out of the room and marching towards the sleeping area.

I've never been in Ewan's room. Privacy at the Mill is taken seriously – it's an unwritten rule that unless someone asks you in, or they're ill, you don't go into their room. Though most are hardly rooms – the long workshop is partitioned off into smaller units for the women. There are three separate rooms in the adjoining barn for the men. When Robbie and I came, Ewan gave up his large room and moved into the one at the end of the corridor that no one wanted: three outside walls and damp all year round, cold as ice in the winter, as it is now. I thought it was generosity, but I'm beginning to suspect he wanted to be away from us, for whatever he's mixed up in.

Familiar clothes are hanging on hooks or thrown on a chair. There's a faint smell of his spicy deodorant. I find a stash of them in his bedside cupboard. It's never occurred to me to wonder how he gets hold of good quality toiletries that have long since disappeared. No one else does. Everyone has indulged him, laughed it off. Treated him like the spoilt boy he is. *Oh, Ewan knows how to get everything.*

On the deep, stone window sill, there's a photo of a young George, his arm around a young woman, only it can't be Tracey, it must be her mother. The young girl in front of them must be Tracey, one hand over her mouth to hide her prominent teeth, the other holding her small blond brother to stop him moving away; his face is a blur but there's that embryonic smile, a child's smile, but recognisably Ewan's.

I search through every drawer, behind pictures and in the narrow wardrobe; its door squeaks and I look round cautiously. My heart ratcheting up, my hands clammy. If he has a phone, if he's in contact with strangers, if… then Daniel stops and I hear a sharp intake of breath.

'Fuck, is this what he's messed up in?' he says. 'Risking all of us! Look!' From under the bed he pulls out a handful of small, sealed brown paper bags.

And it all makes sense. No wonder Ewan is so up and down, relaxed and joking one minute, then tired and short-tempered, desperate to get back to his room, to get outside on his own.

'Of course; the phone's locked!' Daniel's shoulders slump. 'What do you think his PIN could be?'

I shake my head. My mind is blank with fear. I can hardly breathe.

'Ah! The only thing he loves as much as himself is that dog.' Daniel types in the letters, smiles at his success, then scrolls through the phone. I feel my own fingers trying to copy him – that old muscle memory of flicking through messages.

'It's not food or alcohol. What is he trading? How can he get so much? Is he dealing?'

He's shaking his head. 'There's messages from all sorts here. He's in deep. Someone called Jes. Never heard of him.'

Jeston, the fish man from Maryport.

'I know who he is. Let me see.' He passes me the mobile. 'Ewan was very close with him at the market. I thought he was being friendly. Like he always is.'

Then I feel that icy plunge of my stomach – like falling into water.

'What?'

'The day of the raid; he *knew* they were coming. He was expecting them.'

Daniel gasps. 'Listers! Tracey has a heart of gold and her dad means well even if he isn't the brightest, but I thought Ewan was someone who knew what he was about. I can't believe he'd do something so fucking stupid.'

Messages date back weeks, well before the day we all went to the market. The most recent tells Ewan to meet up in the park, near the bandstand, at first light. He isn't trading food or alcohol for drugs; it's information. Ewan has brought NOAH to us.

The safest place is the roof space above the library. Nula and Jamila will hide there, pulling the ladder up with them. Tracey will take Tiny to the ice house, with stacks of straw and hay to muffle any sound. Nula is reluctant to be separated until I tell her it makes sense for the children not to be together. We reinforce the warning systems and defences, but all we can do is wait it out.

For the rest of the day there's no sign of Ewan.

Robbie goes to look for him. 'I'll bring him back.'

'Don't, Robbie.' I'm holding on to his coat. 'We need you here.'

'Who else is there? Someone has to.'

'Please.' But I know he will. He has to help. I can't stop him. 'Hide if you see them. Don't try to fight. Take Victor.'

He kisses me, then his hand is on the door when I add, 'And stay safe.'

The old phrase from the time of the C viruses comes back to me. I was only a child then. I remember Mum saying it when she left us. 'Stay safe, look after your dad, Anna.' But I was only a child. How could I look after him? Now both are gone. My heart quivers to imagine who will be next.

Our early-warning systems work; we hear the whistle from the lookout. We know they're near. Through the mist and snow they come. Four of them on horseback, harnesses jingling. Four of them. What chance do we have? No weapons that can hold back armed soldiers on horses.

They come when we're at our weakest, prepared but ill-equipped – we've sworn we'll never use guns, so we do what we can. We turn out the dogs, but shots blast out over the snow. Fowler falls with a whimper and lies shaking on the ground, then is still. There's a deadening silence. They're in the yard. The uniform I've not seen since the journey here, tattered and mended with added sheepskin for warmth. The gold and purple of NOAH. Horses standing, stamping their hooves, clouds of snow whirling around them. A smell of leather and horse.

They dismount and their feet crunch in step through the snow.

'Where is she, old man? Give us the lass and we'll not hurt you.' The leader pushes past me and looks at Daniel. He takes off his balaclava – it's Jeston from the market, the man selling fish.

Another figure stumbles towards the front of the Mill. He looks as if he's slept in his clothes, or not slept at all.

'Where is she then, Ewan?' says Jeston. 'We said the hill, not down here.'

'Gone. Not enough food for us lot, nivver mind them. We let them go.' Ewan's attempt at a lie is transparent.

Jeston gives a short laugh and pokes a gun into his chest. 'Come on, lad. You'll have to do better than that.'

Ewan stutters. 'I isn't lying. The lasses have gone.'

Without a warning one of the men steps forwards and smacks him over the cheek with his gun. Ewan staggers and falls to the ground, hitting his head against the stone flags of the path. He pulls himself up and starts to crawl away, sliding on the ice, dripping blood. The man kicks him and the others join in, until, at a signal from Jeston, they stop and smile at each other, catch their breath.

Then one of them lunges towards me and grabs my arm. He looks to Jeston: 'This'un, eh? The doc's lass.'

Jeston nods.

Hands tight on my arm.

'We've been watching this place. No one's been out apart from the old fella… Come out now, Nula. We know where you are.' Jeston's voice echoes off the snow-covered hill.

Even the rooks are silent.

'I've got your friend here, the cripple. Big lass with the gammy leg. You won't miss her, will you? We need the pregnant one. Then we're done.'

I hardly have time to take a breath before they're pulling me towards the river, my feet scrambling and sliding in the snow and mud. The crack of ice as they drag me. Pain in every limb.

'No, please. No.' I hear my own voice pleading, then, as the noise of the river gets louder: 'No! No!' A magpie in a whirring fluster of black and white skims the path and in my head I hear the words of the rhyme – *one for sorrow*.

I want to shout to warn Robbie, but I won't say his name. I pray with my whole body that he's hiding somewhere. The choking fear of the flood comes back to me. The river running under the thick crust of ice where green weed is trapped like hair. I slither on loose fragments of slate and down the bank of the river. All senses heightened: a smell of hot metal and wool from their clothes, the oiled leather of their coats, the saddles and harnesses. Breath steaming in the icy air, blown away by the wind. Hands of the one gripping and kneading me. No kindness or pity in his eyes. I'm insignificant, a means to an end. Disposable.

It's how I dreamed it. Cold cutting my skin, the wind hurling sleet and frozen leaves. The sound of the water. Please don't let them let go of me. Please don't hurt me more than this. Under the lid of ice, the river rushes on, dragging everything downstream and over the weir. I will be flung like a coil of rope, unravelling into the water.

Someone is screaming. Nula. Jamila has run out, her mother yelling to her to stop.

'Leave her alone! She's done nothing wrong. Stop hurting her!' Jamila's voice is shrill against the rush of the water.

'Ripe and ready to burst. Here she is,' says one of the men, laughing; they let go of me so abruptly I fall into the snow, inches from the river's edge. My cheek nearly touches the surface of the water where, close to the bank, there are sheets of ice full of tiny bubbles of air. A perfect, brown oak leaf trapped in ice. Jamila tries to help me up but her growing belly slows her. In a split second, they have her by the arm and are dragging her away.

Nula chases them but they push her away; it's Daniel who nearly has his arms around Jamila before he's forced to the ground as they disappear round the corner of the track. Out of sight there are shouts and yells; then Jamila's voice gets fainter until it's silenced altogether.

It's over in minutes. We hear the sound of hooves and harness and they've gone.

Daniel pulls me up.

'Where is he? Where's Robbie?' My heart is hammering in my chest, pulsing in my temples. My palms are sweating and I can't breathe, my legs bruised and cut by my fall in the snow. I see Robbie standing like one of the Antony Gormley sculptures staring out to sea, water creeping up his body as the tide comes in. At high tide he will be covered. He's in danger.

Daniel's voice is grim. 'That's the bugger we need to ask,' he says stopping in the yard where Ewan has pulled himself up to sitting.

Nula sinks to her knees in the snow, her face in her hands.

'Where's Robbie? He was looking for you,' I shout. 'Where is he?'

Ewan is coughing, trying to speak, and I want to shake his big useless body for an answer. But I already know.

Eighteen

Ewan's face is ashen, bruised and swollen. Badly beaten by the NOAH soldiers. He can hardly stand. He's trembling – it could be fear, or withdrawal from whatever drugs he's on. I don't know or care.

'I'm sorry, Anna. Nula,' he says, looking at the ground. 'What I done was wrong. I've betrayed everyone.'

Neither of us meets his eyes.

'It was a bit of fun at first. A nice smoke to take the edge off. I never wanted to hurt anyone. I'm sorry.'

'Where's Robbie? Where is he? What have they done with him?' Without a word, Nula walks up to him and spits in his face. She'll kill him if we don't stop her. And I think he would let her.

'Where's my daughter? Where have they taken her? Where *is* she?'

Ewan wipes his face as if nothing has happened and mutters 'I'm sorry' under his breath.

Nula pushes him. 'I thought we could trust you. You're the same as the rest of them. You selfish, fucking bastard. How could you do this to us? To all of us.'

Daniel, who's been standing with his arms hanging uselessly, makes a move as if he's been shaken awake. He speaks quietly to her and pulls her back.

Ewan keeps his head down. But he's speaking to me. 'I'm sorry, Anna. When all this started, I didn't know. NOAH's losing babies all the time. Doctors won't work for them.'

My heart is beating so fast it feels as if it will take off. My head is spinning; I'm falling, the ground coming up to meet me. I catch hold of Ewan's arm then pull away, breathing deeply to settle myself.

'They want his medical knowledge. I'm sorry, lass.'

Before I have time to respond, there's the sound of crying and Tracey comes into the yard with Tiny struggling and kicking in her arms. 'Oh my god what's happened to you, Ewan? Are you all right? Can you walk?'

'I didn't know what I was getting into. I didn't mean any harm… honestly.'

George explains.

Tracey's face changes from concern to disbelief. 'This time you've gone too far. I can't forgive you for this, Ewan. I'll nivver speak to you again.'

'I hope he knows he's lost a father as well as a sister,' George says, fighting back tears, rubbing his nose on his sleeve. 'Come here, Tracey.'

He puts his arms around her and the baby. 'I'm good for nowt now,' he says. Tiny reaches his arms up to him, smiling. 'Ah, look at babbie.' He takes Tiny's hand in his. 'So innocent. That's how they want to stay.'

Tracey starts to help him back to the house.

'But, Dad!' Ewan is crying like a child. 'They shot my dog. Dad, they killed Fowler.'

'I've nowt to say to you, lad. Nowt.'

Nula breaks free from Daniel and charges at Ewan.

'Is that all you can think about? Your dog! Where's my daughter?' She beats at him and he cowers, covering his face. 'What have you done to her? What have you done to Jamila? Where is she?'

'Daniel?' I say. 'Let's go in. Nula, come inside.'

'Yes, everyone inside. That's enough, Nula. He needs to be punished, but not like that.' Daniel grips Ewan's shoulder. 'Get up and get inside. We've got decisions to make and I don't want you wandering off back to them NOAHs.'

'I know what I want to do,' says Nula, and I try to pull her back again. She shakes me off. 'He doesn't deserve to live after what he's done.'

I put my hand on Daniel's arm. 'Thanks, Daniel. Nula, Tiny's crying. We need to go inside.'

When Tracey hands Tiny to his mother, she holds him so tight it looks as if she'll smother him.

Daniel pushes Ewan roughly into a straight-backed chair and keeps one hand on his broad shoulder, a muscle twitching in his jaw. 'Talk. Go on. This is your chance.'

'Tell us, Ewan,' I say. 'Tell us everything you know. We need as much help as we can get. Daniel, Robbie's not back either. They've got him too.'

Daniel's eyes widen as he glances at me. 'I'm sorry, lass. That's another blow I wasn't expecting.'

His hands grip Ewan's shoulder, knuckles whitening. 'You selfish bastard. If it wasn't for Anna you wouldn't get a second of my time. Go on.'

'I don't know what to say. What I done was stupid. And now it's all a big fucking mess.' Ewan slumps in the chair.

'Well keep your bloody mouth shut then, lad. There's nowt you can say to make this better,' George says. 'I don't know what your mother…' He can't finish, chokes up.

'I was trying to help. Get some nice stuff. Meds and that. I wanted to help.' Ewan's voice is whiny. A spoilt child. 'Didn't I, Anna?'

Our eyes meet. That flash of silver-blue. And I know I have to say something. I can't hide anymore. I've got to do what's right. Or I'll fall and never stop. Down under the water, into the abyss. An image comes to me – Nula rising in fury with a silver axe flashing and sparking. I see the blade slice through the rotten heart-wood of a diseased oak. It crumbles. She offers me the axe then I'm alone in the wood, the axe raised in my hand, every muscle in my arm straining and starting to twitch. I breathe out a long breath.

'If you punish him, you'll have to punish me too.'

'Don't be daft,' Daniel says, his accent stronger with emotion. He moves towards me with a smile. '*You*'ve done nowt wrong. You're like your dad. He'd be proud of you. I know that.'

I take in an uneven breath, as tears catch in my throat at the thought of what I've done, what Dad would say. 'I'm sorry, Daniel. Everyone. He got drugs for Elsa. I asked him because I knew he could.'

'Aye, well we all know he's got his connections.' Daniel takes his hand off Ewan's shoulder. 'And we know who they are now, don't we? Stop blaming yourself, Anna. It's marra here who's brought all the trouble.'

'You need to listen to me. All of you. There's more.' I sit down heavily into an armchair. 'He got me something too, for the pain. For the other things. To stop it getting worse. To help me. I was scared. And stupid. I couldn't do it on my own. I didn't tell Robbie. I couldn't. And now he's gone too.'

'Aye, a few paracetamol and herbal nonsense off the market,' Daniel says smiling grimly. 'We've all done that –'

I interrupt him. 'Not ordinary painkillers. Strong stuff. To stop the nightmares.'

'Bad dreams?' Nula asks gently. 'We all have them.'

'More than that. Worse than that.'

She puts an arm around me. 'I know what you mean. Flashbacks. I get them sometimes.'

'Yes, those too.' I almost wish the river had swallowed me up. To talk about this after so long feels like a terrible confession, and I wish I'd told Robbie. 'Sometimes I see things. Hear things. Like it's real and it's happening now. Not the past. Not dreams. Worse than that. I can't wake myself up. In the daytime and it's happening. Not the past. New things. As real as this, with sounds and smells. Like PTSD, only it hasn't happened yet. Ewan knows. He understood, didn't you, Ewan?'

Daniel is smiling. 'You're a good person, someone we rely on. We've all gone through bad times.'

'It's much worse.' My face is wet with tears now.

'Christ, Ewan, what have you given her? What have you done now?' Tracey comes out with it, her face distorted with anger.

'So what if she's taken a few illegals now and then? She was desperate. I was trying to help. She needed sommat.'

I remember the day he found me up on the hill, how he held me tight, to stop the shaking. The sick taste of death in my throat. How, when I swallowed the pills down, light blossomed in my head, the noises stopped. The sound of a machine grinding through stone finished. How everything was clean and open and full of light.

'It works. That's all I know. I'm sorry. I've let you *all* down.'

The disappointment in Tracey's face is worse than anything. And the clench of tears in her voice – 'Not you, Anna. I can't believe it. You too.'

'So you need to punish me as well, if you're going to punish –'

'No, Anna.' Ewan tries to get to his feet but Daniel puts both hands on him to stop him. 'You knew nowt about NOAH. She didn't, Daniel. I swear. Leave her out of it.'

Daniel breathes out. 'I don't know. I don't know anything anymore. Everything's changing too quickly. This is what happens when we lose trust in each other and have secrets. Didn't we say at the beginning – no secrets?' Daniel shakes his head. 'I don't know what to do for the best.' He looks at us one by one.

Nula is the first to speak. 'You all thought it was me. *I* was bringing NOAH to you. All the time it was *him*.' I've never heard her shout. 'Whatever Anna's done it's nothing compared to *him*!' She points her finger at Ewan. 'Send him *away*. He can look after himself.' She's almost triumphant.

Everyone starts talking. A cacophony of raised voices. George thumps the table. Nula dives at Ewan, scratching him, pushing him until Daniel pulls her off and speaks, finding his voice of quiet calm that cuts under the uproar.

'The ice house. Until we come up with a plan. And because if I have to look at him a minute longer, knowing what he's fucking done, I'll kill him. Come with me, Anna.'

Daniel shoves Ewan ahead, along the path to the ice house. 'Anna, I wish you'd said something.'

All I can do is cry. There are no words.

With the rain and snow, the door to the ice house has swollen. Daniel pushes Ewan in and, as he forces the door shut and secures it with the padlock, we hear him complaining.

'But there's nowt to eat. I'm hungry. And it's cold!'

'Think on what you've done. Plenty of food for thought there. Come on, Anna. Let's get you back in the warm.'

Tracey takes charge. She sends Nula and me to bed. I want to sleep. I want oblivion. I'm aching, cut and bruised, but my thoughts are whirring with a dizzying sickness. Ever since my illness, dread has lurked like a single cancer cell, waiting for the right time: when Nula arrived, I knew it was coming. When they threw me down onto the hard, icy ground, it exploded into growth. They showed me what no one else will say aloud: I have no right to love, or to hope for a good life. I'm worthless. I deserve to lose what I love most in the world. I'll never see him again. Everyone says how strong I am, tall and wide as a barge. A laugh like the heat from an oven door opening. I let myself imagine I was attached to Robbie with threads of steel and now I don't know how to move alone. My bones are like brittle glass.

I don't know if I'm awake or asleep, but in the dream it's dark and I'm running over high ground that crumbles and breaks, looking for him. I'm plunging down into water. Then I'm out, on the ground again. Walking, pushing through bushes. There are trees on all sides and I'm crawling or stumbling. It's so hard to walk, I fall down again, sliding down towards the water. Everywhere I look he's not there, or I catch a glimpse of him disappearing around a bend in the path. I hear him calling for me and I shout back but all I hear is the echo of my own voice coming back to mock me. Like Red Riding Hood I'm in a dark forest – there's a house where the hunter lives and I know I must find him. He'll help me. I must get to the hunter. 'Help me! Please help me!' my voice wakes me. My mouth is dry but my pillow is wet and cold with tears.

I hear her walking around the room, feel the shadow of her figure at the window. Then the light comes in again, falling across the bed. Tracey's voice is so warm it could melt ice. When I open my eyes she's leaning towards me, her smile trembling.

'It's all right, Anna. You're safe. I'm here. Can I get you something?'

The dream stays with me. There's something I need to do. Somewhere I need to go.

'I have to get him back.' I put my hand up.

She takes my hands in hers. They're warm and dry. 'Aye, but what can we do? Women can't do owt with this NOAH lot on our doorstep. I reckon it's best to bide our time till it's all over and run its course. Once everything's settled and sorted out, and there's proper order, he'll find you again. He won't stop looking for you. I know that much.'

'I have to go now. There must be some way of finding him.'

'Don't try to get up. You need to save your energy and get stronger. We need you here. Safe. Do you think you could manage a bit to eat? No? All right then, you get some more sleep and see how you feel later. I'll bring you a hot drink. You stay in bed, right?'

I nod, and she smiles, pats my hand.

'You've had a terrible shock. We all have. But you and Nula the worst. You need to get better, and you won't if you rush off to look for Robbie. I know you want to but let's wait a bit first. Anna, I can't believe my own flesh and blood has helped cause all this misery. It was bad enough before, but he's made it ten times worse.' She shakes her head and wipes away a tear. 'Our dad's taking it hard but he's strong. He'll pull through. I've got him looking after babbie!' She laughs and pulls the covers over me. 'Now all you have to do is sleep. We'll get through this together.'

But I can't get comfortable. I can't stay in bed. The atmosphere of the dream is with me. I kneel up and look out of the window. The same winter landscape. No evidence of the upheaval in our lives. Snow on every branch, covering the ground evenly. More has settled in the few hours since they came, covering the tracks of the horses and the men. It could be a folk tale.

The hunter. The forest. The old childhood story means something. I can feel a nebulous shape at the back of my mind. Red Riding Hood – is that me? Or is it Robbie? And the wolf? That must be NOAH. But the hunter is the one who seemed important in the dream. What did it mean? The hunter? In the story he helps the child. Is he someone who can help me? Someone who has a gun. I don't know anyone with a gun. The only guns are the ones NOAH has. This is going nowhere.

Outside, Daniel comes into view with a heavy pail of milk in each hand. It's late for milking but it has to be done. He disappears into the kitchen then comes out with his violin. Everyone needs a few minutes of consolation. The melody drifts up. He's playing for Elsa. For all of us. In defiance of NOAH. Music can't be stolen away from us. Music. Now I remember – it surges back.

Nineteen

Daniel pleads with me, but I am determined. I wait until dusk then set off.

A sign outside the building sways in the wind. It's faded and the paint is flaked, but you can make out a hunter, rifle over his shoulder, a dog at his heels, a sack bulging with the birds he must have shot. In the years we've lived here it's never sold a gun, but it's known as the old gun shop. When we came for holidays it was only ever a house. It stands on the slope of the hill next to the main bridge over the river where the old road runs down into what used to be the centre of town.

It looks unoccupied; no light in the window, moss curling over the plant pots that flank the door, a mush of leaves clogged in the tiny front garden. Rusting railings, paint peeling off a black door to reveal previous layers blue, red, drab green. Under the porch, the front door is so covered in cobwebs and blocked by a pile of rubbish it's obviously not been used for years. I go round the side and into a back yard. The sun must never reach here; moss covers every surface and my feet slide on the concrete. Through the window next to the back door I can see piles of something – newspapers, magazines or books. So much paper not being used. A waste, I can't help thinking. In the failing light it's hard to see clearly.

I take in a deep breath and let it out slowly to calm my heart, raging against my ribs. I raise my hand to tap on the door, but something makes me turn round – a sound, a change in the constant river noise. It brushes past my legs and scurries into a small square hole in the front door – a cat going through a cat flap, nothing more than that. So ordinary. A cat to keep down the mice and rats. There must be someone here to feed it.

I lift up my hand again. I will knock. I have to. But something grabs me around the waist, forcing my breath out, and there's wool, the smell of damp, something metallic next to my nose. Cold against my cheek.

'What do you want?' a voice hisses. 'There's nothing here for you. Go back where you came from… or I'll cut your throat.'

'I'm looking for the composer,' I say, shaking, but conscious of the absurdity of the words Robbie made me memorise. 'I have a commission for him.'

'Is it for a requiem?' he says.

'No, it's for a…'

The knife moves away from my face and he pushes me towards the door of the building.

'Come in. Here. In here.'

I'm in a room so dark it could be any size – a concert hall, or a lift. I hear the scratch of match and a candle glimmers to life, casting shadows into the corners of an ordinary living room. There's movement above, footsteps on a wooden floor, then something is dragged across the floorboards. Someone else in the building. I wasn't expecting that. They're walking slowly down the stairs.

The man holds the candle up to my face. I can feel its heat. 'It's you. The doctor's lass. From the Mill. Right?'

'I need to get to the coast.' Apart from the day at the market, it's the first time I've spoken to anyone outside the Mill for months. My voice is deadened in this room. It's lined with mattresses. The smell of old, musty bedding. It's so cold in here, colder than outside with the damp of being unheated.

'No one will take you. That leg's a liability.'

'I have to. Please. Rob said you could help.'

The candle is so close to my face I can smell rancid animal fat.

A draft of icy air. Another person in the room. They speak quietly. 'Aye, lad. I can see who it is.' The music man. A further conversation I can't make out.

'We heard about the raid on your place. You've got someone there we were keeping an eye on. We had our suspicions.'

I tell them about Robbie and Jamila. I don't name Ewan.

'Fucking NOAH. It's not worth it. You'll not get far.'

'If you can get me part of the way we can do the rest.'

'We?'

'Another woman lives with us. They took her daughter.'

'Even with someone else you'll not stand a chance.'

'Please. I've nothing to lose.'

'I admire you. Two women on your own. But you'll not get far. There's spies and all sorts.'

They speak in urgent quiet voices again.

'So… we can get you through Buttermere. Mebbe a bit beyond. There's a safe house – they'll give you details when you're on your way. From there, there'll be others to help.'

'But, if owt goes wrong you'll be on your own. Do you understand? We don't want to lose our people either. Network's fragile. One single mistake and it'll all go and we'll have to start from scratch. Once you set off, you can't change your mind.'

'Do you know where you're heading?'

'The coast? That's all I know.'

'Not Maryport or Workington… South. Right down to Barrow.'

'Barrow-in-Furness?'

'Aye. You can't go on main roads. There's road blocks everywhere. It's not safe to go by boat neither – NOAH is patrolling the coast. You need to go cross country. Right? Over the fells, through the Lakes.' He shakes his head. 'But with that leg… I'm sorry.'

'I have to,' I say and irrationally, hope flickers in my chest, like a small candle in the dark. I have to do this for Robbie. 'I've nothing to lose.'

When he finally gives me more details, he's shaking his head. I realise this is the first time I've done something by myself in the post-flood world.

Nula is in her room, leaving George to occupy Tiny. She has folded herself around Jamila's teddy bear and is sitting in a small armchair. In profile she looks like her daughter; I've never noticed how strong the resemblance is. An older version, with short hair. It's not the time to tell her.

'Together we can do something,' I say. 'We can help each other.'

She shakes her head and turns away to face the wall. 'No. You'll have to go on your own. I can't come with you. You go.'

'There are people who can help us. It's dangerous, but there are ways.'

'You're my friend, Anna. I'd like to help you too, but I can't do this.'

'I'm going to go whatever you decide. But you want to get Jamila back. Let's go together.'

She shakes her head again. 'There's nothing I can do to bring her back. You don't know what they're like. I can't do it again.' Her voice is flat, a monotone.

'Nula, you've been so strong –'

'Not this time. No. I'm very tired. Please let me rest.'

When I wake the next morning, I'm ready. Daniel tries to stop me, but he knows I'm not going to change my mind.

I refuse the wind-up torch at first, but he insists. 'You'll need it, lass. Take it.' His hands tremble as he helps me load my backpack.

At the last minute, I go back inside to find my only photo

of Robbie. I can show it to people, to ask if they've seen him.

'I've spent so long building all this up and now it's collapsing around us.'

He gestures to the Mill rising grey against the clear blue of the sky, to the furrowed fields, their dark ridges brown against the remaining snow, and to the hillside, a bulwark that protects us from the worst of the weather. But not from NOAH. There are unshed tears in his eyes and he sighs heavily each time he goes in search of supplies, bringing out apples and oatmeal bread, knives.

'I'll try to let you know where I am,' I say. 'They said I can get a message back to you. The messengers have…'

'Too dangerous. System's been infiltrated. Look at fucking Ewan.' Nula is standing holding a large rucksack. 'When I thought about it, you with no knowledge of NOAH, of course I'm coming with you. I'm going to get my daughter back!' Her voice chokes with tears. She sniffs then brusquely rubs her eyes. 'You'll look after Tiny for me, won't you, George?'

He smiles. 'Right now, that would be grand, lass. La'al un meks me laugh with all his little ways.'

'And I'll give him a hand too,' says Daniel. 'We'll all look after him, won't we, George?'

'Aye. And I hope I do a better job than I have so far with our Ewan.' George laughs bitterly, coughs from deep in his chest, and turns to spit out on the ground.

At that moment, the quiet is torn by a jet roaring over. We all duck, and Tiny starts crying. There have been a few others since the one at the market but only in the distance, too far away to impinge on our lives.

Daniel shakes his head. 'Bastards. Growing stronger by the day. I never thought Ewan would be stupid enough to get mixed up with that lot. Religious bloody fundamentalists.'

'But could it be…?' I say, and Nula gives me a fierce look

to shut me up. Of course she knows about the resistance, but does she know about the EUROS?

George tickles Tiny's toes and he laughs. 'Our Tracey's taken him some food. What did he have to say, Tracey?'

'He's ashamed. He wants to help. But, Anna you can't –'

'Like I'm going to trust *him*!' says Nula, pushing things into her rucksack. 'I know he's your little brother but...'

'He says he can get you across the first flood. He can help. There's folks he knows who do it regular, like.'

'Like people smugglers, you mean?' I say.

Nula forces tools and clothes into her rucksack.

'I'll never forgive him, but he's trying to make amends. He has contacts; everyone knows that,' I say.

Nula won't look at me.

'How can you trust him after what he's done, Anna? Are you soft in the head or something?' Daniel says.

George jabs the air with his forefinger. 'Pay no attention to him. Don't listen to him. Worthless piece of –'

'No, Dad divn't say owt you'll regret. I know what I said on spur of moment but whatever he's done he's my brother. He's one of ours. There's good trying to get out.'

'He thought he was the big man, but he was used,' I say. 'We need to ask him what information he's got. Can you bring him here, Tracey?'

Daniel's mouth shuts with an audible clack of his teeth. The decision has been made, and it's we women who made it.

The atmosphere in the group is uneasy, everyone trying to avoid eye contact. It turns out Ewan has been trying to keep a foot in both camps; he knows more than we ever thought or knew. He warns us about the spy drones, further south, about the weapons NOAH has built up. He confirms what I heard from Robbie about the resistance.

'If you're ill or injured, don't ga to hospital. NOAH military have connections; they patrol hospitals and check lists. You'll be arrested and end up in one of NOAH's own 'safe' houses. It's risky and unpredictable.'

He gives us a map of the Lake District, green, brown and blue areas shaded to show the extent of flooding. What used to be long fingers of water, the lakes and meres, are fat and wide. Like police chalk outlines of bodies on the ground. But there are also regions where the shading is less pronounced.

'What's going on in those lighter areas? Is that where the floods are spreading?' Nula says, reluctantly speaking directly to Ewan.

He bends closely to examine the map. 'No, lass, no. That's what I thought too, but others say it's where water is going down. It's only what folks are saying. We've no proper research. Stick to high ground when you have to. Barra' is south, remember.'

For a moment he hesitates. When he tries to speak again his voice breaks. 'I'm sorry for what I done… To you of all people, Nula. I –'

'It's too late for that. Everything's different now.' She turns away from him. 'Let's go, Anna.'

There's a change: the icy north wind has dropped and, for the first time in months, there's the sound of water: dripping, flowing, a movement of the river, under the ice on puddles. Ice clings to the banks. Nula pushes Tiny, who has become, without me noticing, a great strapping child, into Tracey's arms. We wait for cries of protest but he goes willingly and she distracts him by showing him the water dropping down from the icicles strung along the gutters, splashing into the water butts. He puts out his hand to catch them and laughs.

Soon, the land will be running with water again, and we can get the mill wheel turning. But there's the fear of snow-melt running down from the fells, filling the rivers and swamping the frozen ground. Last year it led to more flooding and we had to move to the upper levels of the Mill. I'm not convinced or reassured by everything Ewan has told us; he's broken the trust we thought we had. But it's all we have to go on.

It's not going to be easy with Elsa hovering between light and dark, her brother recovering from frostbite and a toddler to care for, as well as NOAH on the rise, curfews, and patrols watching the Mill, but Tracey, George and Daniel will do what they can. As we walk along the stony path away from comparative safety, they wave, and Tiny copies them, shouting goodbye and good luck. They wave until we can't see them anymore.

PART THREE

Twenty

'Over there, that's where you need to wait, behind that wall. No lights, and keep your voices down.'

After travelling for a day, night has fallen again. We walk through the woods towards the shore of the reservoir, or what was previously a reservoir. If you lived here you'd recognise the landmarks: the silage stores or church tower visible above the surface of the water; to us, it's only an anonymous area of flooding on our route to find them.

Cold rain is falling quietly but steadily, a fine soaking drizzle. There are patches where the snow has clung on, where we slip and slide. Behind us, the lights of the village where we ate and briefly slept, sheltering in a deserted farmhouse, could be a distant galaxy, glowing dimly. Or they might as well be. We may never come back this way and in a few years it might not even exist, apart from in memory, or unless you could dive underwater and find it.

The full force of the decision we've made hits me, and I'm overwhelmed by a wave of nostalgia for The Mill where I've been part of a community, where I've lived in safety; for a place that has looked after us.

I have to keep reminding myself that this isn't an ordinary day: we're not going out foraging for food, or timber for the fires; we're risking our lives. But neither of us is in doubt. This is the farthest I've travelled since the long journey north three years ago, and forgotten memories have started coming back to me. Mainly of Robbie. Robbie was there then.

~ ~ ~

How little I now have to remember him. One photo. Before the bad weather started and the land began to flood, there were photos everywhere. Digital. Films and videos. Every week, new ways to share images. Millions stored online, in the Cloud. How useless that all turned out to be. If I could go back I'd print them all off, but no one thought like that, there was no need.

Then it all went. The messages. The signals. Electricity only for emergencies. Now all I have is his heartbreakingly beautiful smile, grinning on his Oyster travel card. The leather holder held together by a few stitches, beginning to thin and fray at the edges. The picture is smudged and wearing off, the card brittle and cracking, the plastic yellowing and gritty with dust. In the other half is an old photo of my parents in happier times, on holiday in Crete, standing next to a scooter. Mum's hair blowing back. The sky absurdly blue. Dad's hands: one on her waist, the other steadying the bike. Everyone said she looked like me. I could never see it. What I love about the picture is that under my mother's white cotton dress I was already there, cells dividing, my body forming.

Does Robbie have mine, tucked into the back pocket of his jeans? I remember the day we swapped photos. Walking along the motorway, a few weeks out of London, feet blistered, mouths dry, and that ache of hunger that became so familiar when we no longer had instant access to food. We'd reached a bridge somewhere near Birmingham.

'What's that? That thing down there in the water?' Robbie said. 'Next to all those plastic bags… No, don't look.'

When someone says that I can't help rubbernecking.

Not one but several. Dipping up and down as the wind blew the surface and made waves and ripples in the murky water. Bumping next to the plastic detritus.

I gripped his hand until I felt the bones I knew so well and looked away, but the smell was harder to stomach. We tore up a shirt and tied it around our mouths and noses, more a psychological prop than anything else. Like plague doctors with masks full of sweet herbs to protect themselves, to ward off the stink of the dead and dying.

We walked on without speaking.

'I keep thinking each one is a loss to someone. Someone's son or daughter,' I said.

'If it was you, I couldn't bear it.'

I held his hand tighter. 'We mustn't think like that.'

'I couldn't bear to lose you.' His voice was shaking.

'If anything happens you've got to get to the Mill. Even if it's without me. Promise.'

He nodded.

'I'll do the same,' I said. 'But it's not going to happen. OK?' My laugh came out like a cough.

'Give me your travel card. Let's swap. If we lose each other then we'll have a photo.'

It's hard to believe but, after a few days, we became used to the sight of them. But they're in my dreams, and nightmares. Like logs floating in the plastic soup under the sodden skies.

~ ~ ~

The rain is so fine it hardly makes a mark on the surface of the water, then a cold breeze gets up and ruffles it into small waves.

The snow is gradually melting now that the temperature is rising again. Turning it into a spreading lake; if it doesn't stop, I imagine it forming part of a huge ocean. Like the back of the globe. Our blue planet.

Nula and I are both shivering – the usual cold, and that other constant: fear. There's no sign of a boat. Not a sound or a light. A woman in the village, in the first safe house, told us it might be late.

'It'll be here soon. She said two hours at the most,' I say to Nula.

Even time isn't reliable – timetables, schedules all a distant memory since the flood. For months I clung on to an old-fashioned watch after the battery went, naïvely hoping everything would go back to normal.

We're not the only ones waiting here tonight. A family with three children. One girl about five or six. Pale with blonde hair. And two babies – twins, tightly wrapped against the weather. An ordinary family. Why are they here? What are they fleeing from, or towards?

'It's not coming,' says the father. He turns to go back. 'We've been here for hours.'

The woman looks at her watch, pressing in to illuminate the face. 'It's only half past. Let's wait a bit longer.'

We don't say anything to each other, but both Nula and I decide not to engage in conversation. They'd be a liability, with a child and babies. We need to look out for ourselves. We have the papers.

'Someone's going to notice us if we hang around here much longer.' The man's voice is spiky with irritation. 'There'll be sanctions. The fucking curfew.'

I'm suddenly angry too. I pull at Nula's sleeve. She squeezes mine as if to say 'Don't.'

My stomach flips over. Heading deeper into this surreal world with its uniformed guards and religious rules feels so much more dangerous than anything Robbie and I did on the journey to the Mill. Other people could jeopardise everything.

'I've had enough. They're not coming.' The father turns with the baby bundled in his arms.

And there it is: a glimmer of light through the mist, coming towards us over the water. Like the barge in Tennyson's *Morte d'Arthur*.

'Nula? Can you see?' I'm trying to whisper but my voice squeaks and the family turn their heads. They've been looking in another direction. The father comes back, hugs his wife and apologises. They huddle together and I feel a spasm of jealousy, the solidity and grounding of having children. A future.

The light winks as the rain drifts down, but it's getting closer. A rhythmic splashing. I'd expected a motor, an engine. Only the sound of the wind and rowing.

Nula nudges me and mouths *a rowing boat.* The first water we crossed was in a boat with an outboard motor.

I'm smiling: 'What did you expect? A cruiser?'

The rubber dinghy pulls in, scraping on small stones. Two men, one with a cap, the other his face hidden by a balaclava. I can't believe we'll all fit in. I hand the one with the cap our papers; he gives a cursory look over our passes while sweat drips down my sides and my breath catches in my throat.

'What else?'

Nula rummages in her backpack for the bottle. '99 per cent,' she says.

'Right. Get in. Take it easy.'

After so much time avoiding water, all the warnings, it's hard to allow my feet to leave dry land again. When I hesitate, Nula puts pressure on my head, like a police officer making an arrest, pushing my head down as I get into the police car.

The child is whimpering. 'I'm scared. I don't want to go.' Her father is whispering, doing that reassuring that parents try. Her voice is louder. 'But I can't swim!'

'No fucking noise, right? Or we not taking you,' the one with the balaclava hisses.

It's the mother who stops the child. One slap. That's all it takes. She doesn't look the type. And I think she surprises herself. As her hand falls, she immediately puts her arm around her daughter, willing her not to cry, but the girl is too stunned to respond, and freezes.

'If you don't get in, there's others will.'

The family slowly steps into the boat. It's very low in the water and it rocks violently each time someone gets in. The father helps the child; the mother starts to pass him the babies, one at a time. One of the oarsmen gestures to them, swaddled like Egyptian mummies.

'They won't cry,' the mother answers. 'We gave them enough…'

When I try to catch Nula's eye she looks away.

As we're pushing off there's a rustle behind us from the bushes. We automatically duck.

'Wait! Please wait!' A woman's voice with an eastern European accent. Polish, I think. A couple.

'You're too late. We need to go. We're full.'

'But we can't go back now.' The Polish woman is crying and panting with the effort of running and clambering over rocks and finding their way in the dark, through the woods. 'Here.' She thrusts her papers towards the man who spoke.

He flicks through them and flashes his torch into her face.

'OK. Get in. And shut the fuck up.'

Again, the fine balancing of the boat as they get in. Now we feel much too low in the water. Have they overloaded the boat? Are they risking all of us? We're packed together, balancing on the slippery rubber edge. No space between us, almost having to breathe in turn.

The couple are finally in and we push off into the dark, leaving the whispering trees behind us. How do they know where they're going? The Polish woman holds her bag close to her. The husband leans away, lights a cigarette, offers one to the boatman. He takes it and puts it in his pocket for later.

'Where'd you get the fags?' the other says.

'Last pack. Saved them.'

We shake our heads; neither of us is a smoker.

'How far is it?' the smoking dad asks.

No answer.

'So, where are we going?' he tries.

'Safe house. No more questions.' The man folds up the map that was spread out in the bottom of the boat, and tucks it away in an inner pocket.

'Aren't we going to use the motor?' the father asks.

'What do *you* think?' the man says. 'And no more fucking questions, right?'

I find myself on the verge of hysterical laughter: here we are in a dinghy in the middle of the night, like a nightmarish midnight adventure from *Swallows and Amazons.* We used to hire boats on the lakes here in Cumbria when we were on holiday. Hours spent rowing out to an island then picnicking. Drifting half-asleep in the shallows under the moving shade of willows. Once we were stuck in a storm (the weather could change so quickly), the rain like hard pennies on the lake. In seconds, we were soaked through to our underwear. From a clear day to a complete loss of visibility in minutes.

When I remember that time, I never imagined we'd be here, out in the middle of the flood, on the water again, and I'd be searching for Robbie.

Twenty-One

For hours the only sound is the oars dipping in and out of the water, the squeak of rubber as the men lean forward and pull back, until before dawn, the rain stops and a pale moon can be seen through the mist hanging over the water. I'm stiff with cold and damp and I can't feel my feet there's so much water in the bottom of the boat. Some of us attempt to stretch, but there's hardly room to breathe. The click of joints. An incoherent mumble of the sleeping child clamped tight to her father, a blue teddy in one hand.

Everyone is hungry and beginning to be restless. At least the babies aren't awake yet; I can't imagine what the parents must have given them, but it's something strong. My stomach is empty. I struggle to open the rucksack on my lap and take out cold bread and cheese. A bottle of boiled water. At the Mill they'll be waking up now getting breakfast, heating water for porridge. Someone will be bringing the milk in, steaming in the buckets.

'Right. We need a break. Any of you think you can do it?' The man who is in charge wearing the cap looks at the men, his eyes glancing over the women. I used to be strong, I used to be able to row, with the stamina to keep going for a long time, but not now. I focus on eating my bread and cheese. The father offers, as does the other husband, and soon there's a competition between them with splashing and cursing, the boat rocking wildly.

The man in the cap mutters, 'Do you want us to be killed?' and they ease into a slow, steady rhythm. Now I've eaten, I've finally started to warm up, and my body is heavy, my eyes closing; leaning on my rucksack, my head on Nula's shoulder, I fall asleep to the rocking of the boat and the hypnotic tick-tock of rowing.

'Keep down. Don't move. Not a sound.'

I must have slept through the change back to the original positions; the two fathers are back where they started, squeezed onto the rubber sides of the boat. It's light and we're aground, on some kind of island, only of course it's not an island. Jutting out of the water is the laden roof-rack of a rusting car and a sign saying *Have you paid and displayed?* Arrows point to submerged pay machines. We're in a Lake District car park surrounded by skeletal trees spiking up out of the icy water from where the land slopes up towards the fells.

I'm chilled and stiff, but the shock of sudden waking makes my heart jump and kick, and I feel the clammy cold of the air deep in my bones, in spite of a pale yellow sun, glancing off the surface of the water. I also desperately need to go to the toilet. I'm not the only one: the young girl holding onto her blue bear, with its floppy ears and bedraggled fur, is asking her mother the same question.

'No way. She'll have to wait,' one of the men says. 'They'll be here soon. Can't hang around when they come. This is the changeover, for fuck's sake.'

But after this long night he can't expect a child to cross her legs.

'I'll take her,' I say. 'Come with me.'

I grab her hand; she's undernourished and thin, hardly any weight, and we scramble out of the boat onto the land. I have pins and needles and my feet don't feel as if they belong to me. When we're out of sight we squat on the stony ground. Hot, dark yellow urine steams. The old sensation of the morning air on my bare buttocks, my stomach. The rank smell of last season's bracken. Sun-dappled. A murmur of quiet voices.

It's as we're hurrying to pull up our clothes that the air is torn apart by a series of shots. Screams and cries. Long minutes of trying not to overbalance, then the coughing into life of a motorboat engine. It fades, then there's only the wind rustling the leaves and the faint splashing of the water.

I crouch on the damp earth, my arms wrapped around her small frame, her warm hand in mine. I don't even know her name. I have no idea what she's called. Nothing about her. We stay motionless until, apart from my pulse battering against my chest, there's silence again.

'Don't look,' I say, stroking her soft hair, fear tight around my stomach, my heart beating so fast I can hardly breathe. 'Wait here and don't say anything, OK? You'll be safe as long as you don't move. Do you understand?'

But she's hot and slippery and, in one heavy movement, pulls away from me. In slow motion, it slips out of her hand onto the steaming ground, and I find myself making the observation that her blue teddy bear has been misted with red droplets, each one small and perfect like a holly berry. How could that have happened? I think I'll let her lie on the ground here, where leaves and bracken have fallen to make a soft layer of vegetation. I put the teddy bear in her hands. It would be a good place to sleep.

The air is humming with a burning, metallic smell. I need to go and check what's happened. I know it's going to be bad. But it's worse. The edge of the water where waves were trickling over small pebbles is stained red. The air is thick with diesel and as the wash from the motor boat rushes back, everything lying in the water bobs around.

A sound. The crack of a branch. Whoever did this is here. I'm rigid, frozen to the spot. He crashes through the bushes. His arms are around me. I scream. In that last moment the way I will be hurt, my soft body opened up and unzipped, the way I'll die flashes in front of my eyes. I struggle. I fight back. Then it stops and there's only our muffled breathing and sobbing. I turn myself into her familiar smell and we hug each other hard.

Nula whispers in my ear. 'They've taken everything. The food. Everything.' She wipes streaks of blood off her face. 'I lay down with them all. I pretended until they'd gone.'

'I didn't even find out what her name was,' I say.

'They took the men,' Nula says.

The girl's mother is lying shot, on the shore. The other woman in the water. Two tiny swaddled shapes washing backwards and forwards onto the shore. They never woke up. The men who brought the dinghy too. The boat has gone. All the supplies.

'NOAH,' Nula says.

With very little food or water – only the few things I have in my rucksack – we're going to be hungry. Bread, a couple of rough-skinned apples. Nula reflects the horror on my face; we don't want to, but we don't know when we'll eat again, so we take what we can from the limp, warm bodies. Their pockets. Their bags. How heavy they are as we work together to turn them over to make sure we don't miss anything useful.

There's no map.

'But we might find the safe house,' she says. 'They said it wasn't far.'

'If it even existed,' I say. 'I'm beginning to doubt everything they told us.'

'Which direction?' Nula says. 'I've no idea how far we've come.' She has inside knowledge of NOAH, but when it comes to finding our way down to the coast, I realise her survival skills are limited. It crosses my mind that she must have had a lot of help to get to the Mill.

'We know we have to go south and west. Follow the sun if we can. Stick to high ground as long as there's something to camouflage us. Search for shelter before it gets dark.'

She nods.

'Then find a house to ransack, if we can. At least for today. After that, we need to move at night-time. It will be safer.'

'I don't know. I can't think, Anna.'

'You're hungry.' It's mid-morning now and we haven't eaten. 'Here. Have some of mine.' I give her the bread.

She shakes her head. 'I can't.'

'You have to eat. Remember what we're doing this for.'

She doesn't return my smile. Reluctantly, she tears a piece from the bread and bites into it. Each mouthful is an effort of will. I smile at her again. 'You're doing great. Keep going. It'll make you feel better, give you some energy.'

Now we're on foot our pace is slow, and walking up through woodland with no clearly defined path is difficult, almost impossible; but most of the day and late into the evening we keep moving, only stopping to drink from a stream that chatters whitely over boulders and small stones as it tumbles down the hillside. With every step, there's the dread that we're being followed; though what use would we be? Neither of us has skills or knowledge that would be of value. But we're women. That's enough for NOAH.

We don't stop until it's nearly dark and the first few stars can be seen between the nearly bare branches of the trees.

'Over there… that would be OK,' I say. In a large clearing there's some kind of low building.

Our boots have started letting in water and we're both chilled. Nula is exhausted and ready to drop. 'Let's sleep here, Anna. I don't want to –'

'It's more important to find shelter. We don't know what the weather's going to do.'

'They could be here!'

'There are no lights. It looks deserted. If I don't come back, keep going.'

Absurdly it's a National Trust visitors' centre. Cut off by the flood. Now I'm closer, shapes loom out of the twilight: the carcases of rusting cars. Whoever was here must have left on foot, years ago. I signal with the torch for Nula to come.

'At least we know where we are.' Nula smiles for the first time since NOAH took the boat. 'Thanks, Anna.'

I smile back, but at the back of my mind a small voice whispers: *Yes, but that could mean the flooding is so bad no one can get here without a boat.* I keep the thought to myself. I hope I'm wrong.

It's like finding heaven. In the gift shop are maps, compasses, torches (but no batteries); and a farm shop that had sold local produce: large bags of flour and pasta wriggling with grubs, a brown, stinking slime of rotting potatoes. No gas or electricity, of course, so we couldn't cook it even if it was fit to eat. There are cakes hairy with green mould but, packaged in tins, some stale but edible biscuits and chocolate. We fill our rucksacks then make a meal of white-speckled chocolate and shortbread biscuits with UHT orange juice. A couple of years past its sell by date, but our stomachs are stronger than they ever were before the Flood: we've built up a resistance to less-than-fresh food.

'Like a kids' party.' Nula laughs quietly. 'I'm so, so hungry.'

'Where do you think they've taken them?' I ask.

Her face changes. 'South. To the sea. The Arks, if they're lucky.'

'And if they're not?'

'Let's hope that's where they're heading. I don't want to think about it. All I want to do is finish this, then sleep.' She pushes half a soft chocolate chip cookie into her mouth, then stops, her eyes filling with tears. 'I can't bear to think of her there without me. On her own. With them.'

I put my arms around her. 'We'll find them. We won't give up.'

We push some damp chairs together to make beds, and to keep us off the floor, but it's cold. Nula whimpers in her sleep, grinds her teeth.

As I lie shivering, it comes back – the bodies, like alligators sunk in the water. Those two tiny, swaddled shapes. I try to picture where Robbie is. I think of his hands, helping. I imagine him with Jamila, keeping her calm. I don't pray – how could I? – but I tense my body, willing him to be safe. Willing warmth and safety for all of us.

Twenty-Two

With the map, we plot a rough route and keep to woodland, uphill paths where there's no sign of human life, only the odd pile of bones, scavenged by animals. Sometimes we have to wade through swollen streams, fast-moving water, but we're mostly on higher ground; at least here the clammy fingers of the water can't reach us.

Sometimes we find roads, then it's not such a strain on my leg. Broken tarmac with weeds pushing up through every crack. No one maintains roads. Why would they, with no vehicles apart from the odd cart or bike? Soon they will be gone. *Weather and rain have undone it again* – lines from the Kipling poem I read at school, about walking through a wood where there used to be a road, echo in my mind with each step. Dad said it showed how planting trees could undo some of the damage we've done to the world. But it struck me as melancholy. Everything changes and eventually vanishes. *Now you would never know there was once a road through the woods.*

One day, we come to the gateway of a farmhouse on the edge of a small village; the smell and the industrial buzzing of flies tell us what we dread: NOAH, or someone equally dangerous, has been this way, in the last few months. We gag at the smell. But we need food.'If there'd been anyone else here they would have buried them,' I say. 'You stay out here.'

In the living room, a man and woman, I can only tell by the clothes, of indeterminate age, sitting side by side on the sofa, as if they were watching TV. Squirming with maggots, a scribbling mass of them. It's something you don't ever get used to: that sweet smell of rotting flesh. In here, the drone of the flies is like a building site, or a motor way in the distance. I imagine they had lasted on their few supplies and what they could grow for a couple of years after the flood, but then their crops failed, or someone found them. It's impossible to tell now. They must have sat down together; perhaps they were injured, waiting for the end.

My empty stomach is heaving. The house is full of it. Retching, with my sleeve pulled over my nose, I make my way to the bathroom and open the mirrored doors of the wall cupboard: paracetamol, diazepam, other pills; I look for anything useful. Antiseptic, disinfectant. And cram them all into my cotton bag. Our main concern is water-borne illnesses and the diseases that spread when hygiene is compromised. I find a few tins in the kitchen cupboard. A sodden box of matches and a stub of candle. These people lived a frugal life, expected to get old together. In such a sparsely inhabited region there are few looters, until NOAH came.

Nula calls: 'We could stay in the barn. Or one of the other houses in the village. There's not a sound. There's no one here. I think it's safe.'

A cat winds around my legs.

In the outhouse, the smell is less overpowering: dusty tools neatly shelved, boxes of labelled screws and nails. A smell of old sawdust. A half-finished pine table. A handful of notices pinned up in the kitchen: *Furniture made to order. No job too small.* If he were here, Robbie would take his time selecting from the tools. Before the flood, he'd mastered knocking nails in to hang pictures to decorate our flat. Even then I could see how like his father he was, handling the hammer, feeling its weight, getting the angle right. Skills we never thought he'd be using daily for survival at the Mill.

In a wedding photo they look like any other newly married couple. Ridiculously happy. Unaware of the bleak future.

'Maybe, when everything's sorted out, we can think about getting married,' I imagine saying to Robbie when I find him. I know I'd get that raised eyebrow, neither of us has ever been interested in marriage; but with so much change, so much under threat, who knows what we'd do?

When I show her what's in the cupboards and drawers, Nula hesitates. 'I don't like taking their food and tools.' But we both know that's the old way of thinking; I remember the boat, how we took their food; people who fuss about such niceties are the ones who won't make it.

We leave the farmhouse and go further into the village. Most houses we come to have at least one tin of baked beans; it becomes a joke between us. When we find an out-of-date can of pilchards at the back of a cupboard, we cheer. But we can only carry enough for a few days. In what must have been a house for holiday lets, as well as the tins of food we find bunk beds, bedding and towels. There are even matches dry enough to light, so we collect wood and make a fire with old newspapers. After a feast of baked beans and tinned rice pudding we sit with a candle lit and the moon peering in. All night we're warm.

The next morning, we pocket the matches wrapped in the remains of a plastic carrier bag and take another paring knife. The area is so cut off, we risk moving during the day, before dawn. If we keep up a good pace, we'll get to the next village and find shelter by the time it's dark again. But the weather is changing: black clouds hang over the fells, and almost as soon as it's light, the rain sets in; a cold wind blows down the valley, making the leaves and creamy-white flowers of the rowan trees shiver.

I quickly put my raincoat on and am zipping it up when Nula lets out a cry of rage. Her waterproof has ripped and begun to shred.

'It's useless!' She throws it on the ground and stamps on it. 'For fuck's sake what are we supposed to do now?'

I shelter in the lee of a stunted tree, the rain dripping down its silvery-brown bark, as she kicks at the raincoat until she slides on it and trips. She pulls herself up, hands covered in mud, takes one look at my face, and bursts out laughing. She holds her arms up to the sky and starts whooping madly. '*Blow winds and crack your cheeks!*' Then we're both running round in the rain, jumping and dancing, until we're soaked. She flings herself onto the grassy hillside, panting and laughing. I join her.

For a few minutes we're smiling at each other, occasionally breaking out into a giggle, then she pats my arm; she's shivering. 'We made it this far!' she says, gasping for breath. 'We can find them, can't we? I'm going to bring her back home again!' She hugs me, then puts on a spare sweatshirt from her rucksack and we set off again. For the rest of the day we walk, almost without stopping. By the time it's beginning to get dark again we're both wet and all we want is to find shelter.

I unfold the map. 'Looks like it's over the next ridge.'

'I'll go,' she says and jumps up. The next minute she's standing on top of the hill, outlined against the sky like a film heroine. She waves me on.

'No lights. I don't think there's anyone left,' she shouts.

'Unless they heard you making all that noise,' I say when I catch her up.

'Stay close and keep quiet then,' she says and smiles.

The terrible smell. The sad ordinariness of it. We take what we can, what's useful, then find an empty house with no evidence of human life. They must have left in a hurry: doors open to cupboards, drawers hanging out. It's damp and cold, but only in the way of an unoccupied building. It's shelter, and that's all we care about. There are mice droppings and that smell, flies on food left out on a table. But there are beds. And we sleep.

We sleep for what feels like weeks and when I wake the sun is out and there's a noise downstairs. Nula is sleeping soundly so I creep down and look through the gap in the door.

In the kitchen, a man is sitting at the table eating our food. A long stick is leaning against the chair. I push open the door and stand in the doorway. When he turns to me his eyes are bloodshot and his face red and bloated. The face of a drinker, or at least of a man who is ill. As he chews, sweat drips down from his forehead and onto the table. He grunts a greeting then goes straight back to his food – a tin of beans, with those small sausages (that remind me of a child's fingers). But what overwhelms everything is the urinous, meaty smell of someone who lives on the streets. It hangs in the air like a fog I don't want to inhale. How has he survived like this?

On the table next to him is a collection of small white objects that look like toys. I keep my distance but can see that they're bones and the blanched skulls of small animals, their overlarge eye sockets staring and absent. With one hand he circles his fingers round one of them repetitively.

'What are you doing here?' I say.

He shakes his head irritably and mumbles something incoherent, then carries on eating. I walk away quietly. At the door I turn back to check; since we left the boat we've not seen anyone alive; I think I might have imagined him. Spooning up beans as fast as he can, there are dribbles of tomato sauce in his grey beard. Yes, he's real. He's old, and doesn't look like a NOAH. But who is he? Is he dangerous? He's starving, and hunger makes everyone desperate. And he's a man. If he has enough to eat perhaps he'll go on his way and leave us alone.

'There's a man. Downstairs. Eating. I think he's harmless.'

Nula springs out of bed grabbing a hammer from the floor next to the bed. 'Where's that knife?'

'In my bag.'

'Get it. You might need it.'

She pulls on her damp sweatshirt, shuddering, and runs downstairs. She gestures for me to stay in the hallway, then goes into the kitchen. I can't move. Through the mould-greened window I can make out the rise of hills against a limpid blue sky. The Lakeland fells in their spring colours. A moment caught in a photo. In my hand, the knife is hot. Beads of sweat on the handle. I hope it's sharp; I hope I don't have to use it.

I strain to hear something but there's an eerie absence of noise. Then, like photos on the old iPhones jolting into life, it starts. A creak of floorboards, a muffled shout then, when I expect conversation or something else between them, there's nothing. I force myself to move from the window and push open the door, my fingers tight against the handle of the knife.

Panting, Nula is standing astride the man who's lying on the floor and staring up at her. He looks like the homeless man selling *The Big Issue* outside our nearest Tube, in London. How can we be standing here about to kill him in cold blood?

'Let me go. Please, mate.' He coughs and shakes, from drink or fever.

Nula's hand leaps to her mouth and she turns away.

'Nula, he's ill. Look how he's sweating.'

His shoes are stuffed with dried grass and leaves. When he tries to speak he has to give in to a hacking cough. 'There's no one else… I'm on my own… I promise.'

'He's not going to hurt us. Leave him.'

When she steps back holding the hammer in her fist, her jaw is clenched. 'OK then. Stand up.'

The man struggles to his feet and another fit of coughing makes him bend double. He wipes his mouth on the back of his hand then rubs it off on his trouser leg.

'Got anything to drink?' he says when he catches his breath. 'Booze?'

'Not till you tell us who you are and what you're doing here, eating our fucking food.' This is a Nula I've never seen before. Cold. Fierce. 'Go on. What's your name?'

He can hardly stand. I push a seat behind him as his legs give way.

'Jim,' he says, wheezing. 'Hungry. Starving. Sorry. Took my chance.' He wipes his mouth again. 'Got any booze?'

'First, we want information.' Nula stands rigid, legs apart, but when she sees how weak he is her shoulders relax.

'I'll tell you what I know. But it's not much.'

'We're looking for someone. Anna, where's your photo?'

'I'm on my own. Not seen anyone for weeks. I'm keeping out of their way.'

'Who from?' Nula says, pushing my hand away. 'Wait. Not yet. We need to know we can trust him.' She gets down to his level, eye to eye. 'What do you know about NOAH?'

He turns away and coughs heavily, gasping for breath. Spits on the floor. Shakes his head. 'I've seen what they do. I lay in a ditch for a whole day once to keep out of their way. Don't want anything to do with them and their half-baked theology.'

'What have you seen?'

'Enough to know they're bad news.'

'Show us your arm,' I say.

'I don't think you'll find anything,' says Nula. 'He's OK.'

He shows us – no sign of a tattoo. Or an attempt to remove one.

Nula nods at me and I take out Robbie's photo. 'There's a young girl with him. Heavily pregnant.'

He examines the picture. 'No. As I said, I've seen no one for weeks. Brother? Boyfriend?'

I slide the photo back into my pocket.

'Pregnant, you say?' He shakes his head slowly. 'Daughter? Sorry. So many have disappeared. I hope you find them but you're going to need a lot of luck.'

'We're going to find them,' Nula says. 'You sure you've not seen anything? Heard anything?'

'Look at me. I'm hardly a reliable witness,' he says with a dry laugh. 'I hear things but I can't trust my senses. See all sorts too, but most of that's through the bottom of a bottle.' He coughs, phlegm rattling in his chest. 'Where's that booze you promised?'

Later, when I've found the dregs of a bottle of whisky, we hear his story. He worked for a law firm before all this happened. He stayed as long as he could, too long, and was one of the last to abandon the city and make his way out; the Thames flowing into the streets, pouring down steps and into Tube tunnels – he lost everything.

'No need for City lawyers when London's under the sea,' he says. 'I was James, always James. I had so much. But now I've nothing. You can call me Jim. Even my name's shrunk. All I have is the clothes I'm wearing. And my collection.' He points to the delicate animal skulls on the table. 'It's something to do. Before, I used to collect netsuke.'

He saw whole buildings crashing into the water as the river washed away their foundations.

'I'll never forget that sound: a terrible, deep gurgling into every street and building, rushing against the bridges, hurtling at them until they gave way. The city nosediving under the waves. Like the Titanic.'

He tried to save people. He got friendly with a woman and her child. They came with him to the camps, but when they were processed they were separated; he never saw her again.

'That's how it was, getting worse every second. She had such pretty hair. I often think… Got more alcohol?' he says again. 'And now NOAH.'

'When did you last see them?'

'Not since I was cut off here. Further south. Weeks ago, I think. But time's changed. Every day's the same. My memory's shot at. Feels like the same day dragging on.' He barks his hacking cough again and his face twists with pain.

'Let me look at you, Jim.' Nula gently touches his forehead and stands back. 'Anna's right. You're feverish.'

He grins, teeth yellow against his grey beard, speckled with sauce from the baked beans. He coughs and spits into an old rag then aims it at the bin, overflowing with tins. We were too tired to notice it last night. We let our guard down.

'How long have you been like this?' she asks.

'What? The drink or the cough?'

'Both. And your feet.'

'I enjoy a pint… or two. Helps me relax.' He unrolls filthy bandages and shows us his swollen feet. 'Never heal. Look what colour they've gone. There's an ache here. A pain.' He points to his chest. His heart? I wonder. Or his lungs?

'I'll clean that up for you.' Nula's voice is too calm. Something is seriously wrong. 'Anna, see if you can find more drugs.'

Outside, the air is cool and clear. I can breathe again. There's a garden overgrown with old bean canes, rampant tomato plants and onions that have gone to seed, all left to rot in the ground. Blackened and slimy. I search the village for alcohol, sleeping tablets, painkillers. Eventually, fallen behind the pedestal of a wash basin, there's a blister pack of tranquilisers and in an inaccessible dark back of a kitchen cupboard a large bottle of whisky, saved, I imagine, for better times. I feel a warm rush of success, as if Jim's going to be cured by this haul.

When I get back their voices are a murmur.

'… then you can come with us,' Nula is saying. She's pulled a chair closer to where Jim is sitting.

'I'll only hold you back. I'm too slow. Even with the stick. No. You need to find your daughter.'

'We'll help you, won't we, Anna?' She stands up. 'Jim needs more than we can offer. He needs medical help.'

'I know what's wrong.' Jim's voice is a growl. He coughs again and Nula turns her face away.

'There must be someone with medical training. Somewhere,' I say. But I know how unlikely it is, and so does Jim.

He chuckles to himself then groans with pain and takes a swig from the bottle next to him, but it's empty. 'I'm grateful to you. But tell you what – you go ahead and I'll rest up here. Once I get my strength back I'll follow and catch you up. Did you find any more booze? Painkillers?' He coughs, almost choking. The terrible bubbling cough. He's breathless, his eyes streaming. For a few seconds the room is quiet, then the agonised coughing starts again.

I show him what I've managed to salvage from the village and his eyes light up. 'That'll do the trick.'

'We'll come back for you,' I say to him. 'Once we've done what we need to do. We'll pick you up on our way back.'

His hollow laugh ends in another prolonged fit of coughing. While he fights for breath, Nula whispers to me, 'If we could get antibiotics there's a chance. I've seen this before. It's bad.'

We prepare a sofa in the sitting room that leads off the kitchen. Blankets. Tins with a tin opener. Then we fill buckets with rainwater (no shortage of that). It's like preparing for a New Year's Eve party, the table covered with bottles of booze, only it's a party for one. Or more like a wake.

Nula finds bluebells and puts them in a jam jar. 'See you soon, Jim.'

He gives each of us one of the tiny skulls he's collected: one is a mouse, the other a shrew, he tells us. 'Memento mori,' he says and smiles. 'Once I'm up and about I'll come and find you; if you don't come back first!' he says. 'I'll race you to the top of Scafell Pike.'

We leave him surrounded by his stockpile of Jack Daniels and half-open blister packs of pills. The last we see of him, he's waving at the door of the cottage, leaning heavily on his walking stick, whistling to himself.

The noise of water flowing in a narrow gulley masks the whistling, then, as the path turns, it disappears altogether.

'What chance has he got without antibiotics?' I say to Nula. But I can guess the answer.

'It won't be long…' she says quietly. 'I saw this in the Hulks. They told us TB was a punishment from God for our sins: "*You will be consumed, your lungs filled by your own blood.*" At least he can enjoy himself, and when it gets too much…'

Nula picks up handfuls of loose slate from the path and hurls them into the stream.

Twenty-Three

We must have been walking for over a week; it's hard to tell, like Jim said, when every day merges into the one before. At first, we tried to sleep during the day and move only once it got dark, but hunger has made us reckless; we finished the last soft biscuits this morning. All we have are a few tins from Jim's village. Without fresh supplies, we won't last long. After all this, to give up and give in. It's unthinkable.

I can only walk very slowly now. I use a stick cut down from the woods, but my leg aches with every step, in spite of bandaging my knee. Sometimes Nula lets me lean on her when she sees how I'm falling behind. Sometimes, when we're sleeping, my leg is so painful it wakes me up crying. I think of how Robbie would massage it for me. I try not to think of the drugs Ewan could get for me.

There have been noises. Helicopters passing over in the distance. The occasional whine of a drone. Someone is on the move. The landscape is dull green rolling moors, spotted with the grey stone buildings of abandoned farms. This far from any village or town, we have lost all links to the resistance network. As the snow slowly melts, the sound of water running in the beck trickles and gets louder by the hour. If we first check upstream for dead animals and boil the water, we won't go thirsty.

After a few days we reach high ground again and, after the impassive grey of water, our eyes are filled by the vibrant green of trees, grass and shrubs. Now the snow has melted we sense water on all sides, but so far below us, it's almost benign. When the sun comes out and the rain stops, we're dazzled by minute points of gold reflected from the leaves beginning to emerge from bare branches, by silver from standing pools of water and the streams that run down into the drowned valleys. In the distance, pylons walk away, knee-deep, cables drooping down almost to the water. Taking power from nowhere to nowhere now. Redundant. Villages abandoned. If the water ever goes down will they reappear, along with the rest of this drowned land?

A hundred years ago, Dad once told me, some of the valleys were dammed and villages flooded to make reservoirs to supply the cities further south. Once, when there was a severe drought in the 1980s, he and Mum visited Haweswater; it was so dry they could walk on the muddy bottom of a lake over the exposed ruins of a dusty, mud-covered bridge where people hadn't walked for decades, and next to forgotten drystone walls, kicking up clouds of dust. I think of the precarious balance that we wilfully pushed until it tipped and became unstoppable. Cities, towns and villages all over the planet submerged by the Flood or on fire. If only I believed what Ewan told us, that there were signs that the water is retreating again, the sea withdrawing to where it should be, the world curing itself.

It feels as if we're alone in this watery world, searching for what we've lost. Under the water are cars, whole families trapped. Bloated bodies of sheep. In the distance, what looks like someone waving is only a sapling garlanded with wind-shredded plastic bags. Once, when we're eating, the sound of a motorboat slices through the night and we douse our lights and hold our breath until the silence gradually thickens around us again. We are getting closer and can't afford to take risks. We have to keep going. In spite of helicopters and drones buzzing overhead, we cling onto hope. We talk of immediate needs and focus on what we must do to survive – to find food, somewhere dry and warm. It's only when we rig up shelters in the lee of stone walls or in sheep folds that we allow ourselves to say the names that simmer inside us all day, let them bubble up. We talk about them as if we'll see them soon: Robbie laughing and making jokes, Jamila dancing; it's only if we think of them as alive that we can keep going.

A flock of pearl-grey birds rises suddenly and startles us. Since we left Jim we've seen no one alive, and I'm starting to imagine shadows that slip away behind trees, the whisper of voices. On the fell sides most trees were long ago cleared for grazing sheep, so if anyone comes, we'll see them before they can get near us; but this starkness means we're also exposed. We don't want to meet possible enemies, yet I sense a fine line between our fierce solitariness and a dragging sense of isolation. Sometimes there's the crackle of a twig breaking, a skitter of stones kicked off the path. Every time we turn there's nothing. Only the wind blowing dried husks of grass.

'You're scared of your own shadow,' says Nula.

But I hear the silence that's left when people stop talking, the intake of breath before someone speaks. Like it used to be on the landline, when you could tell from the sound of air taken in, who was calling. Robbie asking me what I wanted for tea; Dad saying he'd be late. Now the intake of breath is female.

'I'm *sure* someone's following us.'

'Let's keep going. Stop scaring yourself.'

As we move south the land is changing, hills flattening in the dark. Soon there are more floods to cross, wider and deeper than anything we've encountered since we left the boat. We reach the main valley from the Dales, over the M6 to Kendal; there are queues of abandoned cars and lorries, the metal blooming with rust, in what looks like builders' tea.

'Now what? There's no way round this.' Nula shades her eyes and looks around.

'We need a boat.'

She sits down. 'Go on then. Magic us up a boat!' She laughs, on the verge of tears.

'What's that?' I point to where wooden pallets have been lashed together to make a jetty. 'People have tried to cross here. I'll have a look.'

There are boats, but nothing we could attempt to use. I push my hands against the wood of a rowing boat and it disintegrates, rotten and waterlogged. There are rubber dinghies, rafts made from old barrels. All half sunk in the mud and water. Abandoned. They've not been used for years. I pull at what looks like a rope, only it's not. It's a dog's lead. I slide and fall onto my leg. I give a futile cry of pain. An old glove. No, a hand. Sunk under the mud there are people here. Children. I don't want Nula to see this.

I drag myself back up and squat down next to her. Neither of us will admit it, but this could be it. The end of our journey.

'Here. I think it's time.' Nula hands me a small bottle. 'Go on. I was saving it to celebrate but…'

The 'whisky' is warming. I can taste apple and smoky autumn bonfires. Last year, George and Tracey made it from a glut of crab apples steeped in alcohol Ewan brought back. I didn't question where he got it from at the time. We sit at the edge of the land, passing the bottle between us, looking down through the murkiness at what's left of the old motorway. The wind ruffles waves on the water. The sky presses down, threatening more rain. I'm so exhausted I could sink down here and never wake up.

I put my arm around Nula's slighter shoulders. 'We got this far, didn't we?'

'What do you want? Are there more coming?' A dark-haired woman in a red tunic, face patterned with mud and armed with an axe, appears as if from the water itself. 'What you got?'

Two of them. They've come round behind us. I pull myself up, ready to run. So does Nula. That's what we planned, but in our weakened state they're too quick for us. And where could we run? We're almost surrounded by water.

Her companion pulls at our rucksacks. My leg gives way and I slip onto the ground.

'Food? Weapons? Drugs?'

Nula doesn't move.

'It's only us,' I say. 'I'm Anna. This is Nula.'

'I said, what you got? What can you give us?' the first woman says.

'A few tins, packets. Nothing else. We're as desperate as you.'

'Don't believe you.' She puts her fingers to her lips and makes a high-pitched, penetrating whistle.

Dogs, teeth bared, ears back, rush towards us.

I love dogs. But these are trained to attack. Nula whimpers and pulls me close. She is terrified of dogs. One jumps at her and she elbows it to the ground, burying her face in my shoulder, trembling.

'Call them off. We don't mean you any harm.' I try to open my rucksack. 'This is all we've got.'

She whistles again and the dogs stop and stand next to her, immediately quiet and unthreatening. Like a nightmare halted.

The other woman, shorter and fair-haired, wearing blue denim jeans, wrenches open our backpacks and takes what food we have left.

'How did you get here?' the axe woman says. 'Where are t'others? Where's your boat?'

'Who are you?' Nula asks.

'What the fuck's that to you?'

'We came on foot. From the north. West Cumbria. We're trying to find someone,' I say. We don't want to give too much away; we don't know who they might be working for.

'On foot? You must have been walking for weeks.' A visible softening behind her aggression. She puts her axe down, leaning it on the ground.

'We've been watching you,' the shorter, fair-haired woman says. She raises her head to meet my eyes.

I exchange a look with Nula.

'We've been caught out before. We had to know if you were dangerous.' Her voice has a glimmer of sympathy, as if she cares. They're women after all. 'Who are you looking for?'

'Family.' We show them our photos.

'Boyfriend?'

I nod.

'And my little girl. She's only sixteen, for fuck's sake!'

'NOAH?' says the woman with the axe.

'They had horses.'

'Ah.' She steps towards us and mechanically we both move back. But she holds out her hand. 'Look.' There's a scar from where a tattoo has been inexpertly erased. She clasps my hand. Hers is hard and grained with dirt, her nails broken.

The other woman nods. 'Me too,' she says.

I show them my unmarked wrist.

'And your friend?'

'If I could burn this off my arm I would.' Nula yanks up her sleeve and shows the tattoo. 'I want nothing to do with them; but they've got my Jamila.' Angry tears come easily. 'I've got to find her.'

The dark-haired woman shakes her head. 'You'll find not many mek it here. Fuck! Did they do that to your leg?'

I explain briefly and the other woman tuts. 'You're brave, mate. It's the sort of thing NOAH would do. They stop at nowt.'

'We've got to find them,' I say. I show her Robbie's photo.

The axe woman shakes her head. She touches my arm gently. 'We can feed you. You can stay. At least tonight. I'm

January, but you can call me Jan. This is Emma.'

'Em,' says the other woman. She nods at us, her thick, fair hair swinging forwards. She doesn't smile.

'Come. It's not far.' January takes our bags, calls the two dogs to heel, and we follow them for about a mile, skirting along the edge of the water. Behind a scrubby rowan tree distorted by the prevailing wind, she drags away branches covering another boat.

We get in, the two dogs curling at our feet. Nula keeps as far away from them as possible. Em pulls the starter cord to fire up the outboard motor and we're engulfed in black fumes. Automatically, both of us look around to see if we're being watched. But the water is like glass, reflecting the low hills and the overarching grey sky. We have to trust them.

Jan keeps up a monologue about where we are, pausing only to point out landmarks, telling us the names of fells, but we're too tired to talk. After an hour, the light is fading again when we reach the remains of a village where a steep road, rising up from the water, leads to a cluster of stone houses and a church with a tower.

'Bastards can only get us if they have a boat,' says Em. She smiles for the first time.

Jan doesn't stop talking as they tie up the boat and we climb the steps behind the church to a building screened by trees and set back from the road. A light flickers next to a sign that says *The Lakes Hotel.* When the door opens, I look down to see a skinny, young girl, about Jamila's age. She's introduced as Megan. She smiles shyly then, after a hug from Jan, disappears down a passageway.

'She's a good lass. Loves cooking,' Jan says, then in a lower voice adds: 'Understands everything you say but she doesn't speak. She will one day.'

'She's happy here. That's what's important,' says Em, quietly. 'We're keeping her as safe as we can.'

'You can have the rooms with the view,' says January, laughing. 'After you've cleaned yourselves up a bit, let's have a glass of wine.'

Soft beds. Carpets. Jugs of clean water.

After my first shower in weeks, I lie on the bed, taking in the strange luxury. When I go downstairs, Nula has had a shower too and stands with her hair dripping onto the quarry tiles of the kitchen. It's the first time I notice how much it's grown since we set off, making a dark halo around her head. There's a rich smell of food and my mouth starts to water.

'This is unbelievable,' she says, sitting down as if her legs have given way. 'I feel like I'm going to wake up and… What is that amazing smell?'

'Lamb,' says Em.

'It must be months since we ate meat, apart from rabbit,' Nula says. 'I thought everybody was vegetarian, since the floods?'

'So why did you take our food?' I say quickly.

When January throws back her head and laughs, her throat is soft and white. 'Wanted to see if we could trust you lasses. If you'd fight! You can have it all back. We've got hams and bacon hanging in the outhouse on the cold side of the house, larders full of cheeses. We're not short of food!'

Nula is smiling more than I've ever seen her smile. She looks radiant.

'We have sheep,' Em says, 'and a ram, so in the spring we have la'al lambs. Without a vet we lose some, but you learn quick when you have to. And there's the wool to collect an' all. I make stuff. To wear and for decoration. I like to keep busy.' She points out a wall where a brightly coloured woven tapestry hangs.

'We're developing permaculture, forest gardening. Hard at first. Lots to go wrong, but we're getting there,' Jan tells us. 'It's going well.'

I'm intrigued at how they ended up living here.

Em explains: 'We met at school. Boarders at a school on the coast. Parents working at Sellafield and wanted the best for us. The ordinary primary school not good enough. We didn't speak like some. I got bullied. Jan befriended me. We became allies. Afterwards we travelled. Learned languages, took a few basic jobs. Travelled more and went to university in Holland. Set up our own business as artists then… the flood. A bad few years. I don't want to talk about it.' Em breathes out heavily and let's Jan take over.

'We struck lucky finding this place. Isolated. When we first came there was so much. Freezers. Walk-in larders full of all sorts. But once the National Grid went, it all rotted. There's tins and dried lentils and that. We've learned how to grow our own, haven't we, Megan?'

The young girl nods and smiles.

'Decades before it became a hotel it was a vicarage with a walled kitchen garden, melon beds.' Em yawns. 'Damsons and apples trained against the walls. One of them places that struggled after the First World War. You find amazing things every time you dig.'

'I worked at Kew, before. School visits and…' I begin and Jan's smile settles on me for a second, like sun coming out through mist; when she turns back to Nula, she grins like a summer's day. I'd forgotten how Nula draws attention; I'm so used to her face. Its familiar beauty.

'Aye, of course. Now, you must stay for a few days to recover…'

'Thank you,' says Nula, 'but one night will be enough. We have to keep going.'

Jan pats her arm. 'It's impossible to go far once weather turns, and it looks like it's going to again.'

'Two nights max,' I say.

'So how safe is it here?' Nula asks. 'We've not seen anything on the ground, but the air…'

'Nowhere's safe,' Em says bluntly. 'Nowhere.'

'A fractured country. Everyone fending for themselves,' says Jan. 'NOAH mushrooming everywhere you look. Like mould. But we're listening, aren't we, Em?'

'A radio isn't difficult to mek.' She frowns. 'Took me a few goes, but I can access new web. If owt happens we'll be first to know.'

Twenty-Four

With full stomachs for the first time in weeks, we fall asleep on warm, dry beds and sleep for hours; we wake to sunshine and the smell of toast, bacon and eggs. A real full English breakfast.

Nula sits up and stretches. 'I can't believe they live like this.' She laughs and pulls open the curtains. 'It's like a dream.'

I open the window to feel the sun on my skin, and look out at the sheep grazing in a field close to the hotel. At the bright yellow daffodils *fluttering and dancing* in the walled garden, at the rows of broad beans and potatoes.

Em is digging up leeks. She smiles and waves. 'Hurry up. Breakfast's nearly ready!'

'I feel like we've been sleepwalking,' I say. 'As if the whole journey's been a bad dream and now we're awake, all the hunger and cold gone.'

We eat until we can't eat any more. Then we sleep again.

Jan directs us to wardrobes full of clothes smelling of mothballs, left behind by previous guests – trousers, waterproofs and sweatshirts. But also vintage sequinned evening dresses, cocktail frocks. Silks rotting. While Megan washes our own clothes, we dress up. It reminds me of that strange time of celebration and anticipation between Christmas and New Year, when all we used to do was stay in and eat and drink. We see each other relaxing, we begin to smile.

Everyone dresses for dinner. Nula takes her time running her hands over dresses in the wardrobe, trying them on then putting them back. She stays at the mirror applying make-up and teasing her hair into tiny twists all over her head.

'Don't you think it's silly?' I say, irritated, when she appears in the sitting room in a full-length dress. Iridescent blue shot with emerald. 'Like pretending we're in a Sunday night costume drama, like everything's a game. Do you think they do this when no one else is here?'

She dances across the room, glass in hand, and stretches out on one of the sofas. Then she's up again, dancing. Delicate arabesques.

'I thought you never danced. You wouldn't let Jamila dance.'

She frowns. 'You need to relax sometimes, Anna. We've been walking for weeks. We need to build our strength up if we're going to get them back. It's only for a short time. You can't imagine how much I've missed dancing. It was my life. I'm going to fucking reclaim what I love. Look at this.'

In the brilliant blue evening dress, she's like a kingfisher darting across the surface of the river. 'I don't care. I'm going to dance and I'm going to find Jay!' She stumbles and sits back on the sofa. She giggles. I see a fragility I've never noticed before; a vulnerability. I realise she's had to take responsibility for others so early in life, she wants to enjoy small moments while she can.

That night we eat another feast, cooked and served by Megan. Lamb from the fells, so well cooked and tender it slides off the bone; it hardly needs to be chewed.

Robbie and I were already semi vegetarian, before the flood; we agreed that meat was unsustainable. When it became scarce, we only ate meat as a luxury, even at the Mill when we had our own livestock. But here at The Lakes we crave meat.

'Megan marinates it in red wine for days, cooks it in the Aga overnight and all the next day. Slow cooking. It's a traditional Greek recipe,' Em says.

Megan lifts the serving spoon towards my dish.

'Thank you, Megan,' I say and let her ladle out another serving. The young girl blushes but doesn't speak. She's like a character in a fairy tale, under an enchantment. Her silence unnerves me.

'You won't find owt like this in NOAH territories, you know. Strictly boiled fish and plain potatoes,' Jan says.

Em grimaces. 'We're embracing life as it should be lived: slowly. Away from the madness of the twenty-first century. Religious extremists. Poverty. Misery. Learning to be proper humans again.'

'No need to rush. All that speed, instant gratification, instant everything. What was that about? No more McD's,' says Jan, laughing. 'I know most folk don't have what we have, and we help when we can. But you have to admit, it's good.'

'I remember Saturday afternoons, coming out of the cinema with my friends. Skinny chips dipped in ketchup. Greasy chicken nuggets. Not everything was bad,' I say, and laugh too.

Jan smiles a slow smile. She pours wine, helps us to more food. 'No going back now, thank God!'

The rest of the long, dark evening is spent by the fire with songs, jokes and music. When Jan plays 'Fields of Gold' on the guitar I can't stop myself singing; Nula dances with Em, their long, silky dresses swishing against the thick carpets. Occasionally a helicopter roars overhead, search beams tracking across the landscape; then we understand why they have blackout blinds, to keep our own light inside and hidden.

'Anna, your voice is gorgeous,' says Jan. 'I could listen to you all night.'

It's so long since I've felt like singing. I smile as I picture the music evenings at the Mill, like something from a previous, diminished life. Then I run my thumb over the rough edges of Robbie's photo in my pocket.

'You've been great hosts, you've saved our lives,' I say. 'But we'll have to leave tomorrow, won't we, Nula?'

She's dancing, and doesn't hear me. She's laughing at something Em says.

'Let's leave straight after breakfast,' I say when we're getting ready for bed. 'We need to get much further south, to find the Arks. I'm ready to go.'

She yawns. 'Good night, Anna.' When she adds, 'Not tomorrow, maybe the next day,' something inside me sinks. It's not what I'm expecting. There's something about these women and their comfortable life, even if it's only slight, that sets my teeth on edge. I'm surprised Nula can't see it too?

She sighs and turns over in bed. Soon she's snoring lightly, leaving me with my own gathering worries.

I wake to the sound of a shot. Then another.

I drag myself as quickly as I can to the window, expecting the worst. Em and Nula are in the field beyond the kitchen garden with the two dogs. The sun is shining brilliantly again. Nula is aiming at cans lined up on a stone wall. She has never touched a gun, but takes to it easily, and within minutes has moved on to birds. She aims for a crow but misses, then immediately raises the shot gun again. The crow drops from the sky, fluttering to the ground. At a command from Em, one of the dogs runs to retrieve it, the black wings limp and drooping in its mouth.

I dress quickly and go to join them. The sun casts long shadows on the wet grass. As I open the gate to the field there's an ear-splitting scream. Nula has hit a rabbit. The squealing of the injured animal cuts through me. She drops the gun and puts her hands over her ears. Unfazed, Em whistles for the dogs and, in a flurry of bared teeth and growling, they finish it off. All that's left is mangled fur and blood. My stomach is heaving.

Before they see me, I go back inside, but Nula comes in, triumphant. 'I killed a rabbit, Anna... Jan found out neither of us can use a gun. She was shocked. Em is teaching me.'

'We used to say we'd never use a gun.'

'We're going into NOAH territory. We won't stand a chance if we can't fight back. We've been naïve.' She's panting with excitement, her eyes bright. 'Em says she'll teach you too. She says a shotgun is for nearer targets – a less precise aim and a wider spread, but with a rifle you can shoot a rabbit right at the bottom of the field.'

'I don't want to use violence,' I shake my head. 'Look at yourself. You're covered in blood; it's barbaric.'

'Oh Anna!' She comes so close I smell her sweat and feel the heat from her body. 'Sometimes you can't stick to principles. I've lived with NOAH. I know what thugs they are. Working for the *greater good*.' She laughs scornfully. 'You've seen how ruthless they are.'

When I don't answer, she goes to wash her hands and face. 'It's better if one of us can use a gun. I'm going back to practise.'

This makes me angry. 'What's wrong with you? Your daughter's pregnant and in danger but you want to stay here and play at shooting? I'm going to pack. I'm leaving today. Please come with me.'

'Not yet. This is a great opportunity. We'll be so much more effective if we can use a gun.'

'We're running out of time. I've got to find Robbie. If you don't come today, I'll go without you.'

'I want to find Jamila. You know that. Of course I do. But if we can handle weapons, we will be safer.'

Jan is in the doorway. She smiles her slow smile.

'It's all my fault. I can show you the best route to the coast.

Let's go for a walk. And we can work up an appetite for lunch.'

'I'll collect some wool,' says Em. She calls the dogs.

I clamber ahead until I have to stop because I'm out of breath. When I look back, Jan has linked arms with Nula and is yanking one of the dogs to heel. Superficially she is warm compared to Emma, but I don't trust her. She reminds me of a dog trained to be obedient and to do tricks to please you but, at the right signal, will go for your throat. If we get on her wrong side we'll be hunted down like rabbits. I need to make Nula come with me. I can't leave her here.

Em walks slowly, collecting sheep's wool caught on the rusting barbed wire. At the top of the hill Jan is pointing out how to reach the coast when there's a sudden downpour; within seconds we're soaked. It's as we're running back that it happens. The rain has made the ground slippery, dislodged pieces of slate. Going downhill is more difficult than going up. I watch each step, placing my feet carefully and slowly, cruelly aware of the weakness in my leg. There's a sharp cry and I look ahead to see Nula sliding and tumbling down the fell-side, arms flailing but failing to make purchase on the scree.

By the time I reach them, she's back on her feet, supported by Jan and Em.

'I can't put any weight on it… my ankle … I'm going to…' She's violently sick.

We make our way back down to the safety of the hotel to dry off. Nula is whimpering with pain. Everything becomes moving water: streams run down the fell sides, washing the land away. Heavy clouds are rolling in from the west and soon the rain starts beating down relentlessly; it's hard to see beyond the edge of the garden, the fells veiled by pewter grey clouds.

Jan and Em tell me to shower and get changed. Look in one of the other bedrooms. People have left all kinds of stuff behind. Find something to wear. It's not a disaster. They'll take care of Nula. They have painkillers. I attempt to think of them as generous, kind, warm. But something niggles at the back of my mind, something wrong that I sense but can't fully explain. Something that means I can never relax. I open the wardrobe to find dry clothes. The last thing I want to wear is one of their ridiculous evening dresses, and after a long search I find a drawer full of shirts and trousers. They're far too big even for me, so I fold up the trouser legs and roll back the shirt sleeves. At least they're dry.

'Christ, what are you wearing?' Jan says when I go into the kitchen where there's a warm smell of vegetable broth.

'I found them.'

'Take them off. Let's find you something nicer.'

'They're fine, and they fit.'

Em comes in. 'Isn't that Davy's?'

Jan frowns and interrupts. 'Sorry, darling… it's a surprise seeing you in his clothes. One of our infrequent visitors. Forgetful boy…' She goes to the cutlery drawer and takes out a handful of knives and soup spoons. 'Food won't be long, will it, Meg?' Her voice is warm syrup. 'Let's have a gin and tonic.'

'Who's Davy?' Nula says. She's sitting on a bench, her leg bandaged and raised with cushions. Her voice is strained but she's smiling; the painkillers must have kicked in.

'Davy? He stopped here on his way north – there's a photo somewhere. Here.' Jan passes her a photo. 'Nice.' She shows me: dark, spiky hair, fair Irish milky skin, freckles, blue eyes.

'Cute, isn't he?' Em says.

'But he wanted to join NOAH.' Jan looks pointedly at Em. 'I tried to tell him, but he was determined to go, wasn't he, Em? He wouldn't listen. Even when I said they'd make him grow his hair and throw away his razor if he wanted to be a true believer.' Her laugh sounds forced.

Em nods and seasons the soup, saying little as usual, but I catch a look between her and Jan which makes me shiver. I picture the crow again, wings fluttering, falling out of the sky. 'You can't set off now,' Em says, as Jan gives Nula another cushion to make her more comfortable.

I nod reluctantly. 'One more day at least, then we have to go.'

She hugs me. 'One more day stronger and more able to fight back.'

Jan insists that Nula drink creamy milk, and bread dipped in bacon dripping with fat with her lunch. It irritates me when she leans against Nula and pats her hand. She does it to me too, but with Nula it's almost proprietorial. There's a greedy look in her eyes.

Em spends the rest of the afternoon dyeing the wool with tinctures from leaves and plant roots, then creates pictures of the local wildlife and views from the large bay windows of the residents' lounge. Jan goes out to attend to the animals.

When I try to tell her how uncomfortable I feel, Nula laughs in my face.

'Jan's generous. She's trying to be helpful. It's her way of showing it. There's no ulterior motive, if that's what you're thinking. She didn't push me over, you know. I slipped. You need to learn to trust people.'

'She makes me uneasy.'

'Anna, you're so suspicious. They're good people. We're close to the territories but I think you're being paranoid.'

'What if they're working for NOAH?'

She laughs. 'I'm not even going to answer that!'

I go upstairs to have some time on my own. I lie on the bed to think. And then I'm walking. I'm on a hill, walking up a track, my feet scuffing on loose shards of slate, the smell of grass, wind blowing in my hair. I look back. There's a sound of shooting.

I look for somewhere to hide, stumble and crouch down behind a stone wall, holding onto my backpack. My heart is racing. Something is terribly wrong. Then I'm swimming up, pushing myself up through layers of consciousness, up to the surface again. My heart is rattling and uneven and I'm gasping for air. For the first time since we set off I've seen something of what's going to happen. Or what might happen. I don't know what it means, but it leaves me with a sense of cold dread.

Shivering, I fall asleep on the bed and only wake when Em knocks on the door to tell me it's time for dinner again. Our third meal here.

When I go down, everything is hazy, out of focus. Nula looks concerned.

Jan wipes my hair away from my forehead. 'You're pale. Come and sit by the fire to warm up before we eat.'

'I'll be OK. Thank you. Strange dreams, that's all.'

'Deep breaths,' says Jan, handing me a glass of red wine. 'Life is challenging now, but we can make the best of it. We won't eat till you feel better.' Her hand is warm when she pats mine.

It takes a long time for the atmosphere of the dream to fade; everything around me shimmers. It lingers as a sensation of pressure against my temples.

Jan makes me nervous, and conscious of every movement, but the smell of the food is irresistible; I'm ravenously hungry. The mahogany dining table is set with a candelabra that casts light on plates of meat sizzling in pools of dark, salty gravy with apple sauce, crisp, golden crackling. Bowls of crunchy potatoes and long, green beans.

As she pours the wine, Jan smiles at me. In the soft

candlelight it glows a deep, cherry red like a stained-glass church window. There must often have been power cuts here, even before the flood; long, dark evenings with limited light. As I pierce slices of meat, grease spatters onto the tablecloth, my lips are coated with it. Nula is laughing, her pain forgotten, slightly drunk already.

Outside, the light is fading; Emma goes to the windows to pull down the blinds and draw across the heavy, velvet curtains. There's the whirr of a passing helicopter but here, in the hotel, we're so isolated and hidden, NOAH soldiers would surely struggle to find us. For once that's not what I fear. There are dark corners and shadows I can't explain. Until Nula can walk, we have to stay.

As we're eating, Jan tells us Emma has heard something on the radio. 'I don't want to alarm you… but – '

'I've picked up information,' Em says. 'NOAH's on the move. They're planning something. It's mebbe a good thing you have to stay till Nula's ankle is better. And till we know what's going on. At least you're safe here.'

When we're getting ready for bed, a penknife falls out of the trouser pocket; it has 'Davy' engraved on it. He must have forgotten it when he left. It could be useful; I push it into the bottom of my rucksack.

Nula is in pain again and her mood has plunged.

'I'm sorry. I feel so stupid.'

'At least we're here where you can recover.'

When I look up she's crying.

'She's nearly eight months now. I need to be with her.'

'We will. We're so close. But we both need to be strong for the last part of the journey. No point trying to change something when we can't.'

She's the strong one. She's had to be. So it's my turn to reassure her. I want to leave this place, these women. But I can't go ahead alone. I need Nula as much as she needs me. When she eventually drops into a deep sleep in spite of the pain, I lie with my head aching. I find myself thinking of the crow, how its wings fluttered as it fell out of the sky, warm and limp in the dog's mouth.

Twenty-Five

During the night, something wakes me. Nula is sleeping soundly, exhausted by crying and the pain in her swollen ankle. I pull open the door, letting in a crack of light. Voices. From somewhere, the hiss and squawk of a radio tuning through the frequencies. It's coming from the small residents' lounge on the ground floor. I edge down the stairs.

'Something I can't quite…'

'Try again.'

'I'm not picking up the signal. They're blocking it.'

'But what *did* you hear?'

'Please, Jan, don't make me –'

I pull open the door.

Their faces are two white masks reflected in the low electric light. Jan is surprised, but she quickly regains her composure; she moves back from leaning over Em.

'Anna, can we get you something? Is Nula –?'

'I heard you talking. It's NOAH, isn't it?'

For once, Em speaks without consulting Jan. 'I'm not sure… the signal is weak. I don't know yet…'

'We need to be careful.' Jan's voice breaks and I realise she is straining to hold back tears.

Em holds her. 'They're on the move.'

'Tell me.'

I remember the vision – the sound of gunfire. It all slides into place. 'You're working for them, aren't you?'

'Of course not.' Jan's laugh echoes. 'We're on your side, lass.'

I pull myself up to my full height. I don't speak. I wait.

Em pulls away from Jan. 'I think it's time,' she says quietly.

Jan shakes her head, but so slightly it's almost imperceptible. In the dim light she looks exhausted, old and vulnerable.

'At first we thought you were NOAH,' says Em. 'We had to be sure. We didn't know if we could trust you.'

'We've been honest with you,' I say.

'We know that now. So we'll be upfront with you,' Em says. 'We had no choice. We've both been in the programme – INCREASE. Here – we showed you old scars, but not these.'

Em pulls up her shirt to show a long, crumpled line knotted horizontally across her lower belly.

'We were forced. Both of us. Minimal medical support. There were complications. Two of mine didn't survive.'

'Three times.' Jan's hand is over her face. 'When we were no use to them they let us go. Put us back to the land. But my little Megan came with me. She didn't meet their standards!'

'We've been lucky. Most never get out of there.'

Em glances at Jan and I realise this is more than a close friendship; these women are lovers. I can't imagine what they've gone through. Nula will understand.

'It couldn't get much worse,' Em says, 'but we're fighting back against this religious madness.'

'There is support from abroad but it's not reliable. This time it's good news, we think. The EUROS joining us, growing in strength now. So NOAH will be desperate because they're under threat and liable to lash out. We're passing information to the resistance.'

'We *are* the resistance,' Em says. 'NOAH calls us unclean, terrorists, but we're freedom fighters.'

'But they must know you're listening. What you're doing is dangerous,' I say.

'If no one stands up to them it will only get worse. It's what you're doing too. You're doing exactly the same,' Em says.

She gives a short laugh. 'Davy was a NOAH spy. We couldn't let him leave.'

'But who are the EUROS?'

'As far as we know a loosely allied group of European and North African countries, trying to quash NOAH before they take over the Med.'

'We know what we're doing.' Jan squeezes Em's hand. 'We made the decision together. We're here to remind them that there are people, women, who won't do what their closed-off policies dictate. We know we're not alone. And we're ready. In the end, good and love will prevail, whatever happens to us as individuals.'

'But you do need to leave as soon as Nula can walk,' Jan says. 'Em picked up something; it's St Donald's in a week's time. A night of feasting then revenge… with NOAH on the back foot who knows what could happen.'

The door to the yard shuts with the smallest click. All the dogs are sleeping, chained up, but when we pass, they stand, wide awake. They're used to us. We've been here for over a week.

'Here boy.' I stroke each of them in turn. 'Good girl. I'll miss you.' Their breath is warm on my hands, their flanks smooth, the muscles and bones strong. At the right command they'll be ready.

On Nula's shoulder the shotgun slides up and down as she moves. It rained nearly all night, washing through our dreams, and now the air is sweet with grass slowly drying; long stems catch our legs. We walk quickly up through the woods then onto a narrow track that leads up to the first of the fells that shelter the hotel. A blackbird begins its morning song, fluting high on a ribbon of sound, and the further we go, more birds join in, as if following a score. The dawn chorus is so much louder than I remember from the old days, before the Flood, before the sea crept up the rivers, and journeys became a way of life. In that innocent time the sound was blended with early Tube trains and a hiss of traffic like the sea; louder when it had been raining, punctuated by the high-pitched wail of sirens. Here, in the south of the Lake District, there's only birdsong and the crunching of our feet over rough ground.

I feel a sense of urgency. But also release. A breeze, almost warm, brings the scent of grass. Small animals, mice or birds, rustle at the base of neglected hedges, surging up and trying to grow back into trees, then the higher we go there's only the march of grey stone walls. Gradually the sky turns from grey to pale blue, then it's light and we can be seen.

We stay near the wall. When Nula stops suddenly and listens, I stop too; we scan the area behind and all around us. She shakes her head and mouths: 'It's nothing. I thought I heard something.'

I know we're both remembering how quietly they tracked us the days leading up to our arrival at the hotel. Walking into that strangely idyllic world.

My stomach is beginning to rumble; I've eaten nothing since dinner.

'We can shelter over there.' I point to the remains of a sheep fold. 'Let's have breakfast.'

'We need to get further away,' Nula says. 'I don't feel safe yet.'

Down at the hotel, the breakfast table will be set with jugs of creamy milk. Fresh eggs scrambled or poached on thick slices of buttered toast. Gallons of coffee or tea. Sometimes apple or pear juice. Em already playing her guitar. The easy chat. I feel the pocket of my backpack for the reassuring shape of the penknife.

'I feel like I've been under a spell,' Nula says, voicing my own thoughts.

'I can't believe I was so wrong about them. God knows

what happened to them under NOAH.'

'I think I can imagine what it was like…'

'I'm sorry.'

'And it makes some give in; others want to fight back. Jan and Em, they're the good ones, like you and me.'

I hug her. 'Thanks. I couldn't keep going without you.'

'But don't rush to imagine the worst, Anna. People generally aren't like that. Apart from a few…' She stops and bends to massage her weak ankle. 'Come on. All I want is to find my lovely girl. My child. Fuck! Who hardly had a childhood.'

We branch south east and now we're climbing steeply. Our boots clump on the stony path, and there's a muffled, hollow sound as if there's nothing underneath us. The sense that we've escaped makes me light-headed, almost drunk, and I march ahead, telling Nula: 'The soil is so thin here, we're only inches above solid rock; it's been smoothed and eroded away over thousands of years. Can you imagine that these fells used to be as high as the Himalayas? During the Ice Age, when the lakes were formed, they left behind huge rocks: the Bowder Stone near Keswick, that one over there looks like…'

A shot rings out.

Nula grabs my hand and we dive behind the large boulder. Now we've left the wooded hillside of the hotel, we're sitting ducks.

Her hand is warm. Pulse beating fast. I'm shaking, I reach round and take out the knife. The compact weight of it in my hand feels good, but what use is it when they're armed? And if it came to it, could I?

Shots echo around the valley below us. Nula gets the shotgun ready.

I remember how cold the barrel was in my hands when Nula persuaded me to hold it. The weight of it, and how terrible it felt to see her only taking shots at the plant pots on the wall at first, then at birds. I never thought we might have to use it.

The dogs at the hotel are baying. I remember the rabbit torn to pieces – scraps of fur, an ear, a smear of bright blood. The dogs' teeth stained with it.

'Anna, if you're on your own, you know how to find the Arks.'

'Of course. I remember it all.'

There's a pause in the firing. Voices. Shouts. Then horses neighing and whinnying. A sound that sends a spike of fear through both of us. We cling onto each other.

Far below we see it happening, like watching a film through a window on someone's TV. So far away it's almost not real. Both of them are dragged out, screaming at the NOAH soldiers. Emma is in her jeans. Jan is clutching Megan, covering her daughter's eyes. There are shots, then Jan's red tunic is trailing on the ground. Then there is nothing at all. Our ears buzz in the sudden silence. The wind whips over and through the gaps in the drystone wall, making a keening, musical sound, like an Aeolian harp. Disappearing towards the coast we see the NOAH soldiers, galloping. A flash of weapons.

Twenty-Six

At last, the landscape is beginning to change: hills are lower and smoother; everything is flattening out. With binoculars we see small towns that have clung on and survived, although they can't be far from the sea. We're going more slowly, as Nula wants to build up the strength in her ankle without straining it again, so we make good progress and my leg is much less of a problem. We take frequent rests.

As we approach yet another valley, we see a building rising from the water. The local pink-red sandstone glows as the light catches it – the ruins of a once great mediaeval church. Furness Abbey. It looks peaceful now, sinking into the silty mud, its ancient wooden footings softening and gradually returning to the earth. The gothic era lingering on, five hundred years after Henry the Eighth dissolved the monasteries. When I look back the way we've come, the Lakeland fells lie in long ridges and fade into blue in the far distance. From here the air has a soft quality, a golden warmth, cut by the salt of the sea. We're close now.

We arrive in the dark only too glad to find shelter. Green algae and moss grow around the old stone of a cottage. It's cool to the touch, spongey and moist. Under a rotting lean-to, piles of logs, stacked ready to burn by the woodsman or shepherd who once lived here, are darkened and covered by a thick carpet of moss. They're ready for the return of the owner, or for someone new, or perhaps to be washed away by the next wave of flooding. Who knows? I keep these thoughts to myself. Not that we dare start a fire in case we attract attention; we sleep back to back for warmth, breathing together. In the night, we are woken by the racket of helicopters clattering overhead, fading into the distance. Loudspeakers chanting NOAH propaganda.

Shivering, we get up before dawn. Today a lid of fog presses down on us, amplifying every sound.

'Did you hear? When it was dark?'

'Yes.' Nula shudders. 'On board I often heard them, mainly bringing supplies. But once I saw...' She breaks off from folding her sleeping bag and puts her hand on the shotgun, propped next to the mattress. 'Once I saw... ' She smiles through gritted teeth, then grasps my hands. 'You know what scares me? That she'll go into labour with no one to help her. If it comes early. Tiny was my second. My body was ready. I knew what to do, what to expect.' She lets go of me and holds on to herself, massaging her shoulder. 'I'm terrified. She's only sixteen. Still growing herself.'

I hug her, but there's nothing I can say to comfort her.

As I look at the bands of green moss around the walls of the cottage, the sun begins to appear, a small white disc behind the grey.

'It's dropping.' I point to the outside of the cottage. 'There's the level where it used to be. I've seen it on a few houses now.' Where they face the waves of incoming weather from the Irish Sea there's a dirty smirch, like a tide-line of green. 'It's true, what Ewan told us. The water's going down.'

Within minutes the sun is bright, burning the pelt of fog away, and it's much warmer. I feel that wriggle of hope: yes, the water is retreating, withdrawing to where it should be at last; and we're nearly there. By the time we gather up our rucksacks and set off, the air is so clean and blue it feels washed and made new again. Nula is feeling it too, and we smile at each other. We can do something. We can change this. The relentless onward rush of NOAH over our freedom can be stopped.

The road dips down as soon as we've left the cottage behind, then there's a quick fork left and it starts climbing again, but gently this time. We turn a sharp corner and there it is – the whole bay fills the view. A score of small green fields, marked out by dry-stone walls with pockets of trees, run down towards the coast where Barrow lies, spread out next to the blue-grey of the sea. Far out, hazy and indistinct (once we get right down to the town they'll disappear over the line of the horizon) is the grid of what was once the largest wind farm in Europe. Out there they turn in the wind we can't feel from here, slowly spinning and cartwheeling in the vastness of the sea between the northwest of England and Ireland.

Nula is motionless. 'All that energy being generated – then it's siphoned off by NOAH. Powering their ships, supply factories, computers, all kinds of systems. People talked about the wind farms, but I never saw them. I wasn't even sure they existed. When we get rid of NOAH that's what we need to build more of. That, and use the tide.'

'At the Mill we're burning wood to cook on a smoky stove, straining our eyes by candlelight. Everyone thinks the national grid is broken! Do you think they've got internet?'

Nula laughs. 'Oh Anna! Everything's easier if you're rich and in control. They can do whatever they want as long as no one fights back. They don't care about us. That's what I hate about them. We're only here to serve their needs.'

'Hierarchies and rules. Propaganda and false promises. I thought they'd stay in their churches and chapels. Then it was too late. We've been so naïve.'

'But it's not too late. That's the point. That's why we're here.' She leans her body next to mine and I feel her warmth and determination flowing into me. 'They've run with the idea of living on the water, but that makes them vulnerable; they have to come on land for food. Over there – the warehouses, full of their supplies. It's the same on every strip of coast, near every waterway.'

Suddenly I'm crying, now we're so close to our destination. So near to finding them. 'Wherever Rob is down there, he'll be fighting them. If he's alive…'

It's Nula's turn to comfort me. She speaks quietly: 'Out from the shore; can you see them?' She passes me the binoculars. 'To the north.'

I wipe my eyes and focus on what look like multi-storey factories, like walls of vast, white waves.

'I've never seen anything so big. When you told me, I thought you meant like cross-channel ferries.'

Nula smiles.

'They're like small towns,' I say. 'Fuck! They must be eating up the energy as soon as it's produced.'

'Cruise ships. Up to three thousand people, each one. Those are the Arks.' She tugs my arm. 'Let's keep going.'

From now on it's a quick descent to the long stretch of land where Barrow in Furness lies, half-surrounded by the Irish Sea. We go slowly, almost not wanting our journey to end, conscious that each step takes us closer to Jamila and Robbie; and into danger.

The Arks begin to dominate the horizon. Until now I've not asked Nula for fear of finding out; I didn't want to think about it until I had to, but now I need to know.

'You said Jamila will be on one of those NOAH ships?' I hesitate. 'Do you think Robbie will be there too?'

'If he does what they want, yes.'

'And if he refuses?'

'You'll need the binoculars again.' She stops and takes them out of her rucksack. 'They're hard to pick out against the sea. Much smaller. The ones with smoke coming out of the funnels.'

There's a blur of grey: mist, smoke, the sea itself; I can't focus. 'Where? I can't see.'

'That way. Further south.'

Through the binoculars, I see three of them. Anchored much further out – the type of vessel I remember from crossing the Channel to France. 'Those rusty old ferries, you mean?'

'Those are the prison ships. The Hulks.'

Twenty-Seven

Our footsteps keep in their usual rhythm, Nula's balanced and even, mine with the step and drag, step and drag. The sound bounces off the walls of houses. By the time we reach the outskirts of the town it's morning. Seagulls trace overhead against the grey-blue sky, and land on the roofs, their gulping cries bringing back memories of childhood holidays (although gulls long ago abandoned the sea to feed from rubbish tips and roost on tower blocks). The sun glitters coldly on the sea, and on the NOAH ships that rise like icebergs out in the bay, dwarfing the rows and rows of red brick, terraced houses. Hundreds of buildings around the bay and on the island must have been lost, invisible now under the sea, but there's more evidence that the water has begun to retreat, revealing the ruins of homes and shops, industrial buildings and retail parks. Like the village under the flooded valley of Haweswater.

Neither of us speaks, both trapped in thoughts that we're too scared to voice. We're so close, but will we be able to find them? Will they be alive?

We keep to the side of the road and cling to the shelter of doorways and walls. There are obvious signs of damage – flood tidelines on the brickwork and paths, and gardens littered with flood debris. A few seem to be occupied. It's quiet, too early for many people to be around. A tortoiseshell cat ambles across our path and lies down comfortably in a patch of sunlight, licking its paws. Then, the air is ripped apart. A fighter jet screams across, then another. We crouch down and press ourselves into the shelter of a tree. I remember, on

Lakeland holidays, how the RAF used to shear through the sky, moving faster than sound, so you had to look up, ahead of where the sound was, to see them.

'Fuck! I've never seen planes here before. Only helicopters,' Nula says.

She scrambles up and reaches her hand down to help me.

'NOAH's new toys?' I say, brushing the dust off my hands. Trying to diminish my fear.

'Fuck, it doesn't get easier, does it?' She grips the shotgun. 'I know it's not much but I'm glad I've got this!'

The end of NOAH? Or something worse? Hope and dread alternate. I try to crush both thoughts and, in silence, we set off again. One foot in front of the other down a steep, stony track. The rhythmic duet of Nula's regular stride; my step and drag, step and pull.

On walls of chapels and churches, posters flap in the constant wind from the sea: *NOAH will make you clean again. Cleanliness is next to godliness. Keep your distance from Uncleans.*

She breaks my thoughts with a wrench on my elbow.

Somewhere below us, someone is whistling. Not a warning, but the old-fashioned, musical morning sound of someone getting ready for the day. A male sound. We keep in close to a high wall. Nula takes the lead. We keep going. The sound echoes off the wall. We can't tell where he is.

Then I see him.

Through a half-open door, a dark-bearded man is shaving the thick hair growing on his cheeks into the regulation NOAH style. Nula is ahead. She hasn't seen him. I'm too terrified to call out and she carries on walking, adjusting the straps of the load on her back, the gun. She's looking for where the sound is coming from.

There's the sound of horses nearby and I catch their smell of warm leather and metal. A seagull, perching on the ridge of a roof, throws its head back and makes its raucous cry, beak hinged wide open. The whistling continues and, from a gate in the wall immediately in front of Nula, another man steps out. In full uniform, gold and purple, armed with a handgun and machine gun. Everything about him gleams. Even his grey-flecked beard. Especially his large copper-brown boots.

Nula freezes then looks up and meets his gaze. Her hand creeps round to the shotgun, but he's taller, much better trained.

'Where you off to so early, lass?' he says, taking the gun off her shoulder like a butler taking her coat. 'I don't think you need that, do you?' He leans back next to the door and holds the weapons casually. 'Got your ID?'

We've researched our story and a whole range of possible scenarios. We thought we were prepared; we thought we'd see them before they saw us. An obvious road block or a checkpoint. Not this casual stopping in a small street on the edge of town.

His sudden appearance throws Nula. She shakes her head and mumbles something I can't hear.

'Show me your ID.' His voice is louder now, harsher, with a hint of boredom.

The whistling has stopped. There's the sound of running water then the door opens next to me and the dark-bearded man comes out, smelling of fresh, good quality soap. I take a step back and stumble, catching a whiff of my own earthy, animal smell. I'm acutely conscious of this.

He laughs then shouts to the armed man: 'There's another 'un here, Drew. Big lass wid a bad leg.' He pulls at me and begins to drag me to where Nula is standing, angry and defiant after her initial shock. I struggle as hard as I can, but he's stronger.

'Where you going at this time of day? Curfew, you know.' Drew's hand reaches for the machine gun. He looks up the road, as if there could be more than the two of us.

'You're hurting her.' Nula's face contorts with anger and disgust. 'Let her go.'

The one called Drew smirks and eyes the younger man. Then nods at him and the whistler releases me. I try to stop myself from shaking by folding my arms across my body. So far we've been lucky, almost as if we'd get through this unscathed. Now it feels as if our luck has run out. He rubs his hand over his smooth cheeks and the length of the beard, hanging down his chest.

Nula stands her ground but, after weeks together, I know she's as scared as I am; thinking hard.

'Let us go, eh?' she says, smiling at each of them but mainly at Drew. 'We didn't know the time. Let us get something to eat then we'll be on our way. We're visiting a sick relative.'

'Oh aye? Heard that'un before,' says Drew.

Another jet roars overhead and the younger man looks up. Is that fear that crosses his face? I'm not sure. He looks less confident. Drew scowls. Then there's only silence. It occurs to me that there should be others nearby. Where are they all?

Nula tries another tack. She goes up to Drew and speaks directly. I can't hear what she's saying. But it works. He puts his arm roughly on her shoulder, then the small of her back.

She turns back towards me. 'Wait for me,' she says.

'No!' My voice is lost among the seagulls' cries.

She shakes her head. 'Stay there. Wait.'

'Lass won't be running far on that leg, I reckon,' says Drew. He laughs and calls back, 'Go on, Seth lad. Now's your chance.' Then they're gone.

Seth's fair skin blushes, then he styles it out and makes to grab my arm. Pulls me roughly, awkwardly, back up the road to his room. I know what I have to do.

The last thing I see are gulls flying high overhead, breasting the blue air. A distant sound of heavy gunfire.

His hands are sweating. He's very young.

He starts unbuttoning his flies. 'Please don't say owt. Please.'

I have to help him. This is his first time. I finish unbuckling his belt for him. The sweet smell of his clean, washed skin. He's so young. Hardly older than Stefan was. Without his uniform he's vulnerable, new and clean. He pulls at my shirt, pushing his fingers until he can touch my skin. But his clean unfamiliarity is strange and I can't help comparing him to Robbie. This should be an act of betrayal but Robbie wouldn't turn a hair. And I know I have to do it, to get to the next stage. But what if they keep us here? Like Nula on board the NOAH cruise ships. I'm scared then and start trembling too. I pull away.

He misinterprets me. 'Please. Then he'll let you go.' His hand on my breast is feverishly hot. 'You're very beautiful. Please.'

I close my eyes. Switch everything off and become a physical being. I remember once in the woods, with Robbie when we were first together, looking up through a network of bare twigs, one gold-yellow leaf hanging at the end of November when the others were in drifts and piles on the ground. One leaf clinging to the grey-white slender branches of a silver birch tree.

He scarcely makes a sound, a sigh pushed out of him as he climaxes. Then it's over.

A tentative, embarrassed smile. He frowns and pushes me away roughly. Points to a bucket of dirty washing water. Hands me a damp scrap of towel. 'Here.'

On a shelf next to the bed there's a writing pad and biro. The remains of a pack of biscuits. I push the biscuits into my pocket.

I scrub at my mouth with the cold water and spit out. The taste of him on my tongue, deep in my throat. Dripping between my breasts. I tug down my shirt to cover myself. The smell of him will go. If this gets us through the checkpoint it's worth it. It's nothing.

'Come on then,' he says. 'You've got to go, you dirty bitch. You're one of them fucking Uncleans I reckon.' He's pulling me out of his room, but his hand is shaking.

I walk out to a sting of white light, the gathering seagulls. The roar of a fighter jet. Nula is already outside.

'Fucking EUROS!' says Seth, turning to me from his vantage point next to Drew.

'Aye, see you, spaz,' says Drew to me, fingering his handgun. From inside the building a smell of frying bacon turns my stomach. I glimpse a shadowy figure, her hands on her lower back, standing at a camping stove. She flips over the rashers. She could be any age. Her hair is covered.

Nula wipes her mouth and spits on the ground. 'Bastard… did he hurt you too?' She pulls me with her. 'You didn't have to, you know. I could've done them both.'

I shake my head. 'We're together in this.'

'Come back this way, lasses. We'll keep you safe.' Seth's laugh is loud and raucous. 'Not bad for a cripple,' he shouts. But I won't forget his pleading voice: *Please. Then he'll let you go.*

We shoulder our backpacks. We don't speak until we look back and can't see them. Then we slow down.

'Did you hear him? EUROS. What did he mean?'

She shakes her head and shrugs. 'A European air force. An army? I don't know. You OK?'

I nod. Out of breath. 'Fuck, he was so young. Too young to join.'

'Do you think he had a choice?'

She pushes up her sleeves and shows me her arms. Dark pink fingerprints blooming on her perfect skin. 'And here.' More around her throat. 'But I've had worse. Fuck him!'

She strides ahead, then stops. When I catch her up her mood has changed. She's crying. 'It brought it back. The smell of those bastard ships – sex, sweat and wine. The queasy stink of the generators. Waiting for the next time we'd have to comply. Months and months of… It felt like it would never end. No one to help us.' She sits on the side of the road. 'I can't go with you, Anna.'

'We're through the checkpoint!' I say. 'You did it before, when you had help from the doctor.'

'I remember it was in his eyes. That glimmer. The answer in his eyes. "I can help you get out of here." That's when I found out about the embryonic resistance. That there was hope.' She rubs her eyes and takes in a deep breath. 'What makes it worse is I'm starving.' She's laughing again as I help her to her feet. 'Why didn't we ask them for breakfast too? That smell…'

We share the biscuits I found and stand, blinking in the sunlight.

'Which way now? The sea must be that way.' I breathe in the smell of seaweed, rust.

'Near the harbour, they said.'

As we near the seafront, the noise of gulls circling overhead is drowned out again by the scream of aircraft, skimming low over our heads. I see, in slow motion, Nula diving for shelter. I'm knocked to the ground, the air is sucked away. There's dust everywhere. Debris. Choking smoke.

'Fuck… they're bombing us,' I shout.

But Nula is groping around, blinded by the filth flying in the air, mouthing, 'Anna, where are you?'

'I'm here. Wait!'

She can't hear me either.

But it's not us. We're not the target. We're not important enough to be bombed.

Nula sees me and starts running back the way we've come,

heading up towards the checkpoint where a pall of smoke hangs.

I follow. 'Wait. Slow down.'

Nula picks her way into what's left of the building and comes out with weapons in each hand. She's smiling. 'Whoever they are, EUROS are on our side,' she says. 'At least for now.'

'Where are they? Are they…?'

Then I see him. His face is unharmed but he's a mess of broken bones, shaken out like a rabbit in the mouth of a dog. As the dust swirls and settles, Nula points to a pile of rubble where a large brown boot is protruding. Drew. There's a sickening smell of blood, burning hair.

It feels like there's a stone in my chest weighing me down. I'm sobbing with shock. Hot tears in my eyes.

But not for long; I hear my own voice: 'There's nothing we can do. Let's go.'

Twenty-Eight

The first safe house isn't difficult to find, exactly as we were told all those weeks ago: a corner shop with its familiar smell of washing powder, cardboard and old vegetables. The shopkeeper, behind the counter, fifties with a short grey beard, tinged with red and an accent that even I find hard to penetrate. We both have to ask him to slow down so we can follow what he's saying. We're shown up several flights of stairs to the loft and have our first shower since we left the Lakes Hotel. When it's my turn, I hear Nula having a murmured conversation with another man. Later I find out that this is 'Jack'; he will do what he can to take us where we need to go. To find them. Nula is beaming when she tells me this, and I feel my heart leap.

Laid out for us on mattresses in a storage room up in the loft is the clothing we must wear. For me, a NOAH-issue robe and headscarf of roughly woven wool that chafes against my body. When I see Nula in hers I'm gripped by a chill, like someone running cold fingers down my back. Hair covered, long baggy trousers, tunic that reaches to her wrists so that her tattoo is hidden, she looks more beautiful than ever, her face framed by the gold and purple scarf, in the uniform of the NOAH people's army, the guardians of freedom.

'What the hell are you doing?' she hisses, and her fist thumps against my upper arm, taking me by surprise, the air knocked out of me like being kicked in the stomach. 'How dare you *look* at me!'

'Nula, what's wrong?' I say, sprawling onto the mattress.

She stares through me as if I'm lower than the dirt on her

boot, then smiles grimly.

'If this is going to work, I'll have to. They all do it and it's better if you're unprepared. More convincing… You've only had glimpses of how they operate. When you see them on their own ground, there's a huge chasm between a NOAH and an Unclean. And they're the ones who fill it with their own beliefs and violence.' She hugs me and smoothes the cloth on my upper arm where I feel a bruise developing. 'Sorry. This is the only way we can access the Arks.'

She goes on to tell me what we have to do.

'I'm a good mimic; I can act and dance. It's what I've been doing all my life. For months I observed their arrogance, the way they move. The way they talk. I know what we need to do. OK?'

When it's early evening, light fading across the bay, we set off. She takes the lead. 'Walk behind me. Don't get any closer. Keep back.'

We trek through the old town until, down a narrow side street, we find it. A typical pub: English beer, fish and chips, toad in the hole on the chalk board outside. Free WiFi. Across the upper storey, bunting with the white background and red cross of St George flutters in the cold wind blowing in from the sea. Inside it's noise, heat and confusion. A smell of food frying in old fat.

The smell of cigarettes and beer hits us, the setting sun filtering through a dense haze of smoke. Last year, so long ago, when we heard they'd lifted the ban, we thought it was a cruel joke – since the international trade embargo, who could get cigarettes? Apart from Ewan sometimes. But here behind the bar, they're on display and for sale.

There are a few people in coarse clothes like mine, but what makes me struggle to breathe, in spite of Nula's apparent ease, are the clusters of raucous off-duty NOAH officials in uniform. Mobiles and guns bulging in pockets or laid on the table, they're smoking and drinking, ordering food. Loud music. Under my robe sweat drips and soaks my waistband, my armpits.

Heads turn when they see us; when they see Nula their eyes linger. She has that effect on everyone; you want to look at her, her dark gold skin, her eyes set off by long curling eyelashes, as if she's wearing make-up. In the cramped pub she stands tall, looks around and gives a nod to a group of NOAH militia. The captain nods back and beckons her over, but she smiles and walks towards the bar. She's good at this. I'm terrified someone will recognise her, but her air of supreme confidence makes people give way to her without asking questions. When she arrived at the Mill she was skin and bone, exhausted, bent under the burden of caring for her children, breastfeeding Tiny. Now she smiles, and leans her arms confidently on the bar, one heavy-soled boot on the brass foot-rail.

The noise of conversation and the greasy smell of fish and chips is overwhelming – I can't stop trembling. I can't remember what I'm supposed to do. I wipe my clammy hands on the sides of the rough wool robe, but it's so warm sweat soon gathers again.

'Sit there. Hold my jacket,' she says, her face ugly with authority.

I sink onto a wooden bench at the side with the other Uncleans, tuck my robe around myself, shivering with what? Fear, hunger? I hardly know. Looking relaxed, Nula speaks to the barman. I will her to remember everything she has to say, in the right order. Half an hour later, she's eating a hot meal washed down with beer and talking to a young NOAH officer whose attempts to put his arms around her are met with gentle refusal. On the hard bench we're given bowls of thin vegetable stew, edible if cold, hardly enough for an adult. I look up, scared by a sudden uproar: Nula is shouting at the barman, almost incoherent with rage. The next minute a young girl, head bowed, gives her a clean cotton napkin and Nula makes a great show of chatting to the young officer standing next to her.

'Fucking dirty Uncleans!' She leans close to him. 'I had a shower but now I'll have to wash again to get rid of the stink of that bitch's sweat and her disgusting breath.'

She pushes something into the pocket of her trousers.

'Get up, girl,' she says to me. 'Coat. Now.'

I help her put on her long overcoat. 'Here you are.'

The blow, when it comes, knocks me off balance. 'Don't speak. Keep your filthy breath to yourself, cripple. Come. Now.'

It's only when we are far away from the pub that Nula touches my arm. 'That went well. I've got it.' She glances behind. 'He's not following us. Too drunk, thank God. I need another shower.'

'You were amazing, Nula. How did you –?'

'I don't know. I can't even remember. I thought about Jamila. Let's get back, then I'll tell you the plan.'

The arrangements for the next day feel flimsy, and when we finally go to bed, I lie on my mattress going over them, hoping for sleep. In the morning we'll meet Jack. He'll take us by boat to the Ark where Jamila, we're told, is being kept for observation on the INCREASE hospital deck. I'm to go as Nula's servant. Jamila is scheduled for an antenatal appointment with one of the 'doctors', who'll advise further tests. Then we'll smuggle Jamila back with us to the waiting boat.

But then Nula adds, 'I'm sorry. No one knows where Robbie is. No one has seen him.' She says this with a lowered voice. 'There are rumours he's in the Hulks.'

'Well, I'll go there if I have to. Somebody must know.'

There are lines of communication, people ready to put

their own lives at risk to stand up for human rights and democracy. Brave people who will resist, even if they're terrified. Just as I am.

I try to sleep. I can hardly breathe. All night I focus on Robbie, as if wanting him so much will conjure him up in this bleak place.

Twenty-Nine

I'll remember it clearly, I tell myself, as if it will be a story in the future. To reassure myself: the gentle swell of the sea and the way the early morning sun highlights the thick, glassy waves. The tremulous silence. The sense of depth below us. How fragile we are in our small craft, as Jack, in NOAH uniform, rows us to the Ark.

It's a mild day with little wind, the water barely rising and falling, but I feel sick. My nerves are pulled to breaking point and the rhythm of the rowing makes me want to curl up in my itchy wool robe and sleep. I did fall asleep eventually, but all night was plagued by jagged dreams, splintered into dark and light: Nula walking ahead with her shotgun, Nula outlined against the exploding fire of the bomb, the young NOAH soldier's trembling hand against my breast. A foot in a brown army boot. A kaleidoscope of pictures spiralling in my head all night until I woke to a perfect image of Robbie, walking into the river, pulling a rope to fix the mill wheel. His smile. An image of the past. But how I long for it to be the future – to pick up our life at the Mill again. For it all to continue as it was before. Before NOAH's actions made that small, precarious life look idyllic.

I never thought I was superstitious until now; I find myself counting seagulls and if it's an odd number, then Robbie will be safe.

On board, I'm told to keep my head down, my eyes lowered, only look at the ground. Not to speak. Otherwise, Nula's hand whips out to hit me. My body is tight with dread. What breakfast I managed to eat before we set off lies heavily in my stomach. Every breath I take, it threatens to come back up. I follow. I sit. I listen.

It all happens in the right order. At first.

Jack says he will wait outside, on guard, then a door opens and a smell of strong antiseptic masks something vile and dark that I can't identify. A woman whispers: 'She's in here.' It must be the doctor. Then, through the strangeness and unfamiliarity, the voice of a tired child. Jamila. I feel the suppressed sob in Nula's voice in my own throat.

Nula whispers to her. 'Don't speak, my love. We're going to get you away from here.' There is such joy in her voice. 'The doctor will help us.'

From under my headscarf, I glance to where Jamila is lying, smiling up at her mother; her face is even younger than I remember, her dark skin clammy. Her belly distended, rounded out like a glossy plum.

'How long?' says Nula.

'I reckon thirty-six weeks,' says the doctor. 'It's not good to move her now.'

'It's a risk, but this is our only chance. She's not safe here.'

'I'd advise against it.'

'There are rumours of an attack. We don't have the luxury of time.'

There follows a muttered, urgent dialogue I can't follow. Then the door is pushed open.

It's Jack. 'We've got to go. As quick as you can.'

In seconds, we're back in the passageway. I'm holding the clipboard with Jamila's medical notes.

'What's she here for?' A man's voice. Aggressive. I can smell the alcohol on his breath. My guts twist in fear.

'My doula,' says Nula. 'She'll help at the birth.'

'You'll let her touch the girl?' He doesn't believe her. 'You'll let an Unclean put her disgusting hands on a child of Noah?'

'Of course not! She'll assist. She's not a medical professional.

She knows the process. Surprising for an Unclean, I know.' Nula laughs.

My hands are sweating so much the clipboard slides out of them and falls onto the floor. Then my head is rocked sideways by a stinging slap.

'Stupid, Unclean trash! Pick it up.' Nula's voice is harsh, laced with contempt.

I fumble my hands down for the clipboard, all the papers blowing loose.

'Hurry up, you useless piece of shit!'

'Why can't she have it here?' The guard is on our case.

'Ow!' Jamila says. 'My belly's gone so hard. I think the baby's coming soon!'

'Let me...' says the doctor. 'A Braxton Hicks contraction. Your body's getting ready. She's young. There could be complications, sir. She has to get to the mainland.'

'Ow it really hurts!'

I don't know if this is part of the plan or the doctor is improvising. But it works.

'She may need an emergency C section. We no longer have the necessary facilities on board, sir.' The doctor sounds authoritative and the guard is unsettled. Perhaps he has children. Or is fearful of a messy birth on his watch.

'Right. Go then. But not you. You stay here. There are plenty of doctors over there.'

'I have to go with her. She needs –'

There's a sound that will repeat itself in my dreams if I ever reach safety. A raw slap of metal on bone.

'Who do you think you are, questioning orders? NOAH can get ten good doctors to replace you, girl.'

The doctor is on the ground bleeding from a head wound. Without thinking, I lean down to help her up but am pushed aside.

'Leave her. She'll learn. Go now. All of you. Before the tide turns... Or I change my mind.'

The rest of us are unhurt, and it goes well. Until we have to put blindfolds on. I'm not expecting that to happen. But yes, I think it's going to plan. Soon we're climbing down, away from the great bulk of the Ark and into the waiting boat. My robe is whipping in the wind and twisting around my legs. Under my face covering, I smell the sourness of my own breath. At last I'm in and, with the sudden release from movement, my heart is battering unevenly.

It seems to be taking Jamila forever to make her way down the metal ladder. Even though I know she's heavily pregnant, I will her to hurry. She's breathing heavily and groaning, but I hear each step and creak, Nula's quiet, encouraging words. I'm aware that I'm waiting for her body to sit close to mine and I pull my clothing in to make space for her. But then, there's a deafening explosion of gunfire that is ringing in my ears when a hand, I think it must be Jack's, forces me down into the bottom of the boat.

All I remember now is noise and confusion. There are muffled shouts and urgent voices. It's Nula – *No, I won't. I won't leave her.*

So, we've failed, I think. After all this, someone is telling her she can't take Jamila.

Abruptly, the voices are cut off as if a door has shut, and I'm falling into blackness; then someone is pulling me up by the hands so hard my arms feel like they will come out of their sockets. I'm on solid ground, groping my way forward. Slowly, I release the knot and push the scarf out of my eyes. I'm on the quayside again. Jack is helping me. But Nula and Jamila have gone.

'It's OK.' Jack catches me as I stumble. 'It's OK, Anna. This is how it works.'

'But is someone with them? How will they –'

'I was blindfolded too.' He looks me straight in the eyes. 'I'm sorry. There's nothing I can do from here. I never have information about forward plans. That's how the system's designed. To minimise the chance of the whole web breaking. You only know a few links in the chain on either side. Never the whole sequence.'

With dizzying clarity I realise it was me Nula was talking about, me she didn't want to leave; she wanted to help me find Robbie. And also, for the first time in weeks, that I'm on my own. 'But I can't…? How can I…?'

My legs are buckling. He smiles grimly and guides me to a bench.

In my mind, I pray they're safe and on to the next stage – the journey back; I try to visualise a happy homecoming. But it's too difficult. Without Nula beside me I feel as if one limb has been excised. I can't stop myself from crying.

'You're stronger than you think. Remember that.' His voice is quiet, understated. 'I'm here. I'm going to help you. You have to trust me.'

But I can't stop the tears.

'I wasn't going to tell you this till later. I'm waiting to hear details, but there's good news.'

'Robbie?'

'Someone saw him two weeks ago. I've sent out more messages to find out where he's likely to be,' he tells me. 'But nothing will happen for a few days. We have to wait. And you have to stay focussed.'

As we walk back to the safe house the air is split by the roar of another fighter jet. We both cover our heads and drop to the ground.

'There's more action in the air than I've ever seen before,' he says. 'There are rumours going round of more skirmishes. Somewhere off the coast. It's all heating up.'

'But who's attacking NOAH? Are they on our side?'

He sighs, then looks at me as if I'm stupid. 'It's EUROS. And before you ask; all I know is that whoever brings down fucking NOAH is on our side.' He winks. 'Can you picture anything worse?'

I shake my head.

'NOAH are getting weaker. And if they're feeling the pressure, they'll be on the defensive. They're likely to do something unpredictable. We've got to be ready. All you need to do is get some rest. Don't leave the room. And,' he says clapping me on the shoulder, 'remember you're strong enough. Look what you've already done.'

He leaves me alone up in the attic of the safe house.

Pacing back and forwards in this tiny space, every fibre of my body resists this last-minute enforced imprisonment. I need to go now and find Robbie. I pace until I'm exhausted.

From the window I can see the lines of roofs and the towering Arks. When the tide is right, we will go back out on the sea and make our way to the Hulks. The last stage of the search for the man I love more than my own life. When Jack comes, I must be ready. This is my only chance. I walk until I collapse onto the bed.

That night there is more bombing but, mercifully, I sleep through the worst of it. I dream I'm on a ferry. The throb of the engine. Smell of rust. Something maroon I take at first to be an ID book slides across the floor. I pick it up; it could be useful, a document to be forged, something to save another life. I flick over the pages like pictures in a story book – the reed beds, bridges, canals and village greens; the rivers, lakes and seashore images of one of the old British EU passports. Dad used to have one. Spotted with mould, pages stuck together, it must have been here for decades. The United Kingdom in all its rural nostalgia, a dream. The memory of a dream. I turn to the photo page, expecting to see Dad's face, but the photo is so faded I have to squint hard to recognise who it is. It's not Dad. It's Robbie. With dream logic I realise Dad has given him his passport. He must be here. Robbie's here. I call Jack. 'He's here. I've found him.' But I can only whisper. My voice won't come out.

I wake when my own name breaks through my dream. Jack is shaking me, pulling me out of sleep. I wake to a vision of hell. Not the red light of dawn. Over the sea are leaping flames. Black, thick smoke. A single circling helicopter.

'There won't be a better time while all this is going on. Campbell is already in the boat. Come on.'

'What's happening?'

'Fuck knows, but it looks like EUROS. The Arks are on fire. It could be the Hulks next.'

'But would they bomb prisoners?'

'Depends on what they know. Everything's changing so quickly. Who knows what NOAH will do?'

'I'm scared,' I say.

'Who isn't?' says Jack. 'Take this.' He presses a gun into my hand. 'Put the robe on. We need to go. There are three of them. I don't know where he's being held. We have to try them all.'

The first of the Hulks is already on fire, and when Jack climbs up to check, he's gone for less than five minutes but it feels like hours. When he appears on deck, he shakes his head and, for a moment, I think that's it: all the prisoners must be dead.

'Deserted,' he says, coughing and wiping his eyes, once he's back in the boat. 'Let's go.'

There's no sign of fire on the second ferry so Jack helps me ascend. The contrast of eerie red light reflected off the sea and the gloom of the interior of the second Hulk is like a blindfold pressing into my eye sockets. Less smoke here, but I can't see where I'm going it's so dark. I can hardly breathe. The gun, deep in the pocket under my robe, bumps against my thigh with each step.

Jack points with his gun towards a rectangle of dark. Gradually it comes into focus – steps lead over a rusting lip of steel, down to the lower decks. The shriek of gulls and wash of waves hitting the ferry's hull slowly fade as we go down, holding onto a rail pitted with rust. Flakes of metal under my fingers. With each movement my feet lift off from the floor with an echoing squeak of rubber. Water, or some kind of cold liquid, drips from the ceiling onto my face. After the night of bombing the ferry is eerily quiet.

There's a deeper rumbling and the engines start, then a few lights flicker on. It doesn't, of course, but I half expect the ferry to move.

Jack shakes his head and mouths, 'Power's on again. Emergency generator.'

Now we're in one of the lounges, sludgy bottles and dusty glasses rattling and clinking with the vibration of the engine; in portholes and windows the view of the glowing horizon goes up and down.

There's no sign that anyone's been here for a long time, but we need to get out of this open space. Everywhere, the smell of rust and age. Piles of rubbish blown and tossed across the floor, collecting under faded and stained furniture. The swell is getting worse and there's a mournful crying, but it's not human, it's the wind moaning through broken windows in the bar.

'Wait there. I'm going to check. We've got to get out of here. The weather's changing. Could be rough.'

He leaves me hidden behind a battered vending machine, where rust-coloured liquid drips into a puddle. The surface ripples with the shuddering of the generator. The bar is deserted, but I hear sounds everywhere, all round me. I remember crossing the Channel to France with Robbie when we were young and free. Looking forward to cheap wine and a plate of garlicky mussels and chips. And now this.

Out of the corner of my eye something red, a flash of silver. A packet, blown by a gust of cold air, lands at my feet. Letters are rubbed off, but I remember the smell, like an image in scent of impossible comfort – potato, oil and salt. A convenience food when convenience was a measure of value. You could pick them up day or night from supermarkets or garages. Everywhere sold them. Advertised by ex-footballers in jokey ads. Plain salted crisps, packaging *not yet recycled.*

Flimsy plastic and foil; it will keep degrading, but never completely disappear. This is what we've done to the world. We've created this monster in plastic. This burning world. We're all Frankenstein.

Jack comes back. 'Looks like everyone's gone. No sign of guards.' He picks up a corkscrew. 'But might need this.'

In the rising storm there's a sudden lurch of the ferry, then a terrible silence.

'Ten minutes, then we're out of here. The dinghy isn't up to it...' he says, then signals for me to listen.

His hearing is better than mine. I hold my breath. From far away there are subdued cries. Noises off. As we walk further along the passageway it becomes shouting. Each step is an effort of will. I don't want to see this. Whatever it is.

Then we're in a large cabin, the air foetid with sweat and dirt. Worse than this; the stench of human excrement. Shackled against the walls are prisoners in dirty, orange boiler suits.

'Let us go, for fuck's sake.'

'Give us something to eat. We're starving.'

Four men, emaciated, unshaven, but not in the NOAH

way. Bruised skin, black eyes. Robbie isn't here. I can't find him after all. I'm too late.

Then a skinny old man, stooped, catches hold of my hand. 'Anna, it's you. Anna. I can't believe you came for me.'

Thirty

Robbie is weak but he can walk, slowly and hesitantly. Jack helps him and the others over the side and into the boat where Campbell puts blankets around them and tells them to sit close together, heads down until we're far away from the ferry. He gives them something to eat, water to drink. Then he revs up the motor. Robbie leans his whole weight on me, his head on my shoulder. He's trembling so violently it goes right through me. I can hear his teeth chattering. I'm wearing the woollen robe over my clothes so I pull it around both of us and tuck him into it. All I can do is hold him and look at him; it's all I want to do.

After the dark of the Hulks, he can't stop blinking in the burning red light bouncing off the waves. His ravaged face is so thin, bones jutting out, but he's here, and I will never let him go. I have so many questions, but they can wait; he needs to conserve his energy. The other men are skeletal too, ghosts of the men they must have once been, sitting passively in the dinghy, watching the windfarms off Barrow fading into the distance as we head north up the Cumbrian coast. I'm preoccupied with Robbie, yet when I look at their gaunt faces I can't help wondering if there will be someone waiting for them somewhere.

The sky is lit briefly by white light and the delayed sound of a massive explosion. I jump, as do Jack and Campbell, as the sound wave punches into us and the boat rocks violently. Behind us one of the Hulks has been hit. The four prisoners hardly flinch, only slump down further into the boat, nodding off to sleep. But they aren't allowed to sleep for long; soon we pull alongside the harbour where slippery concrete steps lead up to solid ground. Campbell half pushes Robbie up, and as soon as he reaches the top, he collapses into the crowds. The sounds of distant gunfire and explosions are masked by voices. When we set off this morning there was no one. Now it takes all my effort to weave our way through the crush of people gathering on the side of the docks.

Robbie's voice is almost inaudible, laced with anxiety: 'There are too many people. Don't let go,' he says. Each bony finger interlacing with mine is familiar, yet icy cold. His hands are never cold. I'm glad of my thick robe to hold around us. After we are all safely together there is a brief conversation between Jack and Campbell.

'This is as far as I go,' says Jack. 'Good luck.'

By the time I turn to thank him he's disappeared into the mass of people, and it's Campbell who leads us through the streets. Buildings are on fire. Soldiers fleeing. Noise. Smoke. Chaos. No one stops us, but the dread is there. I remember the evacuation of London. The same smell of sweat and fear. An atmosphere of barely suppressed emotion that occasionally breaks out in spikes of anger or a shove. Campbell hisses at us to stick together. Keep going.

We reach a building with the old crossed arrow symbol of British Rail. Passenger trains haven't run for years, with landslips and flooding affecting the whole network. We pass along platforms until the crowds begin to thin out and the sound becomes a murmur.

'You wait here,' says Campbell. 'I leave you now. Others will come soon.'

Fear tumbles in my guts. If no one comes will I have to take charge in this alien place?

'Where are we?' I say.

'A siding. You don't need to know more than that. Soon they'll come. Don't worry,' he says. Looks at his mobile. 'Two hours max.'

'How will I know?'

'They'll know you,' says Campbell. 'It won't be long.'

His echoing footsteps die away and the men sit with their backs to a wall. They're falling asleep again. One of them, tall, even more emaciated than the others, slides down, and when they pull him up to stop him rolling onto the tracks he groans, then is instantly asleep again.

There is no clock. None of us has a watch. No mobile. All we can do is wait. Then, as if from nowhere, they appear. Two NOAH soldiers coming towards us. This is it. The end. But when they're close both women smile briefly, and beckon us to come with them. One with an almost plump, doughy face, the other more sharp-featured, vulpine.

We're hurried onto a waiting diesel train, the stink of fuel burning in my throat. We're heading north, following the coast. It's slow, and the engine often stops altogether because the tracks have been bombed. The prisoners sink into sleep. I remember our overland walk – the weeks and weeks it took for Nula and me to make this same journey. This is the first time since she left that I've thought of her. Is she safe? They may not have made it. How likely is it for a woman and pregnant girl? Has she had the baby? Questions no one can answer.

It takes most of the day. We pass the bombed out remains of an industrial complex that looks familiar. Cordoned off with razor wire. Miles and miles of it. The old Sellafield nuclear site, still leaking radioactive waste into the sea here. I will the engine to hurry past, then the land to the east becomes hillier and we reach the red sandstone cliffs of St Bees. The track is too damaged to go any further and we have to leave the train. At least the land is high and well above the sea to the west. They take us to a farmhouse where, even though it's daylight we eat, then crash out and sleep.

It's not until the following afternoon when the two women wake us that I look out and see the land drops again, through woods down to an area of water so dazzlingly bright I can't see how far it stretches. And I'm crying because we've come this far and we're not going to give up, yet how are we going to do it? The tall man has died in the night. The other two are so weak they may not make it. Robbie nods to say he's ok. There's no more food. Nothing. We have to keep moving. Or wait to die. It's not too deep. But we'll have to wade, one of the women says. They've done this before. Many times. There's a rope of frayed, blue plastic tied to a tree to help us in.

I watch the sun flicker through the trees, highlighting leaf buds and emerging white blossom on blackthorn; there is beauty under the sky's blue and white canopy, and the birds are singing a song of survival.

Robbie knits his thin fingers with mine and we hold on tight to the rope to walk down into the water. The initial contact is so cold, I'm gasping and shaking, taking in great mouthfuls of air.

He squeezes my hand. 'We can, Anna.'

We step slowly, each feeling for unevenness with a stick.

The water is soaking up my ankles, my jeans, to my thighs. I stumble and he hauls me back up again.

His teeth are clenched and he's panting. 'Nearly!' He chuckles.

It's like a dream where you do something so strange you wake up laughing because the idea is so bizarre – wading into water with all your clothes on. For so long we've avoided this. We've kept out of water.

Away from the shelter of the woods, the wind is strong, and soon we're breasting the waves, making for a stand of trees where they tell us boats will be tied up. The ground is slippery and uneven, falling away from us. My whole body rebels; this isn't going to work. I can't do this.

'Rob, let's go back. I can't. Please.' I pull his arm. But he only grunts and holds my hand tighter. We keep going towards where the boats are. Now the water is almost up to my shoulders, lapping against my chin, splashing into my mouth and up my nose. Soon we'll have to swim. The sharp-faced woman leads the way. She's started to swim in an efficient front crawl.

Rob grips my hand, pulling at me. 'They said it didn't get deeper than this. Waist-deep, that's what they said.'

'We can't go back. This is it. Our last chance. We'll have to swim.'

He's pulling my arm back, so hard I'm going to fall.

'I can't.'

'What else can we do?' I gasp as a wave hits me full in the face. 'We can't go back there. I'm not going back. There's nothing there. No food. Nothing.'

'Anna, I can't.'

Over the tug of the water lifting us, and vegetation tangling around our feet, his voice is quiet, his body shaking even more than mine. I imagine the bones rattling.

'I never learned.'

'What?'

He shakes his head. 'I can't… you must remember.'

'Of course you can. You're weak, but we'll go slowly. On holiday you liked…'

Then, like a detonation of light in my mind, I see him going for a walk, or lying back in a deck chair to finish the book he's reading; before now I'd never thought of it; whenever anyone suggested a swim, Robbie said he'd rather be doing something else. How did it get to this? This minute when it matters so much: a five-year relationship, living in a drowned world, and I never realised. How did I not know he couldn't swim?

'I'll help you,' I say. But even though he's lost so much weight, he weighs as much as I do. And he's panicking. 'We'll do this together. Please, you have to stay calm.'

Then there's splashing. The rank taste of water. He's like a huge, cold baby clinging to me. Rolling round. Pulling me down. Like Tarzan fighting the crocodile. I'm gagging as I go under. Water burning my throat and nose. The struggle for air. Images flash: sand trickling slowly down through an egg timer – *I am soft sift in an hour glass*. My time is running out and the creature of nightmares squats on my chest, compressing my lungs. Daylight fades above and, for a long time, it's dark, but I won't let go. We're together, sinking down, his hands in mine. Then I break the surface and I'm breathing thin, cold air and my hands are empty. All I can see are his fingers above the water, clutching at nothing; the water closes over him like a trapdoor and I'm scrambling to find him through the water. A thick, cold skin sliding over my body.

He's here. He must be somewhere in here. Where are you, Robbie? Let me help you. Don't hide, my love, let me help you. Please try to swim. The Gormley figures come back to haunt me, drowning as they stand looking out to sea, the tide coming in.

Then arms and hands are hauling me up, prizing me out of the cold depths, like a caught fish. In my own element again, I'm gasping in the bottom of a boat, coughing and vomiting up water. Breathing air. The smell of wood, damp wool, leather, sheepskin. He's holding my hand.

But this hand is warm – I'm a wild beast biting, clawing at him. He's stronger than me. A man, face a mesh of fine wrinkles. Another holding the oars. Both breathing heavily. The older one wraps me in an old coat, and a blanket. My arms are pinned to my sides. A straitjacket for the mad woman. My body jerks with spasms of cold, nausea and fear. There's nothing I can do to stop it. Cold water in my lungs, throat and stomach wants to come back up. I cough out a spume of dirty water. He takes out a flask. Something warm. I feel the younger man lean forward to lift the oars out of the water and pull away from the island of trees.

'We have to go back. Robbie's in the water. He can't swim.'

The man puts his hand over mine.

'What's your name, lass? You've done well to get here on your own. You're safe now. I'm sorry. We've looked all round. T'others have been picked up by another boat. We didn't find anyone else.'

'Please. He can't swim. You've got to take me back.'

He squeezes my hand.

The other man says, 'Mebbe he's got hisself somewhere safe. You nivver know. There's other boats.'

'He would never leave me after we've come so far. I saw him go under and I never saw him come back up. He was with me and I lost him.'

'I'm sorry, lass.'

Once the life force has gone, there's no way of breathing it back in. We are such stuff as dreams are made on… I remember those tiny bundles floating on the water, never waking up, their own lives hardly begun. I will not see him again. Gone under and down. My love. My love. My throat is tight with tears, burned by my own vomit. I'm too exhausted to fight. I sink into myself and let them row the boat. Light is fading from the roof of the sky, until all that's left is the fire of the sinking sun in a mass of purple clouds.

The young man lights a lantern. Again, the sound of oars pushing against the waves, the small boat balanced on the oily membrane of the water. A few stars puncture the darkness of the sky, and their reflections tremble on the inky surface of the flood, then they're covered by cloud; other lights twinkle across the expanse of water; there are more boats. Lamps or torches. The sound of a motor.

'Look,' I say, 'over there. He could be there. They could have picked him up.'

'Quiet, lass.' The voice of the younger man. 'We need to wait.'

He releases the oars and his hand presses hard on my head. Our boat drifts back and he catches the branches of a solitary silver birch, glimmering white as my eyes get used to the dark. He's panting like a woman in labour. Then the motor stops, so suddenly I hear it going on, like an echo. Only the water slapping against the sides of the boat, the hush of a few dry leaves clinging to the tree.

A light arcs over us, catching on the stark trunks and branches, like white bones sticking out of the water. A torch. Sweeping like a lighthouse beam. I count, waiting for it to come back. A signal, repeated.

'It's OK. It's our lot,' the older man says, smiling in the dark. 'They need help. Or they've got information.'

As we get closer we can hear voices. Music. Someone is humming a tune. It takes me back to that last music evening at the Mill. The last time we were all together.

I never made promises lightly
And there have been some that I've broken
But I swear in the days still left…

Despite my parched throat the power of the music forces me to sing – *We'll walk in fields of gold.*

'Ewan?' I say. 'Is that you?'

'Aye, lass, it is. Me and me dad.'

Soon we're level with their boat and I can see it's not only the two of them.

'I'm sorry for everything, Anna, lass. I'm trying to do what's right now.' He smiles that slow smile. 'Hey, look who I found out for a la'al swim.'

At that moment I know I can forgive him everything.

When I'm safely in their boat, Robbie puts his hand under my chin and slowly wipes the tears off my face. Hands I love so much. I feel his heart fluttering against my own ribs.

'Thank you.'

There are tears on his cheeks too. He can hardly speak and he's so cold, so cold, and I'm scared he will never get warm.

Then there's food, something to drink and we're skimming across the black water. I curl up, head on his chest, my face turned so I can see the ink-blue sky; now the clouds have parted it is bright with stars. The Milky Way. For the rest of the night we move almost silently past the towering mass of the fells, their faces turned away from us, contemplating the night sky and the sea. Here, on this terrible lake, we are insignificant.

Thirty-One

By early morning the lake begins to narrow, and the fells are lower, less harsh and high, their tops smoothed and flattened. When we reach Lorton we no longer need the boat. We follow the river west as it hurtles down towards the next valley. Underfoot, there is spongy moss and grass, the road impassable with fallen trees and floodwater. For this last stretch of the journey, we climb up onto the old bypass, silent apart from one cart and horse heading in the opposite direction towards Keswick. Ewan leads the way, helping Robbie.

He places each foot carefully, unlike his old self. Contained. Smaller somehow, with less energy.

'I'm clean,' I hear him tell Robbie. 'You won't find owt. I'm starting again. So much of my life has gone waiting for the next fix. A waste. Whole years I've forgotten.'

Robbie is too exhausted to make conversation.

We make our way down to where the grey stone building rises up in front of us. I smell wood smoke and see the great wheel turning.

'I keep praying she's here,' Ewan says. 'Do you think she'll forgive us? For what I done?'

'Who?' Robbie sighs. Walking takes all his strength.

'Nula. Who else?'

'Don't know, mate. No idea.' Robbie shrugs. 'I can't fix everything, you know!'

It's good to see his sense of humour coming back, but he is so frail I'm scared he'll never recover.

When Tracey comes to the door, red-faced and breathless,

and throws her arms around us, his pallor is even more obvious.

'You made it. You're really here. All of you! You did it, Anna. What did I tell you!' Then she glances back into the dark hallway, pulling away from us. 'I need to…'

Someone must be ill. Very ill, I think, fearing the worst.

But it's not Elsa. She walks out slowly to meet us, her blonde hair scraped back in a ponytail, and stands leaning hard on the gatepost; a smile on her thin face. 'I'll go and tell Dad,' she says, and goes back into the house.

'Did they make it? Jamila and Nula?' Ewan says.

Tracey nods, out of breath, pulling away from her brother.

'Has she forgiven us? For what I done?' Ewan looks down at her, his arms tight around her. 'I'll never forgive myself. It's the worst mistake of my life.'

Tracey's mouth is set. 'Our Ewan, you've got to sort yourself out. It's not up to me. You'll have to work on her yourself, show her what she means to you. I can't do owt, you soft ha'pworth. You're not a kid no more!'

Then there's a noise that makes Robbie get to his feet from the bench where he's collapsed.

A moaning cry that escalates to a wail.

'What the hell! What's wrong, Tracey?' says Ewan.

'I need to go.' She runs, wiping her hands on her overall. 'It can't be long now. Thank God you're here, Robbie. It's going so quickly… Anna can you…?'

Robbie has already stumbled into the house.

I drop my belongings and follow him; he's washing his hands and searching in kitchen drawers.

'Come on, Dad. Let's see if we can do owt. I don't want to listen to that poor la'al lass. It's not going to help anyone.' Ewan and George head for the field where Elsa tells them her dad is hammering in wooden stakes to create a support for the runner beans.

If he wasn't here, we'd have to improvise, and Robbie has assisted at so many births on board I feel a thin sense of safety; but this is a primitive birth without medical help or pain relief. Barbaric and agonising. With each contraction Jamila is transformed into a thrashing animal. Between each wave of pain, she recovers, but is too far away from us now to speak. She's hardly aware of us. Nula wipes her forehead with a towel and, as Jamila leans forward, her arms on the back of a chair, massages her lower back.

'Oh, Mum, it's coming again. Make it stop. I can't do this! Mum!' Her child's voice rises to a shriek.

I put down the fresh towels; there's nothing I can do here.

In the field, Ewan and George have started helping Daniel. He's smiling but looks thinner, worn out by the last few months.

When he sees me his smile broadens and he comes straight over. 'You're safe. I've missed you. We all have.' He squeezes my shoulder and sighs. 'Come on, give me a hug.'

I lean into his warmth and breathe in his familiar smell. He wraps his arms round me.

'You know something,' he says and laughs. 'I reckon I'm getting a touch of old age; it's time for someone younger to take over. I'm glad you're back.'

We watch George and his son stretching wires between the posts.

Daniel gives them the thumbs up.

He moves aside as Elsa leads out a goat with two new kids wobbling on their long shaky legs. 'How's Jamila doing? It's so much easier for animals, isn't it?' As the kids run about kicking their legs up in the air and butting each other, he laughs. 'Look at them. I forget every time how comical they are.'

Elsa comes and links arms with him. 'Come on, Dad. Let's go and have a cup of tea. Stefan's made bread. We all need a break. Ewan and his dad have been up all night!'

Even before we're back in the house I hear it. The small cry. Then, as I walk into the living room, a cheer goes up from Ewan and George.

Nula is holding her granddaughter, wrapped in the soft, yellow blanket she was knitting before Jamila was taken. Her eyes brim with tears when she hands me this impossibly small but perfect human being.

'Anna, you made it. You're here.'

After the drama there's a peacefulness in the room, with all eyes flicking from mother to baby.

Jamila is smiling. 'I'm going to call her after you, Anna. I want her to grow up brave like you.'

'You've been great, Jamila. You're going to be a fantastic mum,' Robbie says.

'Thank you, Doctor Robbie!' Jamila laughs. 'And now you've got to let us look after you!'

He walks carefully out of the room. I hear the tap running as he washes his hands and the quiet plash of the mill wheel turning, the repeating two-note song of a great tit. From the window, petals float down from the apple trees in the orchard like snowflakes. It's been a long winter.

When it's my turn to hold the baby, I take her awkwardly and look at her tiny, red, screwed-up face, her head elongated by birth. I wait for her to cry but instead she opens her eyes – dark blue pools against swollen eyelids. 'Hello, little one.'

Tracey holds out her arms to take her from me. 'A new life here at the Mill. Isn't it marvellous?'

When I give up her small, dense weight, my arms feel empty until Robbie puts his own arms around me, his heart beating quickly.

'One of many, I hope,' Tracey says, as if she can read my thoughts.

Then, as one we duck down, our moment of serenity smashed by gunfire echoing around the valley. We huddle together, Tracey's whole body wrapped round the baby, Nula's arms protecting Jamila.

'So, we've lost after all,' Daniel says. 'After everything we've been through.'

Stefan is the first to get up and edge to the window. He pauses and breathes in deeply. We're all prepared. Ready to go together. We hold hands.

There's a battering on the door.

'I'll go. I've had my life. I'll go,' says George and he stands up, his knees creaking.

'Dad! Let me!'

'No, lass, you stay here with your brother. I said I'll go.'

We hear him move slowly and the doors open.

When he comes back, he's smiling so much you can see his long, yellow teeth, like a wise old rat.

'It's not what you think,' he says, as two soldiers follow him into the room; they put down their weapons and loosen their chin straps.

'Everyone alright in here?' one says in a German accent, her hair covered by a hijab.

'Anyone need medical help?' The other, tall with glowing dark brown skin, looks at our startled faces and takes in the scene. He smiles broadly. 'We heard there was a baby on its way.' He takes his medical bag off his shoulder and kneels down next to Jamila.

~ ~ ~

From the hillside I see a thin ribbon of smoke curling up into the blue of the sky, a twist of silvery grey rising up towards the white clouds passing over, with no threat of rain. There are more fish in the river now and Ewan has been teaching

Stefan how to fish; in an hour we'll be eating again. Eating well. On his way into the mill Daniel has put down sacks of grain and is watching the river flow over the wheel, generating power to grind the wheat; Nula and Ewan are up on the roof of the house fixing the new solar panels we applied for after the liberation; their bodies are so close together, almost welded together.

Jamila and Elsa are chatting and laughing as they shell peas, sitting on a bench in the sun. Later there'll be music and dancing. Nula will dance. We all will. George has the baby in his arms, dangling her toes in the river. I can hear her squealing from here. Our own forest garden is growing – we have soft fruit, nut trees, apple trees; we're working with nature, not against it. We've remembered we're part of nature. At the market we always have something to trade. It's not going to be easy, but everyone agrees with me that we can't be complacent; we have to plant more trees. All through the county, people are coming together to bring about peace, working like us to counter the greedy, the selfish and the ignorant. They say it's the same all over the globe. We have to hope and act as if that's true. That's all we can do.

Robbie has plans to upgrade the irrigation system as well as our plumbing; down in the clearing he is cutting and sawing wood. I register the fall of his arm then the delay before I hear the metal hit the logs, the sound bouncing off the hills. His arms are brown, stronger than ever. As he chops the wood, dust flies up, sparking gold in the sun. Like Vulcan at his forge. He looks relaxed, rhythmically chopping. I imagine the smell of the warm wood – resin from the pines – floating in the air.

'Robbie!' I call and he smiles at me, his hands in the small of his back.

Then, at the same moment, we both look up at the hundreds of trees we've already planted on the flanks of the fells, at the vast sky a radiant blue, where bleached clouds hold tight to their burden of rain; they drift slowly, their shadows briefly darkening our small valley as it settles under the indifferent but glorious sun.

Acknowledgements

Thank you to my wonderful family and all my lovely, supportive friends. The gardeners, yogis, writers, poets and friends from Ealing, St Andrews and Cockermouth. You've kept me going in what has turned out to be a year of ups and downs. Thank you for everything you've said or done: supplying me with bread and berries when I've not been able to walk to the shops, visiting me when I've been stuck at home, and reading (and commenting on) earlier versions of *The River Brings the Sea*. I'm looking forward to celebrating the launch with you! And we can raise a glass to two dear friends, Terry and Ann, lost to cancer this year.